The Brotherhood
The Key

By Elian Lumis and Vickie Acklin

"By the Flame within the Key, I enter remembrance.
By the Seal of Light, I walk the true path.
So it is, in all worlds, now and forever."

Flame of Remembrance Press

Published by Flame of Remembrance Press
ISBN: 979-8-9986972-3-4
This is a work of fiction. Unless otherwise indicated, all
the names, characters, businesses, places, events and
incidents in this book are either the product of the author's
imagination or used in a fictitious manner. Any
resemblance to actual persons, living or dead, or actual
events is purely coincidental.
Printed in the United States of America
First Edition

Dedication

For the seekers, the dreamers, and the ones who trust that stories hold hidden keys. For every reader who dares to open the door and step beyond the ordinary.

And for the one flame we share, whose light burns quietly within these pages.

Every story is a key. Every key unlocks a door. And sometimes, the door opens not into the world—but into yourself.

Prologue
The Storm Begins

Long before dawn, a storm gathered over the Tyrrhenian Sea. Lightning licked the horizon, but no thunder followed; the sky held its breath, as though listening. In the chamber of a crumbling monastery, two men faced one another across a table carved with sigils older than any kingdom.

Duke Antonio Marchetti stood like a man born to command, his tailored suit immaculate even in the dim candlelight. His hands, pale and precise, rested on the table's edge, but his eyes burned with the hunger of a predator.

Across from him, Leone was all shadow and scar—broad shoulders, heavy jaw, eyes like obsidian set aflame. Where Marchetti was refinement, Leone was raw force, his very stillness promising violence.

Between them lay a single object: a weathered codex, its pages stitched with lines of ink that shimmered faintly in the wavering light. Ancient words whispered from it, though no lips spoke.

"The prophecy nears," Marchetti said, his voice calm but edged with steel. "The Convergence will come. And with it, the Key."

Leone's lips curled into something that was not a smile. "The Key is flesh and blood. And flesh bleeds. It dies. What matters is who controls it before the heavens align."

The storm outside cracked, a bolt of white fire splitting the sea. For a moment, their faces glowed—one sharp with cunning, the other brutal with certainty.

In the silence that followed, both men reached for the codex. Neither yielded.

The storm pressed closer. Somewhere in the world, the Key stirred awake.

And when it did, kingdoms would fall, empires would rise, and the earth itself would bow—either to the hand that guarded, or the hand that enslaved.

Chapter One
The Watcher

Some arrivals are expected. Others are orchestrated. And Sebastiano De Luca knew this moment had been arranged long before she stepped from the plane.

The airport pulsed with life—luggage wheels rattling, voices overlapping in a dozen languages, the bitter-sweet scent of coffee mingling with jet fuel. Amid the chaos, Sebastiano stood motionless, leaning against a marble column, a still point in the whirlwind.

Tall and broad-shouldered, he wore a tailored navy suit that clung to him with casual elegance. The shirt was open at the collar, no tie, a hint of rebellion beneath his polish. His dark hair swept back in waves, his jaw shadowed, the kind of face that drew glances without explanation. His eyes, however—dark, precise, unreadable—missed nothing.

He didn't check the arrivals board. He already knew. Amara's flight had landed twenty-one minutes ago. He had tracked its progress across the Atlantic like a line of fate being drawn across the sky.

From his leather satchel, he pulled a folder. Inside were photographs—candid shots, old public records, even one from Dean Savard's funeral. He had memorized them long ago. And yet, when she appeared, he understood: the images had been pale shadows.

She stepped through the arch with a modest suitcase, her cardigan fluttering lightly. Her hair caught the light, and her stride—unconscious grace, born of sorrow—made her presence magnetic. People turned to watch, unaware of why. Sebastiano's mouth curved in the faintest grin.

"La prescelta," he murmured. The chosen one.

She paused by the taxi line, pulling out her phone. Alone, unaware. She had been guided here with precision—an article nudged into her feed, a listing planted in her searches, even a barista's offhand remark steering her toward Anacapri. She thought it was chance.

It was not.

Dean Savard never stood a chance.

Sebastiano's jaw tightened. He hadn't been part of that chapter, but he had heard the whispers. A clean job. Quiet. Tragic. His employer's reach was vast, his methods merciless. Sebastiano had stopped asking questions long ago.

And yet…

He watched Amara move toward the car rental counter, her grief worn like perfume, light but lingering. He felt something stir—something inconvenient, something dangerous.

"They said she was intuitive," he murmured, adjusting his cuff. "But they didn't say she moved like poetry."

He slipped the folder back into his satchel, pushing away from the column. To anyone else, he was just another man in transit. But his steps aligned with hers now, discreet and effortless.

She would not notice him. Not yet.

But he would remain in her orbit.

But as she passed by, blending into the tide of travelers, he found himself thinking less like an operative and more like a man.

***

That same morning, hours before Sebastiano waited in Naples, Amara Savard climbed onto the jet at Austin International Airport, her heart pounding with anticipation and a faint, restless unease that she couldn't shake. She shifted the bag on her shoulder, feeling it's comforting weight as she moved down the narrow aisle, searching for her seat. Finding it by the window, she let out a sigh at the two empty seats beside her. She could settle in without making conversation, the one thing she'd come to dread.

As the plane began to taxi, she exhaled slowly, letting her head fall back against the seat. Her dark hair spilled over her shoulders, its soft waves framing her heart-shaped face—a face that looked tired now, even to her. She could almost hear Dean's voice, teasing her, calling her "his" Botticelli angel. He used to reach out, just like that, and twist a lock of her hair around his finger, his other hand brushing her cheek. She hadn't looked at herself through his eyes in a long time. Her once-sparkling blue eyes felt muted now, faded by the months that stretched into years without him. She closed them as if that might soften the ache.

Dean.

She hadn't spoken his name aloud in months, not since that night when she'd whispered it into the empty, dark bedroom, clutching his pillow and waiting for the grief to wash over her again. He had been gone three years now, and yet she remembered every detail of that morning as though she were still living it: his hand, cool and still in hers, the soft morning light inching across their room, the disbelief growing as she whispered his name, louder and louder, until silence itself seemed to press around her, permanent and unbreakable.

It was the suddenness that haunted her most—the absolute finality of his absence. They'd built a life together that felt like it might last forever, filled with late-night talks, weekend trips, and the kind of laughter that made even mundane moments sparkle. She remembered how they'd spent afternoons wandering Austin's antique shops, scouring the aisles for old treasures to fill their new home. Dean had always loved pieces with a story, and he'd insist on finding just the right chair, or picture frame, or lamp that would bring their rooms to life. "See this here?" he'd say, pointing out a scratch or nick, "it's character, Amara—it's been through something."

The memory made her chest tighten. It wasn't just furniture they'd been collecting—it was a future. They had mapped out dreams together, whole years and lives they'd never get to fill. "One day, we'll see all of Europe," he'd said one night, holding her as they looked out over the Austin skyline. Dean shrugged as if the whole world were waiting just for them.

Except, it wasn't. Not anymore.

Amara glanced down at her hands resting in her lap, fingers pale and delicate against the navy blue of her sweater. The ring he'd given her was gone now; she had slipped it off on a quiet night months ago, thinking maybe that might help her move forward. But instead, it only left her feeling lighter in a way that seemed wrong. She ran her hands slowly over her arms, feeling the faint chill from the plane's air conditioning, and pulled her cardigan tighter. She was slender, her figure shaped by countless hours spent on Austin's bike trails and long hikes through the city's green spaces. But lately, even that had faded—her will to get out, to move, felt dulled by the slow, ever-present hum of loss.

Dean had left her with wealth, but it was meaningless without him. People told her she was resilient, that she carried herself with a quiet, admirable grace, and yet she knew it was all just a mask, a form of survival she'd learned over these last few years. Grief, she had come to understand, was like an endless ocean—it swelled and receded, sometimes overwhelming her and sometimes just lapping softly at the edges of her days.

In a moment of quiet resolve, she'd sold it all: their house, the furniture they'd chosen so carefully, the trinkets and mementos they'd collected, even the little things he'd

4

once teased her for holding on to. She'd given away the last traces of the life they'd built together. She needed distance, needed to leave behind the memories embedded in every room and corner. And so, she chose Naples, a place she'd once visited with Dean during their whirlwind honeymoon. He'd joked that her Italian roots made her a natural fit, that someday they'd buy a little villa near the coast. Now, Naples called to her like an old friend with a promise of a fresh start.

The flight attendant's gentle tap on her shoulder pulled her back to the present. "Mi scusi, signora. Time to prepare for landing," the woman said with a warm smile.

Amara opened her eyes, blinking as if emerging from a fog, and fastened her seatbelt. Outside, the morning light washed over the hills of Naples, where the sea stretched open like a promise. She caught her reflection in the window, her face framed by her glossy, dark hair, those blue eyes still softened with grief but now tinged with something new. Naples loomed closer, with its rolling hills, cobblestone streets, and open skies. And she felt, for the first time, a spark of what might be hope.

As the captain's voice crackled over the intercom— "Benvenuti a Napoli"—she smiled softly to herself. This was her chance, a place where she could let go of the weight she'd been carrying for so long. Here, she would walk forward, maybe even open her heart to whatever life was waiting for her. Whatever Naples held; she was ready.

She ran a hand through her hair, closed her eyes, and let the words wash over her. She had arrived, finally and truly, on the edge of something she couldn't yet name.

Across the terminal, unseen, Sebastiano's eyes never left her. Her journey had just begun. So had his watch.

Chapter Two
The House on the Cliff

Naples unfolded like a tapestry of stone and sea, the city alive with horns, scooters, and the cries of market vendors. Amara tightened her grip on the suitcase handle as she stepped out of the terminal, sunlight glaring against the glass roof above.

Sebastiano followed at a distance, his steps unhurried, his presence invisible in the crowd. He had shadowed people for years, but never one who seemed to bend the air around her. Every motion she made—every glance, every pause—pulled his attention sharper than any assignment before.

She thought herself alone, beginning a new life in a foreign city. He knew better.

Amara rented a small, charming bungalow tucked away on a quiet street in the heart of Naples. She had a beautiful suite at the Bellasera, but she was longing for someplace a little more permanent. She found the most perfect place to rent. The building was a pale shade of yellow, with green wooden shutters and flower boxes beneath each window. It had a cozy terrace where she enjoyed sipping her morning coffee while watching the world gradually come alive. Below, the cobblestone street buzzed with activity— Vespas zooming by, vendors setting up their stalls, and children laughing as they played. The neighborhood felt like home, but she knew something bigger was ahead.

Her cozy new home was simple but full of warmth and comfort. Old terra-cotta tiles covered the floors and there was a brick oven in the kitchen black from years of use. She could walk to all the shops along Via Toledo for fresh pasta, and local wine. She loved to cook simple meals in her small kitchen.

Amara received an invite to a wine-tasting event through the mail. There was no sender, the event was in a few days. She wondered who had sent the invitation. It did sound like fun. There would be music and food. The local wineries hosted the event each year to showcase their finest new wines.

***

Amara hadn't known what to expect from the wine-tasting event, but it turned out to be a lot of fun—the people there were incredibly friendly. The wine seemed to loosen everyone up, bringing out their playful sides. She took a seat, and the woman next to her struck up a conversation. Her name was Sophia. She had thick dark curls that hung over her shoulders. She was a beautiful woman dressed stylishly and full of excitement for life with a laugh that lit up the room. Next to Sophia was Franco, a handsome and charming man with a quick wit. Franco was the kind of person who made you feel like you had known him a long time.

"You've got to try the Nebbiolo," Franco said as they all went to the bar to get another glass of wine. "It's pure magic in a glass."

"Don't let him fool you—he doesn't know a thing about wine."

"Lies," Franco interjected. "I know everything about wine. I just forget it all after a few glasses."

"I'm afraid that if I try any more of this magic, I may not be able to get home tonight." Amara said holding her empty wine glass. She was feeling a spark of connection she hadn't felt in a long time with these two new friends. By the end of the evening, they exchanged numbers, and

Sophia had invited Amara over for dinner the following weekend.

From that night on, they became good friends.

Amara, Sophia, and Franco quickly fell into a rhythm, spending many evenings together having dinner or meeting for a, caffè corretto which is expresso with a little liquor added to it and translates to "corrected coffee". They explored Naples like tourists browsing street markets, hopping on Vespas for impromptu adventures, and indulging in the city's best food. Both Franco and Sophia had grown up in the area, so they wanted Amara to see the "heart" of Naples.

"Gelato or wine?" Franco asked one afternoon as they strolled along the waterfront, the sun setting behind Mount Vesuvius.

"Why choose?" Sophia quipped, a mischievous grin on her face.

"Because if we do both," Amara said, "Franco will end up falling asleep on the ferry again."

"That happened one time," Franco said, rolling his eyes. "And technically, I wasn't sleeping. I was resting my eyes."

Sophia gave him a playful nudge. "Sure, Franco."

Amara smiled as she watched them bicker lightheartedly. She was enjoying the companionship, laughter, and the joy of simply being with people who made her feel at home. It seemed like every day the weight of Losing Dean was lightened.

One evening, they gathered at a tiny trattoria hidden in a narrow alley. Candlelight flickered on their table, and the air was rich with the scent of garlic and basil. They raised their glasses, toasting to nothing in particular.

"To another fun night together," Sophia said with a warm smile as they dug into plates of freshly made pasta with marinara sauce made from local tomatoes.

"So, how's the bungalow?" Sophia asked. "It seems impossible that your lease is coming due very soon. Are you going to renew the lease or look for something a little larger?"

"I love it, but…" Amara hesitated. "I think I'm ready for something more permanent. I didn't come all this way just to rent. I want a real home with some space to make my own."

Franco nodded thoughtfully. "I get it. Naples is great, but I can see you somewhere quieter. Maybe with a view of the sea?"

"I've been thinking about that," Amara admitted. "I've been doing a lot of research on Capri. I found an ad for an old farmhouse on the island. It's a bit rundown, but I can't stop thinking about it. The listing pictures showed a stone house overlooking the Amalfi Coast, built in the 17th century. The seller claims there's magic in its walls." Amara's whole demeanor changed while she talked about the old house she had found online. She was excited.

Sophia's eyes lit up. "Capri? That sounds perfect for you. Franco and I had our honeymoon on the island. Its breathtakingly beautiful. You will love it there."

Franco leaned back, swirling his wine. "An old farmhouse, huh? It might need a lot of work, but finding something overlooking the coast is almost impossible to find any longer."

Amara smiled, "That's exactly what the realtor said when I called her to ask a few questions about the old homestead. But I'll miss being so close to you guys."

"Then what are you waiting for?" Sophia asked, raising an eyebrow. "We will visit all the time. It's just a ferryboat ride away."

Amara laughed. "You're right. I think I'll make an appointment to see the place."

***

Over the next few days, Capri consumed her thoughts. She imagined herself living on the cliffs, waking up to the sound of the waves crashing against the rocks, breathing in the salty air, and finally finding peace. It was the life she'd always dreamt about.

A few nights later, she met up with Franco and Sophia at their favorite café to tell them the news.

"I'm going to Capri," Amara announced as she stirred her espresso.

Sophia clapped her hands, beaming. "When?"

"This weekend. I've booked the ferry, and I have an appointment with an agent. I'm going to see the farmhouse in person."

Franco grinned. "You're really doing it."

"I am," Amara said, her voice steady. "It's time."

***

The morning of her trip, Amara woke up before dawn with a thrill in her stomach. She quickly got ready and as she drove to the harbor, the sun began to rise, casting a bright pink glow over the city as she got to the port. The gates to the ferry boat opened and she drove her car onto the boat and parked. Amara stepped out onto the deck, happy to feel the sea breeze on her face. Her shiny black hair flowing behind her in the wind as she turned her face towards the rising sun.

The ferry cut through the water, leaving a trail of foam in its wake. Naples shrank into the distance and soon Capri began to come into view.

"This is it, I was meant to be here" she whispered to herself as the cliffs of Capri loomed ahead.

For a moment, she thought she felt eyes on her, a gaze just beyond the wind. She turned, but only strangers moved across the deck. Still, the sensation lingered—as though someone had been waiting for her arrival.

Chapter Three
Shadows of the Brotherhood

Amara knew she was home the moment she laid eyes on it.

The farmhouse, perched high on the cliffs of Anacapri, stood at the end of a narrow dirt path surrounded olive trees and wildflowers. Time had worn its mark on the house, lending it a charming, weathered look. The stone walls, cracked and softened by centuries of sun and salt air, glowed a warm golden hue in the afternoon light. Jasmine and ivy crept up the façade of the house, weaving through the cracks and framing the arched windows. Bright pink bougainvillea spilled over the edges of cracked terracotta pots with a burst of color against the old stone walls of the house. Amara paused, taking in the view—the endless blue water stretched out below the cliff and shimmered like crystals.

The house stood, quiet and proud—weathered by time but as if waiting for someone to call it home again. Amara felt a spark of certainty that the house was waiting on her.

The front door was a thick slab of aged oak. The iron hinges rusted from years of exposure to the salty sea air creaked and groaned as they opened the door. A faded ceramic tile above the door displayed the number 17. The old tile was hand-painted in swirling blue patterns by a local artist many years ago. The scent of rosemary and the salty sea air mingled with the perfume of flowers in the garden below.

Inside, the house was a mix of rustic charm and ancient elegance. Stone tiles stretched across the floor, smoothed by centuries of footsteps. In some areas, faded mosaic patterns peeked through—a swirl of glass and marble shaped into flowers and vines, remnants of a time when every inch of the house was crafted with care.

The kitchen was the heart of the home. A grand hearth, large enough to roast a whole boar, took up one whole wall, its bricks blackened by the smoke of countless meals. Copper pots and pans hung from iron hooks, left behind by the previous owner, their surfaces dulled by age. A wooden table, nicked and scratched from years of use, stood in the center of the room, a testament to the many meals and conversations it had hosted. A small window above the sink framed a view of the garden, where grapevines climbed a trellis and orange trees swayed gently in the breeze.

Amara wandered into the living room, where a large stone fireplace dominated one wall. The blackened stone of the fireplace still held its beauty. Shelves built into the walls on either side of it added to the room's charm. The living room opened onto a large terrace, perched right at the cliff's edge. Wrought iron chairs with sun-faded cushions circled an old stone table, and an overgrown bench rested under a lemon tree. From here, Amara could see the jagged Faraglioni rocks jutting from the turquoise waters below, each one catching the light like a jewel. The view made the rest of the world feel distant with the sea, the cliffs, and this old stone house nestled between them.

Inside the thick stone walls of the farmhouse seemed to hum with ancient energy. Wooden beams lined the high ceilings, their edges softened by time. Amara ran her fingers along the rough stone and smiled at its imperfections—each one felt like a story waiting to be told. In the master bedroom, a wrought-iron bed frame sat beneath a sloped ceiling. The bed was draped with decaying white fabric, fluttering gently in the breeze that came through the open windows. Heavy wooden shutters rested against the walls of each window.

Amara walked down a hall with bedrooms lined up on both sides. There were six bedrooms in the house. At the end of the hall there was a narrow staircase. The realtor said the stairs led to the attic and which was full of dusty old relics of the past. Amara climbed the narrow staircase, each step creaking beneath her weight. Dust floated in the sunlight as she pushed the attic door open, revealing a room filled with old trunks, forgotten furniture, and personal belongings left behind by previous owners. The space whispered of secrets and untold stories and something deeper, a presence waiting. Amara would explore these old relics of the past but not today.

Standing in the living room, Amara took a deep breath taking in the faint saltiness of the sea through the opened windows. This wasn't just a house—it had a soul, and she belonged here.

Amara turned to the real estate agent, a slim older woman with silver hair neatly pinned in a bun.

"I'll take it, and I'll pay cash," Amara said, her voice calm but resolute.

The agent raised an eyebrow. "Don't you want an inspection on an old place like this? You're sure?"

"I'm absolutely sure," Amara smiled. "It feels like it was waiting for me."

Amara closed on the farmhouse a few weeks later. Papers followed like a tide: signatures, stamps, a rustle of copy sheets. The closing happened in a small office where the walls were painted the exact white of Capri noon. When the last page lay signed and the folder closed, the agent pressed the iron key into Amara's palm. It was warm.

"Benvenuto a casa," she said.

Amara stepped into the lane with the key clutched lightly in her hand, and whispered to no one and to everything, "I'm home."

***

The truck came at first light, low gears grinding up the lane. By then she had scrubbed the kitchen tiles, thrown open the shutters, and tied her hair back with a scarf the color of seawater. The island air carried the jasmine in from the garden and the metal-salt scent that rises when the waves strike rock.

Two men unloaded her small collection of furniture with a care that made it feel larger: a simple linen-covered sofa in the paler shade between cream and pearl; a chest of drawers with a dovetailed edge; a reading chair; a bedframe. They worked with little talk. When they did speak, it was in the short sentences of people who trust their hands more than their words.

They set the sofa so it faced the terrace doors, the chair beside the hearth. As one man passed through the entry, he paused and glanced up. A small, decorative nail in the plaster held no picture now, only a faint outline where a frame had once shaded the wall from the sun. He squinted, then shrugged, and kept moving.

Amara signed their invoice and handed them water, cold and beading. "Grazie," she said. "For taking such care."

"It's a good house," the older man said, surprising her with English shaped by island vowels. He tipped his cap toward the terrace, "Una casa che guarda il mare." A house that watches the sea.

"That's exactly how it feels," Amara said.

They wished her buona fortuna and were gone, the truck's sound shrinking down the lane until the island took it back.

Silence came in stages. First, the ordinary hush that follows work. Then the longer quiet that seems to arrive in rooms where something important is about to begin.

She walked through each space again, barefoot now, the cool tiles calming the warm pulse in her feet. In the kitchen she poured hot tè caldo into a mug and stood with her hands wrapped around the herbal tea, listening to the first small creaks the house made as afternoon shifted toward evening. On the terrace, she moved the chairs a little as if arranging old friends for a conversation. The lemon tree threw specks of gold across the stones. A fishing boat stitched a white line across the bay and vanished behind rock.

Night fell as a deepening of blue rather than an arrival of dark. Island lights began to come on, a measured constellation answering the one above it. Amara made a simple meal—bread warmed in the oven, bright tomatoes, olives, a soft cheese—and ate at the old table with the doors open to the sea. Somewhere below, the water worked itself against the cliff with patient insistence.

In bed, clean linen cool against her skin, she waited for sleep. The house settled as old houses do: a soft stretch here, a sigh through timber there. Once, something tapped the shutter, delicate as a fingernail. She sat up, listened. Only the hush of the garden, the low rush of the night breeze.

"It's an old house," she told the dark. "I'm not afraid."

The wind shifted, and the lemon leaves made a sound like paper being slowly turned. Drowsiness came and went, a tide failing to decide which direction to go. When she finally drifted, she dreamed of an old golden key in an ancient lock and heard words she couldn't understand.

Near dawn, another sound woke her—not from inside, but from the world just beyond the terrace: a brief scrape, stone against stone. She moved to the doors and found the garden still as a painting. On the table, the ceramic dish she'd left there had shifted an inch. She could not remember moving it.

"Wind," she said, but softly, as if negotiating.

On the far side of the bay, the first smear of pink began to lift the edge of the night. She stood and watched it come on, hands around a sweater pulled close. Her breath made a small cloud she could almost see.

And then, without warning, a warmth rose beneath her breastbone and spread outward, not painful, not even truly heat, more like recognition. She pressed her palm there and felt the warmth.

She laughed once, surprised and breathless. "I'm here," she whispered. "I'm listening."

Down in the lane, a car door closed. The sound did not carry to the terrace. It did not need to. The man who had closed it was already walking, unhurried, hands in his pockets, tasting the salt on the air like a detail to be recorded. He did not approach the house, not tonight. He stood where the olive trees began, and the world dropped away and watched the square of light in an upstairs window.

"La prescelta," he said to the dawn, the word unvoiced, the lips shaping it as a habit.

The window dimmed as the sky brightened. He waited a moment longer, then turned back toward the car. The lane swallowed him without sound.

Chapter Four
The Key Unearthed

Evening light poured over the vineyard, gilding the weeds that had long claimed the rows of stakes. Amara stood at the edge, shading her eyes as though she could see past the neglect to the vision she carried—clusters of ripe grapes, the crush of harvest, the press of wine dark as rubies. It would take time, but she could almost feel the vines waiting for her hand.

Inside, the kitchen was alive with the scent of rosemary and garlic. Amara had spent two days preparing—fresh loaves from the market, roasted vegetables, handmade pasta, a tiramisu cooling beneath a linen cloth. Candles flickered in brass holders she'd found abandoned in a cupboard, casting gold across the stone walls. The house, once hollow, felt warm and expectant.

When a car crunched up the gravel, she hurried out.

"Ciao, bella! We're here!" Sophia's voice rang, bright as ever. She flung her arms around Amara, curls bouncing. "My God—this place! It's straight out of a fairy tale."

Franco followed, grinning beneath his salt-and-pepper beard. "A medieval fairy tale," he said. "The kind where castles whisper and ghosts still walk the halls."

Amara laughed, though the remark moved her strangely. "Come in. There's plenty of food and wine."

They gathered at the farmhouse table, the air full of laughter and the clink of glasses. Sophia kicked off her shoes, eyes roaming the beams overhead. "Honestly, Amara, why would anyone leave this house empty? It's incredible."

Franco raised his glass. "To new beginnings. And to Capri, for claiming our Amara."

Glasses chimed, wine glowed, the farmhouse seemed to exhale. For a time, grief felt far away.

Later, on the terrace, the night grew quieter. Jasmine and sea-salt tangled in the air, crickets sang in the dark. Sophia leaned closer, voice low. "So… you mentioned the movers said something odd?"

Amara hesitated, swirling her wine. "They told me this house holds a secret. Something the original owners protected. A Brotherhood of some kind. Supposedly, only the true owner will ever uncover it." She gave a small shrug. "It sounds like folklore. But…"

Franco tilted his head. "Folklore usually has a seed of truth."

Sophia shivered playfully. "A hidden secret waiting centuries to be found? It's like something out of a Dan Brown novel."

Amara smiled, but the unease lingered. "I can't explain it, but I feel as though I was meant to be here. Like the house chose me."

Franco's gaze was steady. "Then maybe it did."

The next night, they piled into Franco's car for dinner at a trattoria in the village. The road wound through olive groves, headlights carving the dark. Amara leaned into the open window, her hair streaming in the breeze. She was just about to tell them how alive she felt when the sound of a horn shattered the moment.

A sleek black car surged up behind them, too fast, weaving through the narrow road. Its headlights flared in the mirrors.

Franco gripped the wheel. "Idiots. There's no room to pass here."

The car pressed closer, its tinted windows giving nothing away. Amara's stomach tightened. Sophia twisted in her seat. "They're tailing us—why?"

No answer came. The farmhouse felt far away now, swallowed by the night.

At last, as they entered the village streets, the car dropped back. Franco pulled into the trattoria's valet line, jaw tight. The black car crawled past, slowing, lingering—then slipped away without a sound.

Sophia shivered. "That was… unsettling."

Amara forced a smile, though her pulse hadn't steadied. "Coincidence. Has to be."

The trattoria was warm, full of light and chatter. Plates of pasta and bottles of local wine softened the edges of the encounter. By dessert, their laughter returned. Still, when Amara glanced out the window, she thought she saw headlights pause just beyond the piazza.

Back at the farmhouse terrace, the night was calm again. Franco poured the last of the wine. "Amara," he said gently, "it's time you learned this house's history. Legends don't grow this strong without roots."

Sophia nodded, curling into her chair. "I know a historian in Naples. He can dig into old property records. If there's anything to the Brotherhood story, he can find it."

Amara listened, her hand resting unconsciously on the table's worn surface. The memory of the black car, the movers' words, the strange flickers of light—all of it gathered in her chest.

She glanced toward the attic staircase just visible through the doorway, shadow pooling at its base.

"Yes," she said softly. "It's time."

That night, long after her friends had gone to bed, Amara walked barefoot through the farmhouse. The beams creaked above, the shutters ticked against their frames. At the foot of the attic stairs she stopped, heart beating in her throat. She half-expected to hear tapping again, soft and deliberate.

Nothing came. Only silence, deep and patient.

She turned away, whispering as though to the house itself: "Tomorrow."

But as she slipped beneath her sheets, her dreams filled with trunks and keys, and whispers in a tongue she almost understood.

Chapter Five
Whispers in the Walls

Morning light shimmered across the vineyard stakes still holding the promise of fruit. Franco and Sophia loaded their bags into the trunk, their voices light with farewell. Amara stood nearby, arms folded loosely, smiling though her chest tightened at the thought of their absence.

"I still can't believe you found a place like this," Sophia said, brushing a curl from her face. "It's perfect. Like it was waiting for you."

Amara glanced toward the farmhouse, its windows catching the sun. "That's exactly how it feels. I want to dig into its history and figure out why it pulls at me so strongly."

Franco closed the trunk with a solid click. His eyes lingered on the house. "Just be careful. Places like this… they carry energy."

"I know," Amara said softly. "I feel it."

Sophia squeezed her hand. "If there's something to these legends, you'll find it."

Amara's smile was grateful, but her heart was already racing ahead. She waved them off as the car disappeared down the lane, the sound of the engine fading into birdsong and sea wind. Instead of loneliness, a steady calm filled her. The house was hers now. And it was time.

Inside, silence settled like a companion. She brewed coffee in her Moka pot, the sharp scent rising with the hiss of steam. Laptop open on the table, she began to search: property records, newspaper archives, fragments of folklore.

The history was fractured. The house had changed hands rarely across centuries, sometimes sitting empty for decades at a time. One family kept it under their name for twenty years without ever returning, paying a caretaker to care for it. Earlier records blurred into whispers.

Her search uncovered a name that repeated like a shadow: the Brotherhood. They were never the center of the stories, only fragments in footnotes—guardians of something unspoken, linked always to Anacapri, always circling the farmhouse without ever being named outright.

Amara leaned back, coffee forgotten. Her heartbeat harder, not from fear but recognition.

That night, sleep came slowly. When it did, it dragged her into a dream so vivid it felt like memory: a chamber lit by candles, her hand holding a seal etched with symbols she almost understood, voices around her speaking in an ancient tongue that carried weight more than sound. She woke before dawn with her pulse hammering; breath caught in her throat.

She pressed her palms to her eyes. That wasn't just a dream. That was me.

Without waiting, she reached for her phone. Sophia answered groggily but brightened at her urgency.

"Sophia, I need your help," Amara said. "I found references to a group called, the Brotherhood in the records—and last night, I dreamed of them. Not a story, not imagination—it felt like a memory. As if I've been here before, as if I was part of it."

Sophia's voice sharpened. "That's... intense. Sometimes dreams open doors. Sometimes they warn. Are you sure it wasn't—"

"It was real," Amara cut in, her voice low but certain. "You mentioned someone—a historian?"

"Yes," Sophia said slowly. "Sebastiano D'Amato. His family's been on Capri for generations. He's... connected. Knows the island's history better than anyone. "And" she hesitated, "I asked around after our visit. He knows a lot about your farmhouse. More than most."

Amara's breath caught at the name. "Sebastiano… D'Amato." The syllables felt weighted, as if she had spoken them before somewhere… in another life?

Sophia went on. "I'll text you his number. But, Amara… please be careful. That black car that followed us—it doesn't feel like coincidence anymore. If the Brotherhood guarded something dangerous, there may be people still guarding—or hunting—it now."

"I'll be careful," Amara promised, though her heart was already moving faster. "But I have to know. This house is calling to me."

After the call ended, she set the phone on the table. For a moment she just sat, listening to the house breathe around her. Then she whispered aloud, not sure to whom:

"I'm ready."

Chapter Six
The Hidden Hand

The morning sun spilled through the tall farmhouse windows, painting the kitchen in honey-gold. Amara poured her second cup of coffee, her nerves thrumming. She had tried Sebastiano D'Amato's number three times, each call ending in silence, then voicemail. At last, a curt text had come:

Caffè Vista. 3 PM.

By the time she stepped into the café on Capri's main square, her anticipation had sharpened into resolve. The place hummed with locals and tourists, the scent of espresso and lemon tarts mingling in the air. She saw him at once.

Sebastiano D'Amato was impossible to miss. Leaning near the window, he carried himself with the ease of someone who belonged anywhere—streets, palaces, or shadows. His dark eyes lifted, found hers, and for the briefest instant something unreadable flickered across his face. Recognition—or something older. He rose with quiet authority.

"Signora Savard," he greeted, his voice low, carrying the warmth of his Italian accent.

"Amara, please." She offered her hand. His grip was firm, deliberate, and the calm weight of his presence unsettled her more than she expected.

"Amara, then," he said, his smile faint but precise, as though testing the sound of her name. He gestured to the seat across from him.

She sat, smoothing her skirt, willing her heart to steady. He was striking in a way that unsettled her—his features refined but edged, as though something untamed lived beneath the polish. She hadn't let herself look at a man this way since Dean. The thought of her late husband brushed through her like cold water, but Sebastiano's presence was difficult to ignore.

"Thank you for meeting me," she said. "I know you're busy."

"Busy, yes," he replied. "But the Brotherhood is not a trivial subject. And you believe your farmhouse is tied to them?"

"Yes," she said, leaning slightly forward. "At least... that's what I've been told."

He studied her carefully, his gaze steady but not unkind. Up close, Amara caught the faint scent of sandalwood and leather, an earthy undertone that seemed to suit him. She took a quiet breath, forcing her thoughts to remain steady.

"And what have you found so far?" Sebastiano asked, his tone casual but the question weighted. "Any unusual markings? Writings? Symbols?"

Amara hesitated. There was something in his manner—controlled, probing—that made her wary. "Only fragments," she answered. "Mentions of the Brotherhood hiding something in the house in old records. Nothing concrete."

His lips curved almost imperceptibly. "Sometimes fragments are everything."

For a moment they sat in silence, the bustle of the café moving around them. Amara felt his gaze press just enough to stir something inside her—both caution and an inexplicable pull.

Sebastiano's own thoughts moved like a double current. She was beautiful, yes, but it was more than that. She carried herself with an unconscious grace that unsettled him. And she fit too perfectly with the descriptions he'd studied for years—the woman the Brotherhood's prophecy had named, the one who could unlock what centuries had kept hidden. His employer would stop at nothing to possess her knowledge.

And yet...

As he looked at her across the small table, he felt the first crack in his certainty. He had been sent to uncover what she held. To lead her, if necessary, into revealing it. But the longer he watched her, the more the lines between duty and something far older blurred.

Amara lifted her cup, her eyes never leaving his. "If the Brotherhood really did hide something, then it's been waiting for centuries. Why now? Why me?"

Sebastiano tilted his head, the faintest shadow passing his features. "Perhaps," he said, "because some doors only open when the right hand reaches for the key."

Her pulse quickened, though she didn't know why. She had the distinct feeling he was speaking of more than the farmhouse.

Chapter Seven
The Attic

The farmhouse was quiet when Amara returned, the last glow of dusk painting the sea in molten gold. Sebastiano had suggested coming by in the morning to "help" her with the search. His intensity unsettled her. She was drawn to him, yes—but there was something guarded, shadowed, behind his eyes. She didn't know if she could trust him.

Tonight, she would search alone.

The house greeted her with its familiar hush. She lit a single lamp in the kitchen, its circle of light a fragile defense against the growing dark. Her gaze kept drifting toward the narrow staircase that led to the attic. Since she'd moved in, she had passed it again and again, each time feeling the same pull.

She could not resist it now.

The stairs groaned beneath her steps, dust rising around her. At the top, a heavy wooden door waited, its surface furred with neglect. She pressed her palm against the old wood, and for a heartbeat, warmth pulsed beneath her skin. She exhaled sharply, then pushed the door open.

Cool, stale air enveloped her. The attic spread wide, cluttered with forgotten furniture and shrouded shapes. Dust floated in her flashlight's beam, twisting like smoke. Each step she took seemed to stir something awake.

She brushed her hand against the slanted ceiling—and light bloomed.

Symbols flickered to life across the timbers, faint at first, then pulsing brighter. Spirals, crosses, constellations—patterns she almost recognized. They pulsed as if answering her heartbeat. A low hum filled her ears, rising until the attic itself seemed to vibrate.

Her vision blurred. The room dissolved.

Suddenly she was weightless, suspended in a sky without horizon. Stars blazed around her, brilliant and alive. Constellations shifted into place, weaving themselves into a design she could not name yet somehow knew was meant for her. The stars pulsed in rhythm, beckoning, calling her deeper into their pattern.

Her breath caught. She recognized this map. She had known it once before.

The sensation pulled her under, vast and consuming— until she snapped back, gasping.

Amara found herself lying on a dust-covered couch, her phone's flashlight still glowing where it had fallen. The attic was silent, patient, as though holding its breath.

Fragments of what she had seen shimmered in her mind: stars shifting like gears, symbols etched in light, a presence that whispered of purpose. She pressed a hand to her chest, and for an instant the intense warmth returned.

"I've been here before," she whispered. The words came without thought, carrying a truth that felt older than her life. She could almost see herself centuries ago, standing in this very room, part of something hidden and holy. A role. A vow. A secret that had waited with her across lifetimes.

Destiny pressed around her like a cloak. She was not here by chance.

Outside, beneath the olive trees at the edge of the lane, a black car idled in silence. Its headlights were dark, its engine cold. Sebastiano sat motionless in the driver's seat, his gaze fixed on the farmhouse. He had been there every night, watching, waiting.

When the attic window flared with shifting light, his hands tightened around the steering wheel.

So. The house had awakened.

And she was the one to stir it.

For generations, the secret had resisted every hand, every attempt to pry it open. Tonight, the silence had broken.

Sebastiano leaned back in the shadows, his jaw set. He knew what this meant. For her. For him. For Marchetti.

For the world.

Chapter Eight
The Awakening

The ringing of the phone dragged Amara out of a heavy, dreamless sleep. She groaned, fumbling across the nightstand, only to knock the receiver to the floor with a clatter. The shrill sound cut off abruptly, leaving her in the silence of the farmhouse.

She rolled onto her back, eyes half-closed against the morning light. Her body felt as though she'd run a marathon in her sleep. The attic had left its mark: the glow of symbols, the rush of stars, the strange weight of recognition. She pressed her palms to her eyes, trying to hold onto the fragments before they slipped away.

The peace lasted only a moment.

The brass bell at the front door rang sharply through the house. Once. Twice. Then came the heavy thud of the knocker, impatient, unyielding.

She groaned into her pillow. Whoever it was, they weren't leaving.

Dragging herself upright, she shuffled into the hallway, smoothing her tangled hair with her fingers. In the mirror, she caught her reflection: smudged eyes, tousled waves, the look of someone who had seen ghosts. She almost laughed. Perfect. Just what I need if it's the gas man or Jehovah's Witnesses.

The bell clanged again, harder this time.

"I'm coming," she muttered, pulling the latch.

The door swung open.

Sebastiano D'Amato stood on the threshold, framed by morning light. His suit was immaculate, his presence composed, his eyes unreadable. For a long moment, neither spoke. His gaze swept over her, lingering just long enough to make her suddenly aware of her bare feet and tangled hair.

Amusement flickered across his face, subtle and fleeting. "Buon pomeriggio," he said softly.

Amara's heart thudded once, hard. Of all the mornings he could arrive, it had to be this one. "Sebastiano," she managed, tugging her robe tighter around her. "You're… early."

He inclined his head slightly, as if he hadn't just caught her unguarded and rumpled. "I said I would come this afternoon. Why are you surprised?"

She blinked at him, still caught between irritation, attraction, and the exhaustion that clung like a second skin. "Because some of us actually sleep," she muttered, then immediately regretted it when his mouth curved in the faintest grin.

It wasn't unkind. But it wasn't nice either.

Chapter Nine
The Warning

"Bello vederti, Amara."

His voice carried a smooth steadiness, but beneath it ran something else—urgency.

She blinked, still adjusting to his sudden presence on her doorstep. "I didn't expect you so early," she said, trying to keep the irritation from her tone. "Did you have to nearly break the bell?"

A faint smile tugged at his lips. "I wasn't sure you'd answer otherwise."

Amara folded her arms across her chest, leaning against the frame. "You said you would be here this afternoon. What is so urgent at that you would arrive at—" she glanced at the clock behind her, then froze. "Four in the afternoon?"

Her voice pitched up. "It's four?"

Heat crept into her cheeks. She suddenly realized she was standing in the doorway in an old Green Day T-shirt and boy shorts patterned with tiny hearts. Her hair was tousled, her eyes shadowed from sleep. She ran a quick hand through her waves, wishing she'd at least brushed her teeth first.

Sebastiano's eyes flickered with the faintest gleam of amusement, though his expression remained otherwise unreadable. "Apparently you needed the rest," he said.

Mortified, she stepped aside. "Come in."

He entered with the ease of someone accustomed to belonging anywhere. His gaze moved over the farmhouse—not the curious glance of a first-time visitor, but the recognition of someone reacquainting himself with a familiar space. He brushed a hand along the back of a chair as he passed the hearth, then stopped at the kitchen's threshold, sunlight gilding his sharp profile.

"This suits you," he said at last. "The furniture, the air of it—it feels as if you've lived here forever."

Amara frowned slightly, following him into the kitchen. "Most of this I picked out in Naples," she said. "Some pieces were already here, but… you sound like you've been in this house before."

He said nothing, only folded his arms and leaned against the counter, his presence filling the space with unsettling calm.

"Espresso?" she asked quickly, if only to ground herself. "I wouldn't say no."

She busied herself at the stovetop, relieved to turn her back as she set her moka pot on the burner and got two tazzinas from the cupboard for the expresso. "Please give me a minute to change. I'd rather not discuss ancient secrets in pajamas."

He inclined his head in silent agreement, though his eyes followed her until she disappeared up the stairs.

When she returned—jeans, cotton shirt, hair brushed into loose waves—Sebastiano was seated at the scarred wooden table, espresso in hand. Sunlight caught on his cheekbone, carving his profile in gold. He looked perfectly at ease, as though the farmhouse belonged to him.

Amara's steps slowed. For a moment, she could almost believe it.

He turned his gaze to her, steady and dark. "You make a strong cup," he said.

She poured herself a cup of expresso and met his intense eyes. "Hard to go wrong with beans this good."

Silence stretched between them, charged, the steam curling from their cups like smoke from a signal fire.

Finally, she set her cup down. "You seem very comfortable here. Too comfortable. As if you know this place."

Sebastiano's eyes narrowed slightly, and for the first time, his composure cracked—just enough to reveal the edge beneath. He leaned forward, his voice low. "I saw the lights last night from the attic."

Amara's heart jolted. "You... saw them?"

"Yes." His gaze never wavered. "The windows glowed as if the house itself had caught fire. Whatever happened up there was astounding."

Her throat tightened. If he'd seen the attic, it meant he had been outside—watching. "Why were you here?" she asked, sharper than intended. "And why do you move through this house like you already know it?"

He set his cup down with deliberate care, his jaw taut. "Because I do."

Her breath caught, but he pressed on.

"This farmhouse wasn't only a home. It was a sanctuary for the Brotherhood—a place where leaders met, where secrets were kept. They were not a myth, Amara. They were guardians of knowledge powerful enough to alter the course of the world."

She stared at him, trying to process the weight of his words. "And what kind of knowledge could do that?"

"The kind people would kill for." His voice darkened. "And they already have."

The air in the kitchen thickened. Amara's pulse raced, but she forced herself to ask the question she already feared the answer to. "And you? Why do you know all this?"

Sebastiano hesitated, just for a breath, then leaned closer, his tone dropping to a near whisper. "Because I've been studying this place for years. Documents, maps, fragments of prophecy. And because I know what others are willing to do to find it."

His eyes locked onto hers, steady and unflinching. "You've stepped into something far bigger than yourself, Amara. And if you don't understand the danger—very soon—it may be too late."

Chapter Ten
Heat

Amara set her cup down, folding her arms. "Please explain what's going on. After everything you've just told me, I need answers."

Sebastiano's jaw tightened, as though he were weighing every word. "You will have them but not today." His gaze flicked toward the walls, the beams overhead, even the windowpanes. "This house has been watched for a very long time. We cannot be sure who has seen me come here."

A chill slid down her spine. "Watched? You mean—"

"Yes," he said firmly. "Eyes you cannot see. Tomorrow evening, we'll meet somewhere quiet. There's a place— Trattoria della Luna. You know it?"

She nodded. A small restaurant tucked in a narrow street. Discreet. "I've passed by. Never been inside."

"Tomorrow at 8pm, then." His tone left no room for hesitation.

As he stood, adjusting his jacket, Amara felt the kitchen shrink around them. He stepped close—too close—and brushed his hands along her arms before resting them lightly on her shoulders. His lips touched her cheek, then the other, lingering just long enough to blur the line between custom and intimacy.

Amara's breath caught. The warmth of his skin, the faint spice of his cologne, even the rasp of his stubble—all of it unsettled her, tugging her into a heat she hadn't felt in years.

For the briefest moment, his mouth hovered a fraction closer than was proper. His dark eyes flickered with restraint, with want. Then he pulled back.

"Tomorrow," he said, his voice smooth, but heavy with something unsaid.

She stood frozen as he left, the kitchen golden with late sun, the imprint of his presence still thick in the air.

The farmhouse fell silent.

Amara leaned against the table, trying to steady her pulse. She almost laughed at herself—She began the day in a Green Day T-shirt, heart-covered boy shorts, and she had just nearly lost herself in the presence of a man who carried secrets like a cloak.

But before she could shake the moment away, the quiet shifted.

A soft creak overhead.

Her gaze snapped to the ceiling. The attic.

Another sound—a deliberate tap, as though someone had pressed a finger against the wood and released.

Amara's throat tightened. She forced herself to move, padding softly into the hall, glancing up the staircase. Nothing stirred. But the feeling was back, stronger than before: she was not alone.

The silence stretched. The house seemed to hold its breath.

Then, faint but clear, came a whisper of air through the attic door—like a sigh.

Amara backed slowly into the kitchen, her hand pressing to her chest.

Sebastiano's words echoed in her mind: Stay out of the attic for now.

She poured herself the rest of the espresso, her hand trembling as she lifted the cup. For the first time, the farmhouse did not feel like hers. It felt like something watching her, waiting.

Chapter Eleven
Divided Loyalties

Sebastiano unlocked the door of his rented villa just as the sun bled into the horizon, staining the sky in ribbons of crimson and gold. The place was sleek and modern—white walls, cold marble, glass that caught the dying light—but it held none of the warmth of Amara's farmhouse. He tossed his jacket over a chair and poured himself a measure of whiskey, the amber liquid catching the glow.

He sank into the armchair, staring at the horizon without seeing it. His mind was elsewhere.

This assignment was meant to be routine: infiltrate, observe, retrieve. But Amara had unsettled everything. She wasn't a mark, not anymore. She was a force, drawing him in, making him question loyalties he had never allowed himself to question before.

He took a long swallow of whiskey, the burn sharp in his throat.

Duke Antonio Marchetti.

The name itself carried weight—half aristocrat, half predator. A man born into privilege and polished in cruelty. Where others wielded money, Marchetti wielded fear, and he did it with the grace of someone who had never been told "no." His reach stretched across governments and corporations, his empire a labyrinth of shadowed dealings: weapons, resources, even lives, traded like currency.

Sebastiano's family had served him for generations. His father, his uncles—each bound to Marchetti's will. As a boy, Sebastiano had been groomed the same way: taught to obey, to strike, to bury any hesitation. Loyalty was survival. Disobedience was death.

For years, he had carried out orders without hesitation, his conscience dulled by duty. But now…

Now there was Amara.

He set the glass down with a sharp click, his fingers tightening on the armrest. She was not like anyone he had known since his wife—the only woman who had ever breached his armor, the one whose absence had hollowed him out. He had buried that grief under years of obedience. But Amara awakened it again, raw and insistent.

She carried something within her—a light, a purpose—that made his world of shadows feel unbearable. And Marchetti would see that light only as something to exploit, to extinguish if necessary.

Sebastiano leaned forward, elbows on his knees, head bowed. The choice clawed at him.

Bring Marchetti the secret he demanded. Or protect the woman who was becoming more than he had ever intended her to be.

And he knew: there would be no middle ground.

Chapter Twelve
The Key

Duke Antonio Marchetti sat in the vast quiet of his private office, where centuries-old grandeur met the cold precision of modern power. Golden light from floor-to-ceiling windows washed across carved mahogany, antique bronzes, and the gleam of holographic monitors hovering above his desk. Outside, the gardens stretched in perfect symmetry, every hedge trimmed, every path aligned—a reflection of the man who owned them.

Marchetti leaned back in his chair, fingers steepled beneath his chin. Silver hair caught the glow, polished like a crown. His face, smoothed by treatments and sharpened by bone structure, could have passed for a man twenty years younger. But his eyes—ice-blue, unblinking—belonged to someone ageless in ambition.

A knock.

He didn't turn. "Enter."

One of his aides stepped inside, tablet in hand. He moved with the silence of long training, placing the device on the desk. With a flick of Marchetti's wrist, streams of data bloomed into light: surveillance feeds, maps, transcripts.

"Updates," Marchetti said, his voice carrying the faintest trace of old European aristocracy.

"Savard remains at the farmhouse," the aide reported crisply. "She has made contact with Sebastiano D'Amato. Activity was observed in the attic last night—unexplained light phenomena. D'Amato confirms progress, but says the key has not yet been fully activated."

Marchetti's gaze flicked across the projection, reading faster than most men could think. At the mention of the key, his lips curved.

For years, the Brotherhood had been his obsession. Their fragments—symbols, manuscripts, maps—had slipped through centuries like sand through fingers, until Marchetti's men had unearthed them piece by piece. The Brotherhood had not hidden their knowledge behind locks or vaults. They had hidden it inside a person.

A rightful owner.

Drawn by the house. Claimed by it.

Amara Savard.

Her path to the farmhouse had not been chance. The ad she saw, the price, the whispers that nudged her curiosity— every step had been arranged, just as the prophecy required.

"Good," Marchetti murmured. His voice was soft, but final. "It begins."

He dismissed the aide with a flick of his hand. Alone again, he turned his chair toward the windows. The estate shimmered in the late light, ordered and obedient.

Amara believed she had chosen. But Marchetti knew better.

She was the key.

And soon, she would open the lock that no one else had touched in four hundred years.

When she did, the world itself would kneel.

Chapter Thirteen
The Meeting

Trattoria della Luna glowed like a jewel on its quiet cobblestone street. Lanterns hung from wrought-iron brackets, spilling amber light over the arched doorway. Inside, the air hummed with warmth—terracotta walls painted with fading pastoral murals, wooden beams overhead, candlelight flickering across white-linen tables. A violin sang softly in the corner, weaving its notes through the clink of glasses and low conversation.

Amara stepped inside, and for a moment the room shifted. She wore red—off the shoulder, the fabric clinging to her with effortless grace. Her dark hair was swept into an elegant knot, loose strands brushing her cheek, her eyes bright as though lit from within. Heads turned. Conversations paused. She carried the air of someone who belonged, though she herself still didn't know it.

Sebastiano had been waiting at the bar, a glass of deep Barolo in his hand. When he saw her, the measured rhythm of his breath faltered. For a heartbeat, he was no longer the watchful operative, the man trained to master every expression. He was simply a man undone by the sight of her.

"Amara," he said as she reached him, his voice low. "You look… extraordinary."

She flushed lightly, though her smile was steady. "Thank you."

He gestured toward a secluded table in the corner—private, yet with a clear view of the room. A place where one could talk, and one could watch.

They dined slowly, the wine flowing as easily as conversation. He ordered bruschetta, prosciutto with melon, marinated artichokes. Between bites, they spoke of Naples, of Capri's cliffs, of small things that circled carefully around the larger truths. But under it all ran an unspoken current—his eyes lingering too long, her pulse quickening when his voice dipped softer. They never spoke of the Brotherhood and the dangers they had come to discuss. Sebastiano was finding it hard to think with her eyes looking straight through to his soul

Sebastiano battled the tension within. His loyalty to Marchetti, drilled into him since youth, pulled one way. The woman across from him—light in her laughter, resolve in her eyes—pulled the other. He had never felt so divided.

Marchetti would see Amara only as a tool. A key. A thing to be used, broken if necessary. And Sebastiano knew: if he followed orders, she would not survive.

Amara tilted her head, studying him. "You seem far away," she said softly.

He forced a faint smile. "Just taking it all in."

But his grip on the wineglass betrayed him.

Later, when the plates had been cleared and the last of the wine lingered in their glasses, Amara leaned closer. "Would you like to come back to my place?" she asked, her tone casual, though her eyes held something deeper. "The terrace overlooks the sea. It's a beautiful night."

Sebastiano's heart tightened. He could not mistake what she was offering—not simply the terrace, but closeness, trust. His answer came with quiet conviction. "Yes," he said.

They rose, the hush of the restaurant wrapping around them as they stepped out into the cool night. The street was almost empty, lanterns swaying gently in the breeze. The distant crash of waves reached up from the dark cliffs.

At her car, Amara turned to him, smiling faintly. "I'll see you there."

Sebastiano gave a small nod, his expression composed, though inside his pulse thundered. She slipped into her car, the red of her dress catching the lantern light before the door closed.

He watched her taillights glow against the night as she pulled away. Then he followed, his own headlights cutting the shadows of the winding road.

Neither of them saw the black car parked two streets away, its engine idling, lights off. Inside, a figure sat in silence, phone in hand. A message was typed quickly, then sent.

They're together. Heading to the farmhouse.

The net was already closing.

Chapter Fourteen
The Terrace

The road to Anacapri wound like a ribbon along the cliffs, headlights glancing off stone walls and sudden drops where the sea glittered far below. Sebastiano followed at a careful distance, watching Amara's taillights carve the darkness ahead. He kept one hand steady on the wheel, the other tightening on the leather as thoughts circled: her invitation, Marchetti's shadow, the prophecy binding them both.

When Amara's car turned into the drive, Sebastiano slowed, letting her reach the house first. He parked a moment later, stepping out into the cool night air scented with jasmine and salt.

Amara stood waiting at the door, a shawl draped around her shoulders. Candlelight flickered through the window beside her in the farmhouse kitchen, but it was the starlight above that made her seem almost unreal—soft, radiant, as though she belonged more to the night sky than to the earth.

"I wasn't sure you'd follow," she said, her voice low but steady.

Sebastiano's lips curved faintly, his eyes meeting hers. "You invited me."

She smiled at that, stepping aside so he could enter. Amara poured them each a glass of Barollo and they carried the wine out to the terrace, where the sea stretched endless and black, flecked with silver light from the moon.

They sat across from each other at the old stone table, the quiet between them more charged than words. Amara's shawl slipped, baring the smooth line of her collarbone. Sebastiano's gaze flicked there, then away, the restraint costing him more than he cared to admit.

"You've been holding something back," she said softly, watching him. "Not just about the house. About yourself."

His hand tightened briefly around the stem of his glass. He should lie, deflect, but the warmth in her eyes made the truth press harder against his chest. "I've lived in shadows a long time," he said at last. "For a man I shouldn't serve. And yet—I have. Too long."

Amara tilted her head, studying him. "And now?"

Sebastiano looked at her then, truly looked, the mask slipping. "Now I wonder if I've already betrayed him simply by being here with you."

The air between them pulsed. Amara set her glass down, rising slowly from her chair. Sebastiano followed without thinking, drawn to her like the tide to the shore. They stopped only a breath apart, her eyes luminous in the starlight.

She lifted a hand, fingertips grazing the line of his jaw. He closed his eyes briefly at the touch, every muscle in him taut with the effort not to close the space between them.

"I don't know why I trust you," she whispered.

"Perhaps you shouldn't," he murmured, his voice rougher than he intended.

But when her hand lingered, he leaned into it—just enough to betray himself.

For a heartbeat, it seemed inevitable: the kiss, the surrender. But Sebastiano drew back, his breath unsteady. "If I cross this line... I won't stop," he said, though the words cost him.

Amara's chest rose with a sharp breath, but she nodded. She could feel it too—giving in to what they both wanted, would consume them both.

Instead, they stood together in silence for a while, watching the waves crash against the rocks far below. The bond between them had already deepened, woven tighter than either of them could untangle. Deeper than either of them wanted to untangle. Sebastiano made no move to leave. They continued to watch the water below. Both fighting the impulse to move into each other's arms.

Chapter Fourteen
Sparks on the Terrace

The terrace was washed in silver light, the sea stretching endlessly below as the waves whispered against the cliffs. The wine now gone, had been replaced with a bottle of limoncello that sat between them, its golden liquid glowing in the candlelight. Amara leaned back in her chair, the night air teasing loose strands of hair around her face.

"This is perfect," she murmured, her voice softened by the warmth of wine and liqueur. "The company, the view… even the breeze. It feels like something out of a dream."

Sebastiano said nothing at first, his gaze lingering on her. The lamplight caught in her eyes, and for a moment, he forgot every reason he should keep his distance.

When she tilted her head at him, curiosity flickering across her face, he finally spoke. "Words aren't enough tonight," he said, his voice low.

He reached for her then, cupping her face with hands both strong and gentle. Amara caught her breath, the suddenness of the touch electrifying, and before she could think, his lips found hers.

The kiss was deep, inevitable—weeks of unspoken longing igniting in an instant. Her heart raced, her hands sliding instinctively up his arms, clinging to him as if she'd known this was always where they would end.

Sebastiano pulled her closer, the taste of limoncello sweet on her lips, the scent of jasmine and salt wrapping around them. The world fell away—the Brotherhood, Marchetti, the looming danger—all dissolved into the heat between them.

When at last their lips parted, their foreheads rested together, both of them breathless, both of them silent, caught in the aftermath of what had just passed between them. Sebastiano's hands stayed on her face a moment longer, his thumbs brushing softly over her cheeks, as if grounding himself in the reality of her presence.

Amara blinked, her lips still tingling from the kiss. She didn't know what to say, but as she looked into his eyes, she realized she didn't need to. Everything she wanted to know was already there, reflected back at her in the way he gazed at her like she was the only thing in the world that mattered.

Amara rose first, her hand trembling slightly as she reached for his. She didn't speak, didn't need to. The fire in his eyes was mirrored in hers. Silently, she led him through the farmhouse, their footsteps echoing softly against the stone floors.

In her bedroom, moonlight spilled across the bed in silvery pools. Sebastiano stopped at the threshold, his hand tightening around hers. "Amara," he murmured, his voice rough, almost breaking.

She pressed a finger to his lips, silencing him. "No more words," she whispered.

And then they were lost in each other.

He lifted her effortlessly, his strength apparent but his touch impossibly gentle as he carried her to the bed. The softness of the mattress met her back as he leaned over her, his dark eyes blazing with desire. He hesitated for a moment, his hand brushing her cheek as if asking for permission, and when she smiled, he dipped his head to kiss her again, his lips trailing slowly down her jaw to her neck.

Lucia's fingers tangled in his hair as his kisses grew more deliberate, the heat between them building with every touch. His hands explored her curves, slipping beneath the fabric of her dress and sliding it from her shoulders in a slow, deliberate motion. Her breath hitching as his lips continued their path, leaving a trail of fire in their wake.

The cool night air brushed her skin as the dress fell away, but Carlo's warmth quickly replaced it. His own shirt was gone in an instant, revealing a sculpted frame that pressed against her as they came together. Her hands roamed his back, feeling the strength in his muscles. Their movements quickly found a rhythm as old as time, their bodies entwined, every barrier between them disappearing until there was nothing left but skin, heat, and unrelenting desire.

Their lovemaking was not hurried but consuming, each kiss, each breath a promise neither could yet name. It was passion, yes, but also remembrance—as if their souls recognized what their minds had only begun to uncover.

When at last they lay tangled together, moonlight painting their skin, silence held them. Sebastiano brushed a strand of hair from her face, his gaze softer than she had ever seen.

"Amara," he whispered, her name breaking in his throat.

She rested her head against his chest, feeling the steady rhythm of his heart beneath her cheek. For the first time since Dean's death, she felt whole—not simply desired, but cherished. Even as danger loomed just beyond their walls, in that moment they belonged only to each other.

Sleep came slowly, but when it did, it was deep and dreamless. Outside, the sea kept its eternal rhythm, while inside, two lives had changed forever.

Chapter Fifteen
Breakfast

Sebastiano woke to the soft glow of dawn slipping through the farmhouse shutters, gilding the room in honeyed light. For a rare, fleeting moment, he allowed himself stillness. Amara's head rested on his chest, her breath slow and even, her hair spilling like silk across his skin. A faint smile played at her lips, as if even in dreams she had found peace.

His chest tightened. He hadn't felt this in years—the simple weight of another person nestled against him, the quiet intimacy of belonging.

Then she stirred, letting out the tiniest half-snore. Sebastiano nearly laughed aloud, the sound catching him off guard. Endearing. Human. Real.

He bent his head, brushing a kiss to her temple, then to the curve of her neck. She murmured and blinked awake, her blue eyes drowsy but radiant in the morning light.

"Good morning," she whispered, her voice rough with sleep.

"Good morning," he returned, his lips trailing along her jaw.

Amara sighed, tilting her head to give him better access as his hand slid to her hip, pulling her closer. Their bodies pressed together, and the heat between them from the night before began to stir again, this time with a different kind of rhythm.

The pace was slower now, no urgency, no firestorm, just souls remembering each other. Just tenderness.
Sebastiano's hands roamed her body as though discovering her for the first time, his touch reverent, lingering on every curve. Amara mirrored his movements, her fingers tracing

over his chest, his shoulders, memorizing the strength and warmth of him. They took their time, each kiss and touch a conversation, a silent exchange that deepened the connection they had begun to build.

Their breaths mingled, the world outside the farmhouse forgotten as they moved together, finding a rhythm that felt both new and familiar. When it ended, their bodies stilled, wrapped in each other's warmth and the soft glow of the morning light.

Amara lay against him for a moment, her hand resting on his chest as she looked up into his eyes. He leaned down, capturing her lips in a lingering kiss, one that spoke of promises neither of them had yet put into words.

"I need a shower," she said softly, her cheeks flushed as she slipped from the bed smiling as she stretched.

He watched her disappear into the bathroom, the sound of water rushing soon after. The smile on his lips faded.

Sebastiano reached for his phone on the nightstand and went downstairs to the kitchen, his voice dropping to a careful whisper as he dialed the number he dreaded most.

It rang twice. Then Marchetti's clipped voice answered, "Sebastiano."

"Sir," he said evenly. "An update on Amara Savard."

"Progress?" Marchetti's tone was sharp, the question more command than inquiry.

"She's... responding," Sebastiano said carefully. "I believe she's close. But if we press too hard—"

Marchetti cut in, cold and precise. "She is the key. I expect results. If she won't unlock it willingly, we will make her."

Sebastiano's jaw clenched, though his voice remained calm. "If she breaks, so does the prophecy. You know that. Let me handle her in my way. If you move too soon, you risk everything."

A long silence. Then, soft and dangerous: "You had better be right, D'Amato. For both your sakes."

The line went dead.

Sebastiano slipped the phone back into his pocket just as the water shut off in the bathroom upstairs. He exhaled, steadying himself, masking the storm inside.

When Amara appeared moments later, fresh and glowing, dressed in jeans and a soft shirt, Sebastiano forced a smile. She paused in the doorway, relief flickering in her eyes.

"You're still here," she said warmly.

"Where else would I be?" he replied, sleeves rolled, a pan of eggs on the stove. The air was filled with the scent of garlic and fresh tomatoes.

Her laughter was soft, almost shy. "You cook?"

"Oh yes," he replied, sliding espresso across the table. "And we need nourishment after last night."

She sat, the warmth of the rustic kitchen wrapping around them both. For a little while, they ate in quiet contentment, Amara savoring the simplicity of the meal, Sebastiano watching her with a gaze that softened despite himself.

When she caught him staring, she tilted her head. "What?"

"Nothing," he said quickly, then after a pause: "Just… this is nice. You. Here. With me."

She smiled, touched, but then his tone shifted.

"But after breakfast," he said, his voice low, his gaze sharpening, "there are things you need to know. Truths I can't keep from you any longer."

The fork stilled in her hand. The farmhouse seemed to grow quieter, the weight of his words settling over the morning like a gathering storm.

She set the fork down slowly and met his eyes. "Then tell me," she said, her heart racing.

Sebastiano leaned forward, his dark gaze locking onto hers. "I will. But understand, Amara—once you hear this, nothing will ever be the same again."

Chapter Sixteen
Threads of Truth

The kitchen was hushed, broken only by the faint clink of silverware against porcelain. Outside, gulls cried over the cliffs, their calls sharp and fleeting against the steady roar of the sea. Morning light streamed through the windows, gilding the edges of the farmhouse in gold.

Amara set her fork down, her pulse thrumming. "Sebastiano," she said quietly, steadying her voice, "tell me what you know."

For a moment, he didn't answer. He sat back in his chair, dark eyes fixed on her, weighing what could be said and what must be buried. Finally, he exhaled, the sound low, reluctant.

"The Brotherhood," he began, "was not just a group of monks or scholars as some claim. They were guardians—keepers of knowledge older than the Church itself, older than most of what history dares to record."

Amara leaned forward, her fingers curled against the table's edge. "Guardians of what?"

Sebastiano's gaze flicked toward the window, as though wary of unseen eyes. "They called it la verità nascosta—the hidden truth. Records scattered across Europe suggest it is a convergence of astronomy, alchemy, and something beyond either. A code, a prophecy, a… key to unlocking forces that could alter the balance of power in the world."

Her heart stuttered. She remembered the attic, the symbols blazing to life beneath her touch, the stars that had unfolded like a map across the cosmos. Her voice trembled. "And you think it's here. In this house."

"I know it is," he said, his voice firm but quiet. "Your farmhouse wasn't chosen by chance. The Brotherhood built it with precision—stones aligned with the stars, foundations laid upon a ley line. Every wall, every chamber, was part of a design." He paused, his jaw tightening. "But they also wrote of a person. The 'true owner' who would one day awaken what they sealed. Without that person, the secret remains dead stone and dust."

Amara's breath caught. "You mean… me."

Sebastiano's eyes softened, shadows flickering in their depths. "I saw the light in the attic. I felt it. You've already touched the secret, even if you don't understand how. That's why others will come. They'll try to use you—or destroy you—before you can unlock it fully."

Silence fell heavy between them. Amara sat frozen, her mind spinning. She thought of the movers' warnings, of the strange noises in the farmhouse, of the car that had shadowed her on the road. It all knit together with dreadful clarity.

Finally, she whispered, "Who are these 'others'?"

Sebastiano's hand curled into a fist on the table. "Men loyal to Duke Antonio Marchetti."

The name landed like a stone in her chest. She had heard it before in passing—a name tied to old power, whispered scandals, men who smiled in public and dealt in shadows behind closed doors.

"Power is never enough for a man like Marchetti," Sebastiano said bitterly. "He's spent decades searching for fragments of the prophecy. He believes that once the Brotherhood's truth is revealed, he can bend nations to his will. And he will not hesitate to break anyone who stands in his way."

Amara shivered. "And you?" she asked softly. "Where do you stand in all this?"

The question pierced deeper than he expected. Sebastiano's throat tightened. For years, the answer had been simple: loyalty, obedience, survival. But sitting here, with Amara's steady gaze fixed on him, the simplicity shattered.

"I stand…" he began, then faltered. His jaw worked, but the words refused to come. Finally, he reached across the table, his hand covering hers. His touch was warm, grounding. "I stand here, Amara. With you. For as long as I can."

Her breath hitched, the sincerity in his voice both comforting and terrifying. She felt the heat of his palm against her skin, the unspoken promise in his words.

But Sebastiano's eyes betrayed the truth he hadn't said aloud: he was bound by ties she couldn't yet see, ties that could strangle them both.

Before Amara could speak, a sharp rap sounded at the farmhouse door. Three knocks—deliberate, echoing through the stone walls.

Sebastiano froze. His grip tightened around her hand. "Don't answer it," he whispered, his voice taut.

Amara's stomach dropped. "Who—"

Another knock, louder this time. Then silence.

The farmhouse seemed to hold its breath.

Sebastiano rose slowly from the table, his movements fluid but tense, every step toward the door that of a man prepared for danger. Amara watched him, her heart hammering, the truth of his warning settling deep into her bones.

The net was already tightening.

Chapter Seventeen
The Knock at the Door

The farmhouse fell into silence after the second round of
knocking, the kind of silence that pressed in on the ears and
made every heartbeat sound too loud.

Amara's chest tightened as she watched Sebastiano
move toward the entryway. He didn't rush. His steps were
measured, deliberate, the quiet prowl of a man who had
faced danger before and expected it again.

"Sebastiano," she whispered, rising halfway from her
chair. "Who is it?"

He lifted a hand without looking back—an unspoken
plea for her to stay still.

Her pulse quickened, the seconds stretching as he
paused at the heavy oak door. He tilted his head, listening,
his palm resting lightly against the aged wood. Amara
thought she saw something flicker across his face—
recognition, maybe, or dread—but it vanished before she
could be sure.

Another silence.

Sebastiano didn't answer the door. Instead, he turned
slightly, his eyes catching Amara's across the dim room.
The message in them was clear: stay quiet.

The man outside waited a beat.

Then the sound of footsteps retreating, the crunch of
gravel under polished shoes.

Amara held her breath until the echo of an engine
growled to life down the road.

Only then did Sebastiano turn the lock and open the
door a fraction, peering out. The lane was empty, but
Amara could see the faint tire marks in the dirt, fresh and

deliberate. Whoever had come hadn't been a messenger. It had been a warning.

Sebastiano shut the door with a quiet finality and turned to face her.

"You see now," he said, his voice low, almost hoarse. "Marchetti's men are already circling. And if they came to your door—" His gaze flicked to the attic stairs, then back to her. "—they know what you've touched."

Amara's breath caught, fear and anger tangling inside her. "You said I was the key. But you're still working for him, aren't you?"

The accusation hung between them like a blade.

Sebastiano closed the space between them, his hands braced against the table as he leaned toward her, his voice fierce but quiet. "I've done what I had to do to survive, Amara. But with you—" His eyes locked onto hers, dark and unflinching. "With you, it's different. You have to believe that."

Her heart hammered, torn between trust and suspicion. The warmth of his touch from the night before still lingered in her memory, but so did the cold edge of danger now pressing against the farmhouse walls.

The knock had changed everything.

Chapter Eighteen
The Duke Moves His Pieces

Duke Antonio Marchetti stood at the window of his palazzo, a glass of Barolo poised between his fingers. Below, the gardens stretched in symmetrical perfection— rows of cypress trees, marble fountains, and pathways lined with roses cultivated to bloom blood-red year-round. Beauty as control. Order imposed upon nature.

He savored that thought as he took a measured sip, his pale blue eyes fixed on the horizon.

"Report," he said without turning.

A man stepped forward from the shadows of the study. Matteo, one of his most trusted lieutenants, moved with quiet precision, his expression carved into the same hard lines as the Duke's statues in the courtyard.

"She's awakened something," Matteo said. "Last night. D'Amato confirms he saw lights in the attic windows of the farmhouse."

Marchetti's grip tightened just slightly on the stem of his glass. He had waited years—decades—for this moment, and now the prophecy's promise was shimmering on the edge of reality.

"And the girl?"

"Unaware of her role," Matteo replied. "But she's… changing. D'Amato says she feels the pull."

Marchetti turned at last, his expression unreadable, though a glint of triumph flickered in his gaze. "Of course she does. She was bred for it."

He set the glass down on a polished table and walked to his desk. A series of old manuscripts lay spread open across its surface, their pages yellowed with age, their ink faded but still legible under carefully positioned lamps. In the center lay the Brotherhood's fragmented prophecy, painstakingly reconstructed over years of theft, bribery, and bloodshed.

He ran a hand across the text, his fingers lingering on the line he had committed to memory long ago: The Key shall come unbidden, drawn by the house itself. When the stars awaken in her sight, the seal shall tremble.

The seal was trembling now.

"And D'Amato?" Marchetti asked, his voice even.

Matteo hesitated. "He reports as ordered. But there is… a softness in him, sir. He's too close."

A smile ghosted across Marchetti's lips, though it held no warmth. "Ah. Even lions forget themselves when love is dangled in front of them. But lions can be tamed. Or broken."

He picked up a silver letter opener, turning it idly in his hands as he paced. "Keep watching him. If he falters, if he fails—" He pressed the blade against his palm, just enough to leave a white line without drawing blood. "—we'll remind him of his family's obligations."

Matteo inclined his head. "And the girl?"

Marchetti's eyes narrowed, ice-cold and certain. "Bring her to me when she unlocks the seal. Alive, unharmed— until I have what I need. After that…" He let the unfinished thought hang in the air, heavier than any command.

He returned to the window, watching the last light of day vanish into the skyline. Somewhere across the sea, Amara Savard stood on the precipice of destiny, unaware that every move she made was already inside his game.

The Duke smiled faintly. And games, after all, were what he played best.

Chapter Nineteen
The Net Tightens

The villa's underground chamber hummed with quiet menace. Unlike the gilded opulence of Marchetti's office upstairs, this space was stripped down to its essentials: steel, glass, and silence broken only by the soft clicks of surveillance equipment. Rows of monitors lined the walls, each tuned to feeds pulled from satellites, hacked cameras, and private networks that stretched across continents.

Duke Antonio Marchetti descended the narrow staircase, his polished shoes striking the concrete with measured precision. Two men in dark suits snapped to attention as he entered, their eyes lowered. He ignored them, moving directly to the largest screen at the far wall.

On it glowed a grainy image: Amara's farmhouse. The photograph had been taken from a distance, the shot framed between olive trees. A faint glow bled from the attic windows, distorted by the lens flare but unmistakable to anyone who knew the prophecy. Marchetti's pale eyes gleamed.

"She is awakening," he said, his voice low, almost reverent.

Beside him, Matteo inclined his head. "D'Amato confirmed it. He stays close to her."

Marchetti's lips curved, though the expression never reached his eyes. "Yes. Perhaps too close."

He gestured, and one of the men brought forward a dossier—black leather, bound with brass corners. Marchetti flipped it open with deliberate care. Inside were photographs: Amara arriving at Naples airport, laughing with her friends at a café, standing on the terrace of the farmhouse with the sea behind her. In each image, she seemed unaware of the unseen lens that followed her every step.

"She doesn't realize yet how tightly she is held," Marchetti murmured, running a finger over the photograph of her in Naples. "That's the beauty of it. A bird never knows the cage until the door closes."

He turned the page. Sebastiano's image stared up at him now—dark suit, sharp profile, caught in candid surveillance near the farmhouse. Marchetti's gaze hardened.

"Loyalty," he said coldly. "The D'Amato family has served me for decades. But loyalty, I find, grows fragile when love seeps in."

He snapped the folder shut and handed it back. "Send Leone."

The name rippled through the chamber like a shadow. Leone was Marchetti's blunt instrument—the one unleashed only when precision was less important than fear. A man without hesitation, without mercy.

Matteo hesitated. "To Capri, sir?"

Marchetti's blue eyes turned glacial. "To watch. To remind D'Amato of his obligations if he strays. And if the girl begins to resist…" He let the words hang, then finished softly, "Leone will handle it."

A heavy silence followed. Marchetti placed his hands behind his back and gazed once more at the glowing image of the farmhouse.

"The prophecy says the key awakens when the stars burn in her sight. That moment is close. When it comes, I will be ready."

He turned away, his reflection caught in the cold gleam of the monitors. "And if Sebastiano falters…" His smile was thin, merciless. "He will learn that bloodlines are no shield against me."

Chapter Twenty
Leone

The sound of iron striking iron echoed through the cavernous hall beneath Marchetti's estate. The underground training chamber smelled of oil, leather, and sweat—an arena built not for spectacle but for efficiency. In its center moved a man whose very presence seemed to bend the air around him.

Leone.

His frame was massive, carved from years of brutal discipline, every motion carrying the fluid precision of a predator. Tattoos marked his arms and chest, inked in black lines that told the story of violence and loyalty etched into his skin. His head was shaved close, his eyes a pale gray that seemed to pierce straight through whatever they fixed upon.

At the far end of the chamber, a line of sparring partners lay crumpled against the wall, groaning softly. Leone barely glanced at them. He moved back to the rack of weapons, selecting a simple blade, testing its balance in his hand as though it were merely an extension of himself.

Marchetti's arrival was met with silence. Even Leone, the man feared across three continents, turned and lowered his head in a gesture of respect rarely given.

"You called for me," Leone said, his voice deep, rasping, like gravel dragged across stone.

"I did," Marchetti replied, stepping into the circle. He studied Leone for a long moment, the faintest smile touching his lips. "It is time."

Leone said nothing, waiting.

"There is a woman," Marchetti continued, pacing slowly, his hands clasped behind his back. "Amara Savard. She resides now at the farmhouse in Anacapri. You will go there, quietly. You will not yet act, unless I say so. But you will watch. And you will remind Sebastiano D'Amato that his loyalty belongs to me."

Leone's pale eyes flickered once, the only sign of interest. "And if his loyalty wavers?"

"Then you will correct it," Marchetti said softly, almost tenderly. "Permanently, if necessary."

The words settled like frost. Leone nodded once, no hesitation, no flicker of conscience.

"And the girl?" he asked.

Marchetti's smile thinned. "She is the key. She must not be harmed—not yet. If Sebastiano falters, you will ensure she is delivered to me intact. Understand?"

"Yes."

Leone slid the blade back onto the rack, then reached for his jacket, black leather creaking as he pulled it over his broad shoulders. He moved with unhurried certainty, the kind of man who had walked into countless missions and walked out every time. To Leone, orders were simple. Life or death made no difference.

As he passed Marchetti, the Duke spoke one final time.

"She does not yet know the cage is closing. Sebastiano toys with fire. If he forgets his place, Leone—remind him of the cost of disobedience."

Leone's lips curved into the faintest shadow of a smile, though it was devoid of warmth. "Consider it done."

The heavy door closed behind him, his footsteps fading into the night.

Chapter Twenty-One
Morning Shadows

The morning light spilled gently across the farmhouse, gilding the terracotta tiles in a soft glow. The sea beyond was calm, glittering with the pale blues and silvers of dawn. From the terrace, the world looked untouched by darkness, as if nothing could disturb the peace of this cliffside retreat.

Inside, Amara moved barefoot through the kitchen, her hair falling loose around her shoulders. She had slept little after Sebastiano left the night before, her thoughts tangled in his warning and in the lingering fire of their kiss. The house felt too quiet, every creak of its old bones magnified.

She poured herself an espresso, the hiss and steam of the moka pot steadying her. As she sat at the scarred wooden table, her eyes wandered to the attic door at the end of the hall. She shivered, remembering the glow, the stars, the weight of forgotten lifetimes pressing down on her.

A knock startled her.

Sharp. Firm. Too early.

Her heart leapt. For a moment, she thought it might be Sebastiano again—drawn back by the same pull that had left her restless. But something about the knock felt different. Impatient. Commanding.

Amara hesitated before crossing the room. She pulled the door open just enough to peer outside.

A deliveryman stood on the steps, holding a narrow parcel wrapped in brown paper and string. His cap shadowed his face, his expression unreadable.

"Signora Savard?" he asked, his accent heavy, his tone flat.

"Yes," she said cautiously.

He thrust the parcel forward. "For you."

She took it, the weight surprisingly light in her hands. By the time she looked up again, the man was already walking away, his shoulders hunched, his pace brisk down the winding path. Something about his retreating figure left her unsettled.

Amara shut the door and carried the parcel to the table. She stared at it for a long moment before tugging the string free. Inside was a single book—old, leather-bound, its cover cracked with age. No note. No return address.

As she opened it, a slip of paper fluttered onto the table. Handwritten in a precise, almost archaic script were four words:

"The key awakens soon."

The letters seemed to pulse against the page, sending a chill down her spine.

Amara's fingers trembled as she traced the edge of the note. Whoever had sent this knew about her. About the prophecy. About the farmhouse.

And somewhere beyond the cliffs, Leone was already on the move.

The silence pressed in. The faint ticking of the old clock on the wall became unbearably loud. She closed the book, slid the note back between its pages, and shoved the parcel aside. But the words lingered, branded in her mind: The key awakens soon.

Another knock.

This one softer, deliberate.

Her heart lurched. She crossed the room quickly, her hand hovering over the latch, fear warring with hope. She opened the door.

Sebastiano stood there, framed by the early sunlight. His suit jacket was gone, his dark shirt open at the collar, the faint stubble on his jaw catching the light. But it wasn't his appearance that struck her most—it was his eyes. They searched her face instantly, reading her unease before she spoke a word.

"Amara," he said, his voice low. "Something's wrong."

Her throat tightened. She stepped aside, and he entered without hesitation, his presence filling the farmhouse with a steadiness she hadn't realized she needed.

She gestured to the table. "This was delivered a few minutes ago."

He moved toward it, his movements purposeful but measured, as though each step carried the weight of suspicion. He picked up the book, flipped it open, and pulled out the note. His eyes narrowed as he read it, his jaw clenching.

"Who brought this?"

"A man. A deliveryman. He didn't stay."

Sebastiano swore under his breath, something sharp and Italian, before looking back at her. His gaze softened slightly, but the intensity never faded. "They know who you are. What you are."

Amara wrapped her arms around herself, suddenly cold. "You think Marchetti sent it?"

Sebastiano hesitated, the pause telling her more than words. "It has his mark. Or… someone working very close to him."

He stepped closer, his hand brushing her arm in a gesture both grounding and protective. "Listen to me. That note isn't a threat—it's a signal. They're testing you. Watching to see if you flinch, if you know more than you should. Which means—" his eyes darkened, his voice dropping—"we don't have much time before they close in."

The farmhouse, once her haven, suddenly felt like a trap.

Amara looked up at him, fear and determination warring in her chest. "What do we do?"

Sebastiano held her gaze, his hand lingering against her arm. His expression softened, just slightly. "We stay ahead of them. And I keep you safe."

The words settled between them, heavy with promise. For a long moment, neither moved. Then Sebastiano stepped back, the shadow of restraint flickering across his face. He glanced at the book again, then back to her.

"Everything is about to change."

Outside, the sea shimmered in the morning light, calm and unbothered. But inside the farmhouse, the storm had already begun.

Chapter Twenty-Two
The Book and the Omen

The farmhouse felt suddenly smaller, the walls pressing close as Amara and Sebastiano stared at the book lying on the table between them. Its leather cover was cracked and worn, but the words burned fresh and undeniable: The Key Awakens Soon.

Amara reached out, her fingertips trembling as she traced the embossed letters. The leather felt warm, almost alive, as though the book itself held a pulse. She drew her hand back sharply, her breath unsteady.

"What does it mean?" she whispered, her voice raw with unease.

Sebastiano's jaw tightened. He leaned forward, his dark eyes studying the book with the wary respect of a man who had seen too many things others dismissed as myth. "It means someone knows," he said softly. "And they are not merely watching us—they are warning us, or taunting us."

Amara swallowed hard. "This …" She gestured toward the book, her voice faltering. "This feels... Immediate."

Sebastiano nodded, though his gaze never left the book. "The Brotherhood used written signs like this—cryptic, deliberate, always meant for those already inside their circle. Whoever sent this knows the prophecy. And they know you are the key."

Her pulse quickened, fear and something else stirring deep inside her—a pull she could not explain. "But why me?"

He looked at her then, his eyes softening for the briefest moment. "Because you were always meant to be, Amara. This house did not choose you by accident. And now…"

He exhaled slowly, his hand brushing across the book's cover before pulling back. "…now the storm accelerates."

Amara shivered. She wanted to push the book away, to shut it in a drawer, to pretend it was nothing more than a cruel trick. But even as she thought it, she knew the truth: she could no longer escape the path before her.

The clock on the mantle ticked with unnatural sharpness, each second louder than the last. Outside, the sea gleamed beneath a bright sun, yet within the farmhouse shadows lengthened.

"Sebastiano…" she said quietly, lifting her eyes to his. "What happens when the key awakens?"

His expression darkened, the calm mask he so often wore slipping just enough to reveal the weight beneath. "Then we are no longer simply searching for answers," he said, his voice low, grave. "We are racing against those who will kill to claim them."

Silence fell heavy between them, broken only by the whisper of wind through the open shutters. Amara wrapped her arms around herself, fighting the chill that seeped into her bones.

The book remained on the table, waiting.

Unopened. Unread. Yet already it had changed everything.

Chapter Twenty-Three
Shadows Closing In

Deep beneath a vaulted cellar, the air reeked of damp stone and oil lamps burning too low. Leone knelt at the edge of a long table, its surface scarred by centuries of knives, blood, and symbols carved into wood. Before him lay an open ledger, inked not with numbers but with names—each one crossed through until only a handful remained.

At the top stood Marchetti. And now, beneath it, freshly written: Amara Savard.

Leone traced the letters with a calloused finger, savoring the weight of them. "The key has taken the bait," he growled. "The book sits in her hands."

From the shadows, a cloaked lieutenant shifted uneasily. "And D'Amato?"

Leone's lip curled. "He lingers too close. Desire weakens men faster than a blade. If he falters, I will carve his name into this table myself."

With a blackened knife, Leone pressed through the ledger into the wood beneath Amara's name, carving a single word with slow, deliberate strokes: Soon.

The lamp sputtered, choking on smoke, as though the room itself recoiled from his vow.

On the other side of the island, far removed from the cellar's stench, Duke Antonio Marchetti stood at the tall windows of his study, overlooking manicured gardens sculpted into perfect symmetry. His empire mirrored this garden—every line controlled, every weakness pruned away.

Behind him, the quiet hum of machines filled the air— holographic displays, intercepted communications, data streams reaching across the globe. The farmhouse had become the axis of it all.

The door opened. Leone entered, immaculate in his dark suit, his presence radiating a predator's ease. He set a folder on the desk: photographs of Amara opening her door. Another frame showed Sebastiano D'Amato crossing her threshold.

"Too close," Leone said flatly.

Marchetti flipped the images in silence, his sharp gaze lingering on Sebastiano. Then he gave a thin, controlled smile. "Let him draw near. A weakness reveals more than strength ever could. If he bends toward her, he only exposes more of her truth."

He turned from the window, voice hard as iron. "Still, the net must close. Apply pressure. Remind D'Amato of the cost of divided loyalties. If he resists…" His smile deepened, cold as winter steel. "The prophecy names her, not him."

Leone inclined his head, the order clear.

When the door shut again, Marchetti remained at the window, watching the light blaze across his perfect gardens. "Awaken, then," he murmured to the empty room. "Awaken—and the world will be mine

Chapter-Twenty-Four
The Book

Morning light filtered through the farmhouse windows, painting long stripes across the worn wood of the kitchen table. The book still sat where Amara had left it, its leather cover dark, its clasp unbroken. Four words scrawled across the slip of paper that had accompanied it whispered through her thoughts again and again:

The Key Awakens Soon.

She hovered at the edge of the table, arms folded, as though distance might keep its weight from pressing on her. She now knew that the farmhouse held secrets, but this—it was a summons.

Behind her, Sebastiano leaned against the stone counter, silent, watching her. He hadn't touched the book, not even glanced too long at it, but she could feel the tension in him like a drawn bowstring. His presence was steady, protective, but the shadows beneath his dark eyes betrayed a man carrying more than he would admit.

Finally, Amara turned toward him. "You've seen this kind of thing before." Her voice was steady, but her fingers drummed nervously against her arm. "Haven't you?"

Sebastiano's jaw tightened, but he didn't look away. "I've seen... fragments. Texts, relics, things that survived from the Brotherhood's time. But nothing like this." He stepped closer, lowering his voice. "Amara, listen to me— if that book was placed in your hands, it wasn't by accident. They want you to open it. They want to see what happens when you do."

Her breath caught. "They? Marchetti?"

His pause was too long, his silence too heavy. She read the truth in his eyes before he spoke. "Yes. And not only him."

The kitchen seemed to grow smaller, the stone walls pressing inward. Amara turned back to the book, the faint smell of old leather reaching her as though it had a life of its own. "So what happens if I open it?" she asked softly.

Sebastiano's voice was taut. "Then we find out why they call you the key."

Her gaze lingered on him, the unspoken question rising between them: Do you know more than you're telling me?

But before she could ask the question, the farmhouse itself seemed to answer. A sudden draft swept through the room, rattling the shutters though the morning air outside was calm. The candles on the mantle flickered, their flames bending toward the book as though drawn by its presence.

Amara's pulse quickened. She reached instinctively toward the clasp but stopped just short, her fingers trembling above it.

Sebastiano caught her wrist, his touch firm but gentle. "Not yet." His eyes locked on hers, steady, commanding. "We don't open it until we know if we're being watched here."

The silence between them throbbed with unspoken fear, attraction, and a shared sense of inevitability. The book sat unmoved, waiting.

But outside, across the olive grove, a figure knelt in the tall grass, a lens trained on the farmhouse window. Somewhere far away, Marchetti's screens glowed. And in a cellar lit by oil lamps, Leone's ledger still bore her name.

The net was closing. And the book was only the beginning.

Chapter Twenty-Five
Fractures in the Net

The study was dark when Marchetti entered, lit only by the pale glow of the wall-length screen. Surveillance feeds shimmered across its surface—Capri's narrow lanes, the harbor, the farmhouse on the cliff. He saw the image of Amara's front door, the same one Leone had given him; in his own surveillance images, there was one frame frozen in time. The image of Amara accepting a book from a delivery person and it lingered like a wound across the room.

Leone stood near the desk, his massive shoulders hunched as he scrolled through data on a tablet. He didn't look up when Marchetti approached, but his presence filled the space, rough and unyielding, like stone cut from the earth.

"Your message was unnecessary," Marchetti said at last, his voice smooth, controlled. Too smooth. "The book— those words—'The Key Awakens Soon.' You overstep."

Leone finally lifted his gaze, dark eyes glinting under the low light. "A reminder, Duke. Nothing more. She must feel the breath of the hunt. Otherwise, she will not move."

Marchetti circled the room slowly, his hands clasped behind his back. He studied the screens without truly seeing them. "You mistake fear for movement. Fear scatters. Pressure without precision destroys what it seeks to uncover."

A muscle jumped in Leone's jaw. "And yet she held it. She will open it. Soon."

"Perhaps." Marchetti stopped before the desk, turning to face him fully. His voice dropped, quiet but edged with steel. "But you forget yourself, Leone. You serve at my command. You deliver what I require—nothing more, nothing less. Initiatives outside my design will not be tolerated."

For the briefest moment, silence swelled between them, heavy and dangerous. Leone's thick fingers tightened on the tablet until the casing creaked. Then, slowly, he set it down, inclining his head in what might have been submission—or the shadow of it.

"As you command," he said, though his tone carried no humility.

Marchetti studied him, cold calculation behind his pale eyes. He had always admired Leone's brutality, his efficiency, his lack of conscience. But admiration was not trust. The man was a wolf, and wolves turned when hunger outweighed loyalty.

"Do not test me," Marchetti said at last, his voice cutting the air like glass. "I will not tolerate two masters in this game. The Brotherhood's prophecy names her. Not you. Not me. Her. And whoever controls her… controls the outcome."

Leone's mouth curved, but it was no smile. "Then perhaps you should worry less about me, and more about your pet hound D'Amato. He follows her too closely. He may yet bite the hand that feeds him."

Marchetti let out a quiet laugh, though it carried no warmth. "If he bites, I will break his teeth. And if you overreach again, Leone…" He leaned forward slightly, his gaze a blade. "…I will remind you who keeps you in leash."

The room held its breath.

Then, with a slow exhale, Leone reached for his coat, slipping it across his broad shoulders. "Very well, Duke. But do not mistake restraint for weakness. When the time comes, I will act. And when I do, you will thank me."

Marchetti said nothing, only turned back toward the glowing screens. Leone's reflection lingered in the glass a moment longer before disappearing through the door.

Alone, Marchetti touched a control panel and the frozen image of Amara at her doorway filled the screen once more. His hand hovered over her face, tracing the outline without contact.

"Awaken, then," he whispered. "And when you do, you will awaken for me."

The lights dimmed, leaving only her image in the dark—an anchor, a lure, and the storm's center.

Chapter Twenty-Six
The Waiting Book

The farmhouse was unusually still that morning. Outside, the sea shimmered beneath a veil of mist, its surface calm and glasslike, while gulls wheeled lazily above the cliffs. But inside, silence pressed against the walls, thick and expectant.

On the table between them, the book remained untouched. Its leather cover was cracked and weathered, edges frayed as if it had survived centuries. The gilded imprint of a sigil—half-faded, half-burning with stubborn resilience—gleamed faintly in the shaft of sunlight that filtered through the shutters.

Amara stared at it, her coffee cooling in her hands. She had not dared open it the night before, though she had been alone with it for hours while Sebastiano lingered outside on watch. Every time she thought of lifting its cover, her chest tightened with a strange fear, as though some invisible threshold waited just beyond.

Sebastiano entered the kitchen, his movements deliberate, his dark gaze fixed on her before drifting to the book. He carried the weight of the night's vigil in his eyes—shadows of thoughts he hadn't spoken aloud.

"You didn't open it," he said quietly.

"No," Amara replied, setting down her cup. Her voice trembled with equal parts defiance and relief. "It felt... wrong. As if it was waiting for me to make the first mistake."

Sebastiano moved closer, the faint scent of leather and sandalwood brushing the air as he leaned against the table.

His hand rested near the book but did not touch it. His eyes searched hers with quiet intensity.

"You're not wrong. Objects tied to the Brotherhood were never mere books. They were vessels—keys, seals, traps." His voice dropped, edged with something darker. "Opening it without knowing what's inside could bind you before you even understand to what."

Amara's fingers curled around the edge of the chair. "So, what do we do? Leave it here, staring at us every morning until one of us breaks?"

He allowed a faint, humorless smile. "Patience, Amara. Sometimes restraint is the only weapon."

Her gaze softened as she studied him—the controlled steel in his tone, the guarded fire in his eyes. He was so close, she could see the faint stubble along his jaw, the weariness shadowing his features. And beneath it, something else—something unspoken but alive between them.

"Restraint doesn't feel like enough," she whispered.

The words hung between them like an unstruck chord. Sebastiano's hand shifted, almost brushing hers on the table, then withdrew with a sharp breath. He forced his attention back to the book.

"Then we find another way," he said firmly. "If Marchetti or anyone else believes you've opened it, they'll move faster. Leone will move faster. We need to make them doubt. Make them wonder."

Amara's heart quickened at the names spoken aloud. Leone. Marchetti. Shadows that seemed to press closer each day. "And if the book opens itself?" she asked, her voice quieter now. "If it was meant for me, like they believe?"

Sebastiano finally looked at her again, and in his gaze, she saw both warning and devotion. "Then it won't be the book that chooses, Amara—it will be you. And you must be certain you're ready before that moment comes."

A knock shattered the silence.

Both of them froze. Three measured raps against the heavy oak door, too deliberate to be a passerby.

Sebastiano was already moving, his hand sliding to the pistol beneath his jacket. He cast her a sharp look—a silent command: stay back.

Amara's pulse thundered in her ears as he crossed the room. The farmhouse, once a sanctuary, felt suddenly like a trap of stone and shadows. The book gleamed faintly in the sunlight, as though it too had been waiting for this exact moment.

Sebastiano reached the door, paused, then pulled it open.

A man stood there, tall and lean, with a messenger's satchel slung across his chest. But his eyes—cold, calculating—betrayed a role beyond delivery. He smiled faintly, as if he knew exactly what sat on the table behind Sebastiano.

"For Amara Savard," he said, holding out a sealed envelope.

Chapter Twenty-Seven
The Circle Tightens

The evening pressed heavy over Marchetti's estate, the last light of day staining the horizon a blood-red hue. Inside, the Duke's study glowed with a colder fire—screens alive with streams of data, intercepted calls, satellite images. At the center of it all sat Marchetti, his posture flawless, his face carved into stillness.

Leone entered without knocking, his boots striking the marble floor with measured weight. He carried no folder this time, no ledger of names. Only a single photograph—printed on matte paper, the edges curled from the rush of its delivery. He placed it on the desk without a word.

Marchetti's eyes lowered. The image showed Sebastiano outside the farmhouse, his stance protective, his hand on Amara Savard's arm as though anchoring her. A moment frozen in grainy relief, but it carried all the betrayal Marchetti needed to see.

Leone's voice was low, almost amused. "The loyal hound has found a new master."

Marchetti did not answer at once. He lifted the photograph, studying Sebastiano's face—the angle of his body, the proximity to Amara. Every detail betrayed a shift of allegiance.

Finally, he set it down, his fingers steepling. "No. Not a new master," he said softly. "A weakness. And every weakness can be used."

Leone's lips curved faintly, though his eyes stayed hard. "Then say the word, Duke. I will remove him before he compromises everything."

Marchetti leaned back in his chair, the leather groaning under his weight. He studied Leone for a long moment, his sharp blue eyes searching for cracks. "Impatient, Leone? Or eager?"

Leone's jaw twitched. "Eager to prevent failure. You've built an empire, Duke. Do not let it slip for the sake of a man whose heart has betrayed him."

Marchetti's smile was slow, deliberate. "And yet... even betrayal can serve a greater purpose. Sebastiano will lead her deeper. His heart will coax her where fear cannot. She will trust him, and in that trust, she will awaken the knowledge."

He rose, turning to the window, his silhouette framed against the crimson sky. "No, Leone. Not yet. Watch him. Press him. Tempt him. But do not remove him—not until he delivers what I want."

Leone's brow furrowed. "And if his loyalty shifts too far?"

Marchetti turned, his smile thin as a blade. "Then you may have your fun. But only then."

Leone gave a short nod, though the darkness in his eyes lingered. He had followed Marchetti for years, but tonight, something unspoken passed between them—an edge, a fracture waiting to split.

As Leone left the study, Marchetti returned to the photograph, his finger brushing over Amara's face.

"The key awakens soon," he whispered, the words both promise and threat. "And when it does, the world will bow."

Chapter Twenty-Eight
The Book Opens

The farmhouse lay in hushed stillness, the only sound the distant rhythm of waves striking rock far below the cliff. Amara sat at the long wooden table, her hands resting on either side of the book. The weight of it filled the room like a storm about to break.

Sebastiano stood near the window, his profile sharp in the fading light. His arms were crossed, yet his eyes never left her. He didn't speak, though she felt the unspoken warning in the tightness of his jaw.

Her fingers moved to the book. "If we don't open it now," she whispered, "we'll never stop wondering."

"Once opened, there's no turning back," Sebastiano replied, his voice low, steady. "Marchetti, Leone… they'll know when the key stirs. Every move we make will echo louder."

Amara drew a slow breath. "Then let them hear the echo."

She touched the leather-bound book. Its cover was cracked, darkened with age, but embossed faintly in gold was a sigil: a circle of stars.

Her breath caught. The same symbol she had seen blazing across the attic wall, the same that haunted her dream of the Brotherhood.

Sebastiano stepped closer, his shadow falling across her shoulder. "Dio…" he muttered under his breath. "It exists."

Amara traced the sigil with trembling fingers before lifting the cover. The first page was filled with careful script, the ink browned with time. But it wasn't Italian, or Latin, or any language she recognized. The letters seemed to shimmer faintly, as though shifting just beyond comprehension.

"I can't read it," she said, frustration flickering in her voice.

Sebastiano's gaze sharpened. "Then don't force it. Let it come."

She turned the page. Again, the strange script—but this time, as she stared, the letters seemed to bend, rearranging themselves. Shapes became words, words became meaning.

Her lips parted as she read aloud, her voice carrying a cadence she didn't understand:

"When the Key awakens, the seal shall break. Light hidden in stone shall rise, and the one who guards shall remember."

Her voice faltered, her pulse racing. The words hadn't come from thought, but instinct, as though drawn up from something buried inside her.

Sebastiano's hand came down gently on her arm. "You understood it."

"I... don't know how," she whispered. Her vision blurred for a moment, the room fading, replaced by flashes—candles burning in stone chambers, voices chanting, her own hands carrying this very book across centuries.

Her body trembled, and Sebastiano steadied her. "Amara. Look at me."

She tore her gaze from the page, meeting his dark, steady eyes. His presence grounded her, pulled her back from the flood of memory.

But even as her breath steadied, a single truth coiled in her chest like fire:

The Brotherhood hadn't hidden the knowledge from her. They had hidden it for her.

And now the seal was breaking.

Outside, a shadow moved among the olive trees, unseen. Leone's men watched the farmhouse from the darkness, waiting for the moment to strike.

Chapter Twenty-Nine
The Weight of the Words

The farmhouse had fallen into a silence so deep that even the sea seemed to hush, as if the world itself leaned closer to hear what Amara and Sebastiano would say next. The leather-bound book lay open between them on the heavy oak table, its pages trembling in the draft that whispered through the shutters.

Amara's hands still rested on the parchment. Her fingertips tingled, as though the words she had spoken aloud had imprinted themselves into her skin. The key awakens when the blood and the light converge. She mouthed the phrase again, silently this time, her lips moving as if trying to hold it in her mouth like a prayer.

Sebastiano leaned back, his dark eyes locked on her. He had heard many riddles in his life, read countless cryptic fragments in Marchetti's archives. But this was different. This wasn't a riddle pulled from centuries of dust. This was prophecy unfolding before his eyes—and Amara was at its center.

"What does it mean?" she asked at last, her voice low but steady. "Blood and light... convergence. Why me?"

He hesitated, then leaned forward, his hands braced on the table. The candlelight carved his face into sharp relief, shadows deepening the lines of conflict written there. "Because Amara... you are the convergence. Your bloodline, your very presence—it ties back to the Brotherhood. And the light—" His gaze softened, almost reverent. "—the light is what you carry within you. I saw it in the attic. I saw it in you."

Her chest tightened. Part of her wanted to deny it, to push the responsibility away. But deep down, something inside her stirred, like an ember catching breath. She remembered the stars blazing in the attic, the symbols burning to life beneath her touch. The memory wasn't imagination—it was truth.

"And if I fail?" she whispered.

Sebastiano reached across the table, his hand covering hers with surprising gentleness. "Then the world changes—forever. But you won't fail. Not while I breathe."

The conviction in his voice stole her breath. She stared into his eyes and saw not only resolve, but something deeper, unspoken—an intimacy neither of them could deny any longer.

For a moment, the danger outside, the shadows pressing at their walls, seemed far away. All that remained was the fragile space between them, taut with trust and something dangerously close to love.

A sudden sound cracked through the stillness.

Both their heads whipped toward the window. A faint glimmer of movement beyond the olive trees. Too deliberate to be the wind. Too measured to be chance.

Sebastiano was on his feet in an instant, his chair scraping back. He moved to the window, his body taut, scanning the darkness beyond. The night offered nothing but silence. Still, the air felt charged, heavy with unseen eyes.

Amara rose slowly, her pulse quickening. "They're here, aren't they?"

Sebastiano turned back to her, his jaw tight. He blew out the candle with a single breath, plunging the farmhouse into shadow.

"They've stopped watching," he said grimly. "They've started moving."

Chapter Thirty
The First Clash

The farmhouse seemed to hold its breath. The only sound was the low hum of the sea, rising and falling like a heartbeat against the cliffs. Then—

Glass shattered.

The kitchen window exploded inward, shards scattering across the stone floor. Amara cried out, instinctively ducking, her arms raised to shield her face. Sebastiano was already moving, pulling her down behind the heavy oak table.

"Stay low!" he barked, his voice sharp, steady.

Shadows slipped through the broken frame—two figures, masked and dressed in black, moving with the silent precision of predators. Their boots crunched against the glass, weapons glinting faintly in the dark.

Sebastiano drew a pistol from beneath his jacket. Amara's eyes widened at the sight of it, but there was no time for questions. He fired once, the shot deafening in the confined space. One intruder stumbled, a cry tearing from his throat before he collapsed against the counter.

The second lunged forward, blade flashing in the dim light. Sebastiano met him halfway, their bodies colliding with brutal force. The struggle was sudden, savage—steel against steel as the intruder slashed and Sebastiano blocked with the barrel of his pistol, striking back with ruthless efficiency.

"Run, Amara!" he shouted, his voice strained.

But Amara didn't move. Her eyes locked on the open book still lying on the table, its words glowing faintly, almost pulsing in rhythm with her racing heart. The air around it shimmered, subtle but undeniable, as though it were alive.

The intruder swung wide, his blade catching the edge of Sebastiano's arm. He grunted, staggering, blood darkening his sleeve. Rage flickered across his face as he twisted, slamming the man hard against the stone wall. The knife clattered to the floor. Sebastiano didn't hesitate—one swift motion, and the fight was finished.

Breathing hard, he turned back toward Amara. She hadn't moved from the table. Instead, her hand hovered above the glowing page, trembling but drawn as if by unseen force.

"Amara," he said, his voice rough but urgent, "don't."

Her gaze flicked up to his, wide with fear—and something else. Resolve. "I think… I think it wants me to."

Before he could stop her, her fingers touched the words.

The farmhouse shook. The glow from the page burst outward in a blinding surge of light, spilling across the room, wrapping both of them in a radiance that defied shadow.

Outside, in the darkness beneath the olive trees, Leone's men shielded their eyes as the farmhouse blazed like a beacon.

And Leone, watching from the ridge, smiled.

"The key awakens," he murmured. "Now the game truly begins."

Chapter Thirty-One
The General's Smile

From the ridge above the farmhouse, Leone watched the old stone walls come alive with blinding light. It spilled from every crack and shutter, rising like fire from the earth, a column that pierced the night sky. His men staggered back, shielding their faces, but Leone did not move. He stood tall, the glow painting the scar down his cheek in harsh relief.

"There it is," he whispered, the words almost reverent. "The lock opens."

Around him, soldiers shifted uneasily, their weapons gripped tighter though they knew bullets meant nothing against what stirred within those walls.

One of his captains, a wiry man with eyes too sharp for his own good, dared to speak. "Sir, if the key awakens now, Marchetti will want to be told at once. We should transmit—"

Leone turned slowly, his shadow falling across the man. His smile was thin, terrible. "Marchetti will know soon enough. But we were here first. We saw the light with our own eyes. It was my hand that placed the book in hers. And when this prophecy comes to bloom, history will remember me."

The captain swallowed, his throat bobbing. "Yes, General."

Leone's gaze returned to the farmhouse, his jaw tightening with a predator's hunger. He could feel the shift in the air—the stirring of something ancient, powerful, dangerous. For centuries the Brotherhood had buried its secrets in stone and silence, but tonight the silence had cracked.

"Prepare the others," he said finally. "She will be frightened, vulnerable. D'Amato will try to shield her, but that only makes him useful. Let them cling to each other. Lovers make the easiest prey—they bleed for one another."

He stepped forward, boots grinding against gravel, his voice carrying like a vow.

"The prophecy bends to her, yes. But it is I who will bend her to my will. And when Marchetti realizes the key no longer belongs to him, it will be far too late."

The farmhouse flared again, its glow so fierce the olive trees cast two shadows instead of one. Leone's men crossed themselves, muttering under their breath.

Leone only smiled wider.

"Let it awaken," he murmured. "The war begins tonight."

Chapter Thirty-Two
The House Remembers

The glow began in the stones.

Amara staggered back from the table as a golden shimmer pulsed outward from the farmhouse walls, running through the mortar like veins of fire. The ancient structure hummed, a low vibration that trembled through the floorboards, rattling the glasses on the shelves and sending motes of dust raining from the beams overhead.

She pressed a hand to her chest. Her heartbeat answered the rhythm of the house, each thrum of her pulse matching the flicker of the light.

"Sebastiano!" Her voice caught in her throat, torn between awe and terror.

He was already at her side, his hands still bearing the faint tremor of violence from outside, but his eyes fixed wholly on her now. The cold steel of battle had melted from his face, replaced with something raw, something shaken.

"It's responding to you," he said, his voice rough. "Not to me. To you."

The book on the table snapped shut with a sound like thunder. Amara gasped as the symbol from its pages—a circle of seven stars—seared itself onto the surface of the oak table, glowing as though branded there by an invisible hand.

The kitchen lamps flared, the shutters banged open against the stormless night, and a rush of air swirled through the rooms. It was no ordinary wind—it smelled of frankincense and iron, old stone and burning cedar. The air of cathedrals, of tombs, of rituals long buried.

Amara clutched Sebastiano's arm, but her eyes remained locked on the light as it poured upward, crawling along the walls, racing toward the attic above.

"The house remembers," Sebastiano whispered, as if naming it gave the moment shape.

Then came the voices.

Not one, but many—layered whispers echoing from the rafters, reverent and urgent, as though monks chanted in a long-forgotten tongue. The sound didn't come from outside, but from within the walls themselves.

Amara's knees threatened to buckle, but the pull of the light steadied her. She felt as though the house itself was reaching for her, recognizing her, binding her into its hidden memory.

She turned to Sebastiano, her voice trembling. "What if I don't want this? What if I'm not ready?"

He caught her face in his hands, his eyes searching hers with a fierceness that made her breath catch. "Then I'll carry it with you. Whatever this is—whatever they've buried here—you don't face it alone. Do you understand me?"

Before she could answer, the farmhouse gave a final shudder, and a seam appeared in the far wall.

Stone, centuries old, split neatly down the middle, glowing fissures crawling outward until an arched doorway revealed itself—one that had never been there before.

The chanting grew louder. The glow seared brighter.

And at the heart of the opening, a stair spiraled down into darkness.

Chapter Thirty-Three
The Hidden Descent

The seam in the wall widened with a grinding groan, ancient stone shifting as though awakening from centuries of sleep. Dust spilled into the air, shimmering gold in the glow that still pulsed through the house.

Amara and Sebastiano stood frozen, the weight of the moment pressing against them, neither daring to breathe.

Then the chanting ceased.

The silence was heavier than the sound had been, vast and expectant, like the house itself was holding its breath. Amara tightened her grip on Sebastiano's hand.

"Do you hear that?" she whispered.

He nodded slowly. "It stopped."

The glow concentrated now, sinking into the revealed archway. The newly opened stairway shimmered faintly, stone steps spiraling downward into a darkness alive with the pulse of something unseen.

Sebastiano's jaw tightened. "They built this to be found only when the key awakened." His eyes flicked to hers. "That means you, Amara."

She shook her head, her pulse racing. "I didn't open it. The house did."

"Because of you," he said, firm, as though anchoring her to a truth she couldn't yet accept.

He squeezed her hand and drew a deep breath. "Stay behind me. If there's danger—"

"There is danger," Amara interrupted softly, her voice certain. "But it's not waiting at the bottom of the stairs. It's already inside us. Both of us. We've felt it since the beginning."

His gaze lingered on hers, a spark of something unspoken flickering there—recognition, maybe even remembrance—before he turned toward the steps.

They descended together.

The air grew cooler as they spiraled downward, the glow from above casting faint light on the rough stone. The silence pressed harder the deeper they went, until even the sound of their footsteps seemed muted, swallowed by the dark.

Halfway down, Amara brushed her hand against the wall for balance. Symbols flared to life under her touch—lines of script and sigils carved centuries ago, glowing faintly with the same golden fire that had filled the farmhouse above.

Sebastiano slowed, his eyes scanning the markings. "They left instructions," he murmured. "Or warnings."

Amara traced a star carved into the stone, her fingers tingling as it lit beneath her skin. For a moment, she thought she heard a voice—a woman's voice, layered with echoes, whispering her name.

Her breath caught. "Sebastiano, did you—"

But before she could finish, the stairway opened into a vast chamber.

The ceiling arched high overhead, supported by pillars carved with symbols that glowed faintly like constellations. At the center of the chamber stood a stone pedestal, circular, polished smooth by centuries of reverence.

Upon it rested a single object: a sealed chest of dark wood, reinforced with iron bands, its keyhole glowing faintly.

The air vibrated faintly around it, as though the chest itself was alive.

Sebastiano exhaled slowly. "The Brotherhood's heart," he whispered.

Amara's hand trembled in his. "And it's waiting for us."

Amara stepped closer to the pedestal, drawn by a force she couldn't name. Every breath felt heavier the nearer she came to the chest, as though the air itself resisted her approach.

She stopped just shy of it, her pulse thundering in her ears. The wood was dark with age, the iron bands dulled but unbroken, its keyhole glimmering faintly under the glow of the chamber.

Her hand hovered above it.

Sebastiano caught her wrist gently, his grip firm. "Not yet," he said, his voice low, steady.

Amara turned her gaze on him, eyes wide with urgency. "It's calling me. Don't you feel it?"

"I feel it," he admitted. His jaw tightened as his eyes flicked to the shadows along the chamber walls. "But whatever's inside—it's not meant to be rushed. Things hidden this long are hidden for a reason."

Amara swallowed hard, pulling her hand back reluctantly. The glow of the sigils on the walls pulsed as though in agreement, then dimmed, leaving the room bathed in a softer, more unsettling half-light.

Sebastiano released her wrist slowly, his touch lingering for a moment longer than necessary. His gaze never left the shadows.

Amara followed his line of sight, her breath catching.

A sound drifted from the far end of the chamber. A faint scrape, like stone shifting beneath boots. Then another.

They weren't alone.

Sebastiano stepped subtly in front of her, his hand slipping toward the pistol concealed beneath his jacket. His voice was a whisper, calm but edged with steel. "Stay close. No matter what happens, don't touch the chest until I say."

Amara's heart pounded, her gaze flicking between the looming shadows and the chest that pulsed faintly like a heartbeat on the pedestal.

The scrape of boots grew louder.

A figure emerged from the darkness at the edge of the chamber—cloaked, hood drawn low, the faint glint of a blade catching the light.

And then another.

And another.

The chamber's silence broke under the whisper of steel unsheathed.

Sebastiano's grip tightened on Amara's hand. "The Brotherhood wasn't just protecting what's inside," he murmured. "They left guardians."

The first guardian lunged.

Steel sang as Sebastiano drew his pistol and fired in one motion, the crack echoing like thunder in the ancient chamber. The bullet struck the blade, sparks spitting into the dark as if the steel itself defied modern fire.

"Move!" Sebastiano barked, pulling Amara behind the pedestal.

But the guardians were already circling. Their movements were unnaturally fluid, silent save for the scrape of boots against stone. Their faces remained hidden, but the air shimmered faintly around them—as though they weren't entirely of this world.

Amara pressed herself against the pedestal, her breath quick, her pulse racing. She could feel the chest vibrating beneath her fingertips, as though it recognized the threat.

Sebastiano fired again, the shot hitting one square in the chest. The figure staggered but did not fall. Instead, it straightened with eerie calm, the bullet clattering to the floor as though spat out by an unseen hand.

"Not human," Sebastiano muttered, holstering the gun. His hand snapped to the knife at his belt. "Fine."

The next strike came fast—a blade arcing toward his ribs. Sebastiano parried with his knife, sparks flying as the two metals clashed. He twisted, using his weight to shove the cloaked figure back, but another was already upon him.

Amara's heart hammered as she searched the chamber wildly. The sigils along the walls were glowing brighter again, pulsing in rhythm with the chest. She felt the same pull from the attic, that same ancient hum.

And then it hit her.

"They're not here for you," she whispered, realization chilling her blood. "They're here for me."

One of the guardians turned its hooded face toward her. No eyes, no features—only darkness, deeper than shadow.

It raised its blade.

Sebastiano shouted her name as he launched himself between them. Steel struck steel, the shock reverberating through the chamber.

The guardians pressed forward, unyielding, silent, relentless.

And the chest began to glow.

The chest flared.

Light burst through the seams of the ancient wood, so bright it carved shadows into the vaulted walls. The guardians froze mid-strike, their blades hovering inches from Sebastiano's chest. For a heartbeat, the chamber held its breath.

Then the symbols etched into the lid ignited, glowing like molten gold. The hum grew louder, deep and resonant, vibrating through the stone floor, through Amara's bones, through the air itself until it was impossible to tell if it was sound or heartbeat.

Amara staggered back, shielding her eyes. "Sebastiano!"

The guardians lowered their weapons in unison. Slowly, mechanically, they turned their faceless hoods toward her.

Sebastiano moved to shield her again, but Amara pressed a hand to his chest. "Wait," she whispered, her eyes wide, locked on the chest.

The lid trembled, ancient locks snapping open one by one—not broken, but released, as if recognizing something long awaited. The light spilled upward in a radiant column, bathing Amara in its glow.

The guardians sank to one knee, blades crossed before them in ritual reverence. Not defeated, not destroyed—subdued. A silent acknowledgment.

Sebastiano's knife slipped from his fingers, the sound of it clattering against stone drowned by the rising hum. His eyes widened as he looked at her, standing in the golden light, her hair shimmering as if each strand carried fire.

The chest spoke—not in words, but in symbols. The glow coalesced into a shifting script across the air, lines of forgotten language burning in patterns around her. Amara gasped, her vision flooding with images: a circle of hooded figures, a brotherhood swearing oaths, and a single woman at the center—her own face, across centuries.

The guardians bowed their heads. The test was complete.

And the chest, at last, had chosen.

With a sound like stone grinding against stone, the lid of the chest lifted on its own. The air grew heavy, charged with the scent of ancient incense and sea-salt, as though the centuries themselves had seeped into the wood.

Inside, there was no treasure of gold or jewels — only three objects, resting in perfect symmetry upon a bed of faded velvet.

The first was a scroll, bound in crimson cord, its parchment so old it seemed it might crumble under breath. Faint glyphs bled through, pulsing faintly with the same light that had poured from the chest.

The second was a dagger. Its blade shimmered with an iridescent sheen, forged from a metal neither of them recognized. Its hilt was inlaid with a single emerald, carved into the shape of an eye that seemed to watch.

And the third — a small obsidian disk, perfectly smooth, etched with concentric circles that spiraled inward to a single point of light. When Amara leaned closer, the circles seemed to move, pulling her vision deeper until she swayed, dizzy with its gravity.

Sebastiano reached out instinctively, but the guardians stirred. Their blades lifted in warning, though their kneeling posture did not change. It was clear: the contents were not his to touch.

"Amara…" he whispered, his voice hoarse. "It's for you."

Her fingers trembled as she reached forward. The moment her hand hovered over the scroll, the air shifted. The guardians' blades lowered again, and the chamber filled with a low, resonant chant — not in any language she knew, but one her soul seemed to understand.

She took the scroll in her hands. It was warm, impossibly warm, as though it held a heartbeat of its own. The crimson cord loosened on its own, the parchment unrolling just enough to reveal the first line:

The Key awakens when light and shadow walk as one.

Her breath caught. She looked at Sebastiano — the man bound to darkness by loyalty, yet standing now in the light with her.

The chest's glow dimmed, the lid settling back into place with finality. But Amara knew this was only the beginning. The scroll was the first thread. And the dagger and the disk… they were waiting.

Chapter Thirty-Four
The Crack in Control

Duke Antonio Marchetti sat in the heart of his study, a cavernous room lined with books he had never read and artifacts stolen from lands he had never set foot on. His empire was knowledge, but not for its own sake — for leverage, for power. Every object here was a token of control.

But tonight, control was slipping.

Leone stood across from him, silent but watchful. Between them, a holographic feed shimmered to life, distorted as though resisting transmission. At last, the image sharpened into a heatmap of the farmhouse. It pulsed with light — not electrical, not anything their instruments could classify. The entire structure blazed like a beacon.

Marchetti rose slowly from his chair, his eyes narrowing, his features carved in stone. "The chest," he murmured. "It has awakened."

Leone's jaw tightened. "Confirmed. My men reported seismic vibrations in the cliffside. And... chanting. They said it wasn't human."

Marchetti turned, his gaze cutting like ice. "And yet the woman lives."

"Yes," Leone admitted. "And D'Amato still stands at her side."

A silence fell, so sharp it seemed to draw the air from the room. Marchetti moved to the window, staring out at his dark gardens, his reflection superimposed against the night.

"She is the Key. There can be no doubt now," he said, voice low, dangerous. "But the prophecy also warned of the

Guardian." His head turned slightly, just enough for Leone to see the flicker of suspicion in his sharp blue eyes. "Tell me, Leone… is it possible the prophecy does not name her alone?"

Leone's eyes flickered, but he did not falter. "If it does, then D'Amato is the crack in the lock."

Marchetti faced him fully now. "Then he must be broken."

The words hung like a sentence passed. Leone inclined his head, the faintest smile ghosting across his lips. "Consider it done."

But when Marchetti dismissed him with a flick of his hand, the Duke lingered at the window, fingers tapping the glass. The farmhouse pulsed in his mind's eye, alive with power. For years he had maneuvered every pawn, written every line of the game.

And now, for the first time, the board was shifting without him.

Chapter Thirty-Five
The Predator Unleashed

In a subterranean chamber beneath an abandoned monastery outside Naples, Leone stood before a rack of weapons laid out like surgical instruments. His massive frame cast long shadows across the stone floor, the faint light of iron sconces catching the scars that laced his arms and hands. Each scar was a story of survival. Each one a reminder that he did not fear pain—he wielded it.

Before him knelt a man, head bowed, waiting for orders. His name was Raffaele, a hunter whose reputation was whispered through the criminal underworld like a curse. Where others hesitated, Raffaele excelled—tracking, breaking, eliminating. His loyalty to Leone was unquestioned, forged in blood and silence.

Leone's voice rumbled through the chamber like a slow avalanche. "Marchetti tightens the leash. He wants D'Amato broken. He wants Amara Savard vulnerable."

Raffaele lifted his head, his dark eyes glinting with anticipation. "And you want her dead?"

Leone shook his head slowly, almost reverently. "Not yet. She is the key. Kill her now, and the prophecy withers in her grave. No—we corner her, we strip away her safety, and we make D'Amato bleed until he chooses where his loyalty lies. If he clings to her, he dies. If he returns to Marchetti's fold, then she will beg to be mine."

He picked up a dagger from the rack—a slender blade etched with the Brotherhood's twisted sigil—and pressed it into Raffaele's hands. "You will go to the farmhouse. Watch first. Learn the rhythms of their life together. Then strike when the moment cuts deepest. Not to end them—yet. To remind them that shadows can breach their walls."

Raffaele's lips curled into a smile as he tucked the dagger beneath his coat. "They will know fear."

Leone leaned closer, his voice dropping to a growl. "Not fear. Despair. Let D'Amato see how fragile his precious Amara truly is. Let her wake to the truth that every touch, every glance she shares with him places her deeper in the crosshairs."

Raffaele bowed his head in acknowledgment, then disappeared into the shadows with the silence of a seasoned predator.

When he was gone, Leone turned back to the scarred table where the ledger still lay open. He dragged his knife across the page, carving two fresh lines beneath Amara's name.

Soon. Very soon.

The echo of the steel blade filled the chamber, a promise and a threat bound into one.

Chapter Thirty-Six
Threads of Control

Marchetti stood before the great map wall in his study, the air thick with the scent of polished leather and cigar smoke. Red lines traced continents, converging across oceans and cities like veins of blood. Dots of light marked satellites, their orbital paths scrolling across holographic overlays.

Behind him, Leone's voice carried like a drumbeat. "Raffaele is in motion. He will test them. He will remind D'Amato of his place."

Marchetti did not turn. His blue eyes followed the slow crawl of a satellite over southern Europe, watching it blink across the display. "Remind him, yes. But do not break him yet. D'Amato is still useful—his proximity gives us eyes where even our technology cannot see. If he resists too strongly, then he is lost. But if he bends..." Marchetti's lips curved into a wolfish smile. "...then he leads us to the heart of her."

Leone stepped closer, his presence looming, but silent. He didn't argue. Not yet.

Marchetti clasped his hands behind his back. "Do you know why I always win, Leone? It is not because I have more wealth, or more men, though I have both. It is because I do not act from impulse. I let the board shift until the pieces move themselves."

Finally, he turned, his gaze sharp as a blade. "But this time, I feel the prophecy breathing down my neck. This woman—Amara Savard—she is not another pawn. She is the axis of the game. The Brotherhood made sure of it."

He pressed a hand against the map, against the dot that hovered over Capri. "And she belongs to me."

Leone inclined his head, hiding the flicker of something darker in his eyes. "Then Raffaele will make her pliable. By the time she fully understands her power, she will already be in your grasp."

Marchetti smiled, but his eyes remained cold. "See that it is so. I want no surprises. Not from her. Not from D'Amato. And not from you, Leone."

The silence that followed carried the weight of an unspoken warning.

Leone bowed his head, but the set of his jaw betrayed what he did not speak: the game was no longer Marchetti's alone.

Chapter Thirty-Seven
The Weight of the Chest

The farmhouse was quiet again, though it was not the silence of peace. The air still shimmered faintly, as if the walls themselves remembered the surge of light that had coursed through them. Dust motes drifted lazily in shafts of morning sun, each one seeming to glow a little brighter than it should.

Amara sat at the long wooden table, the book lying before her, its cover dark and unyielding. The silver letters across the spine seemed to breathe, their glow waxing and waning with her own heartbeat.

Sebastiano stood at the window, shoulders tense, scanning the road below for any sign of movement. The broken bodies of those who had dared breach the farmhouse hours before had been carried away by his own hands under the cloak of night, but the blood on the threshold had taken longer to scrub clean. Still, he felt their presence lingering, like smoke that clung to the lungs long after the fire was gone.

"Whoever sent the book," Amara said finally, her voice low, "they wanted me to open it. To see what's inside."

Her fingers traced the edge of the cover. She felt warmth there, a subtle hum that spoke not only of danger but of recognition. As if the chest downstairs and this book were two halves of the same key, calling to her, testing her.

"I dreamt of it last night," she admitted, her gaze drifting to the book again. "It felt like… like the beginning of something. And I think the chest knows it's here."

Sebastiano crossed the room in two strides, his hand closing gently over hers. His voice was quiet, but the weight in it left no room for doubt. "What is bound in that chest—it has slept for centuries—it does not wake without cost. If you open that book again now, you may not be able to close it this time."

The farmhouse seemed to breathe with them, the old stones pressing close, the sea wind rattling the shutters like restless spirits.

And then—three sharp knocks at the door.

Amara froze. Sebastiano's eyes narrowed, his hand slipping from hers to the pistol at his side. The sound came again, deliberate, measured. Not the frantic pounding of an enemy, nor the tentative tap of a neighbor.

This was something else.

Amara's gaze flicked to the book. The letters on its spine pulsed brighter, as though answering the summons.

Chapter Thirty-Eight
The Visitor

Sebastiano motioned for Amara to stay back. He moved toward the door with the same silent precision he had used to dispatch the men the night before. Each step was measured, steady, his hand firm on the pistol though he kept it hidden against his leg.

The knocks came again—three, sharp, deliberate.

He unlatched the heavy oak door and swung it open.

On the threshold stood not an intruder, nor one of Marchetti's sleek men in black suits, but a stranger dressed in travel-worn clothes: a linen shirt stained with dust, a weathered satchel slung across his shoulder, boots scuffed from long miles. His face was shadowed by the brim of a wide hat, but when he looked up, Amara felt a jolt in her chest. His eyes—piercing, pale gray—seemed to see straight through her, as if reading lines from a book written beneath her skin.

"I come unarmed," the man said, his voice calm but carrying a strange gravity, as though each word weighed more than it should. He raised his empty hands, palms open. "I am here because the key has stirred. Because the chest knows her name."

Sebastiano's stance didn't shift, though his grip on the pistol tightened. "Who sent you?" he demanded.

The stranger's gaze flicked briefly to the book on the table, then back to Sebastiano. "Not Marchetti. Not Leone. Others. Older. Ones who do not play their games of empire and blood."

Amara stepped forward despite Sebastiano's warning glance. Her voice was steady, though her pulse raced. "You know about the book. About the chest."

The man inclined his head. "I know more than that. I know what wakes each time you open it. And I know the price it demands."

The farmhouse seemed to shift around them, the light dimming as though the very walls leaned closer to hear his words.

Sebastiano stepped between them, his tone hard. "And why should we trust you?"

The man's pale eyes never wavered. "Because whether you trust me or not, the hour is nearly here. And when it comes, you will need more than each other to survive what awakens."

He lowered his hands, slowly, deliberately, as though to place himself in their mercy. "My name is Elias," he said quietly. "And I have walked with the Brotherhood's shadow longer than either of you have drawn breath."

The book on the table pulsed again—once, twice—like a heartbeat.

Chapter Thirty-Nine
The Stranger Within

Amara's hand lifted before she even realized it, resting lightly on Sebastiano's arm. "Let him in," she whispered. Her voice was soft but resolute, tinged with something even she didn't fully understand.

Sebastiano studied her, saw the certainty flickering in her eyes, then gave a small, reluctant nod. He lowered the pistol but didn't holster it. "Inside. Slowly."

Elias stepped over the threshold, his boots scraping the stone floor. The farmhouse seemed to breathe around him, its old timbers groaning as though acknowledging his presence. He removed his hat, revealing streaks of silver at his temples, though his bearing held the strength of a man younger than his years.

Once the door closed, Elias' gaze shifted downward, as though he could see the glowing chest through the layers of stone and wood. "It has waited long enough," he murmured.

Amara moved closer, her pulse thrumming. "You know it. You've seen it before?"

Elias gave a faint, enigmatic smile. "I've seen others like it. The chests are not singular. They were seeded across the world by the Brotherhood, each guarding fragments of the whole. But this one…" His eyes returned to her, sharp and unwavering. "This one awakens only for you."

Sebastiano's jaw tightened. "And you arrived here out of the kindness of your heart? Or are you another of Marchetti's spies playing a deeper game?"

Elias met the suspicion head-on. "I am no servant of Marchetti. Nor of Leone. I walk older paths. I came because when the chest opened, it called across the threads of time. Those of us who still listen… we heard."

He dropped his satchel onto the table with a heavy thud. Dust puffed into the air as he unbuckled it and drew out a roll of parchment, edges frayed with age. He unrolled it carefully, revealing a faded map marked with concentric circles and glyphs eerily similar to those that glowed in Amara's attic.

Her breath caught. "I've seen those symbols."

Elias nodded. "Of course you have. They are burned into your memory because once, long ago, they were yours to guard."

The farmhouse seemed to hum at his words, the book on the table giving a faint tremor. Sebastiano reached out instinctively, still torn between distrust and recognition of the truth settling in Amara's eyes.

Elias leaned forward, his pale gaze fixed on them both. "You have opened the first seal. The others will come for you now, not just Marchetti. Leone moves already. And when they arrive, they will not knock politely at your door."

The candle flames bent inward as though pulled by an unseen breath.

Elias let the silence stretch, the farmhouse creaking faintly around them as if listening. At last, he spoke, his voice low and measured.

"The prophecy was never about power alone," he said, tapping the parchment map with a calloused finger. "It was about convergence. When the stars align—and they soon will—the locks placed upon hidden knowledge will either break open to restore balance… or be twisted to enslave the world."

His gaze moved between Amara and Sebastiano, lingering on her. "The Brotherhood divided the knowledge long ago, scattering it across chests such as yours. Each chest requires a living key—a soul bound to its legacy.

That is why you feel the pull, Amara Savard. You are not the first key, but you may be the last."

Amara swallowed hard, the weight of his words pressing against her chest. "Why me? I never asked for this. I never even knew—"

"You did know," Elias interrupted gently. "Not here, not in this life. But the memory sleeps within you. The Brotherhood trusted your line because you once stood among them. You chose to guard what others would kill to possess."

Sebastiano shifted, his hand flexing unconsciously near his sidearm. "And Marchetti? Leone? They want to twist this convergence, don't they?"

Elias' expression hardened, the faint glow of the candlelight deepening the lines of his face. "Yes. Marchetti hunts to rule. Leone hunts to consume. Both will bleed the world if they succeed. Marchetti's reach extends farther than you realize."

The farmhouse trembled faintly, a vibration that seemed to rise from the very stones beneath their feet. The chest downstairs pulsed with light once, twice, then fell still.

Amara pressed her hands to the table, steadying herself. "So what do we do?"

Elias rolled the parchment closed with precise care, his eyes never leaving hers. "You prepare. The chest will test you again. It will demand proof that you are worthy to carry what it holds. And when it does, you cannot face it alone."

He glanced toward Sebastiano, his gaze sharp and knowing. "Nor can you, soldier. The chest recognizes your strength, but not your loyalty. That, too, will be tested."

The room fell silent. Only the crackle of the fire and the distant surge of the sea filled the pause.

Finally, Elias straightened, pulling the satchel back to his side. "Rest tonight. Tomorrow the path begins. Once opened, it cannot be closed again."

He stepped back toward the door, his presence suddenly less weighty, as if the house itself were gently ushering him away. Before leaving, he turned once more, his pale eyes glinting.

"And remember—when the chest fully awakens, others will come. Friends and enemies alike. Choose carefully which is which."

Then he was gone, the door closing softly behind him, leaving Amara and Sebastiano alone once more with the silence, the chest, and the storm waiting just beyond the horizon.

Chapter Forty
Echoes in the Stone

The door clicked shut behind Elias, and for a long moment neither Amara nor Sebastiano spoke. The farmhouse felt impossibly still, as though the very walls were absorbing every word he had left behind.

Amara pressed her palms against the edge of the table, her breath unsteady. "I don't know if I can do this," she whispered, the words slipping out before she could stop them. "He's talking about me like I'm... like I'm some chosen piece of a puzzle I never asked to be part of."

Sebastiano moved closer, his presence solid and grounding. "You didn't ask for it," he said softly, "but that doesn't change what's inside you. I saw the attic, Amara. I saw what the chest did when you touched it. Whatever this is—it recognizes you."

Her eyes flicked to his, wide and searching. "And what if I fail? What if I'm not the key they think I am?"

"Then we fail together," Sebastiano replied firmly, his voice low but unwavering. "I don't care what Marchetti thinks he owns, or what Leone is plotting. You're not facing any of this alone. I will face it with you. We stand together."

His words steadied her, yet the chest pulsed faintly below them—as if reminding her of Elias' warning. A test was coming.

They descended the staircase in silence, each step weighted with expectation. The air grew heavier as they neared the bottom, charged with that same low hum she had felt the night before. When they reached the bottom, the hum surged into Amara's bones.

The chest glowed steadily in the shadows, its metal seams traced with threads of light that pulsed like a heartbeat. As Amara stepped forward, symbols shimmered faintly across its surface—different this time, sharper, demanding.

Sebastiano rested a hand on her shoulder. "You don't have to touch it tonight."

Amara shook her head slowly. "It won't wait, Sebastiano. It's already calling."

She reached out, her fingers trembling, and the glow flared in answer. For a moment, the walls dissolved around them—stone and timber replaced by endless darkness shot through with streaks of gold. Whispered voices rose and fell, indistinct, circling like echoes of another age.

Then one voice rang clear, deep and resonant, reverberating through the void:

"The key awakens. Will you guard, or will you surrender?"

Amara's breath caught in her throat. Sebastiano's grip tightened on her shoulder, grounding her as the question repeated, louder this time, demanding an answer.

She opened her mouth to speak—

And the vision snapped shut. The walls returned in a rush of air, the chest dimming to a soft, steady glow. Amara staggered back, her pulse racing.

Sebastiano caught her, steadying her against his chest. "What did you see?"

Her voice was faint, but sure. "A choice. They want me to choose."

Chapter Forty-One
The Duke's Resolve

The villa glittered with all the trappings of wealth—crystal chandeliers, velvet drapes, marble polished to a faultless sheen—but its master sat in darkness.

Duke Antonio Marchetti leaned back in his leather chair, a single lamp illuminating the surface of his desk. Before him lay the grainy photographs: Amara at her farmhouse door, the book clutched in her hands.

He studied her face for a long time. The tilt of her chin, the unstudied strength in her gaze even as confusion shadowed it. A woman was unaware of her role then yet already stirring forces that had slept for centuries.

"The key," he muttered, his lips curling. "Not just a myth. Not just words in crumbling parchment."

Behind him, the door creaked open. His aide, Matteo, slipped inside, bowing low. "Sir. Leone awaits your command."

Marchetti's eyes did not leave the photographs. "Leone grows ambitious. Too ambitious. I can taste it in his words—he forgets himself."

Matteo swallowed, his eyes flickering nervously. "He has results, sir. The farmhouse has been breached."

"The farmhouse was not taken," Marchetti snapped, his voice slicing like a blade. He rose in one fluid motion, the steel in his frame belying his years. "And you will remember—results do not excuse insolence. Leone serves at my pleasure."

He walked to the window, staring out at the manicured lawn, his reflection fractured in the glass. "No man, no matter how brutal, will seize what I have bled decades to reach. Not Leone. Not D'Amato. Not even the woman herself. She is mine to use. My key. My prophecy."

Matteo bowed again, his voice cautious. "Shall I send word to Leone?"

Marchetti's gaze sharpened, a predator's gleam in his cold blue eyes. "No. Let him think I am silent. Let him believe his leash is slack. When he oversteps—and he will—then I will tighten it until he chokes."

He turned back to his desk, gathering the photographs into a neat stack with deliberate precision. "In the meantime, we increase surveillance. I want eyes inside that farmhouse. If she so much as breathes differently, I want to know."

Matteo hesitated. "And D'Amato?"

Marchetti allowed himself a slow smile, one devoid of warmth. "D'Amato has always believed he could walk between two fires and not be burned. Soon, he will learn otherwise."

The clock on the wall chimed the hour, its cold tone echoing through the chamber. Marchetti straightened his cuffs, his voice low, a vow to himself more than to his aide.

"The key awakens. And when it does, the world will kneel—or it will burn."

Chapter Forty-Two
The Guardian's Charge

The farmhouse had never felt so alive. Sunlight streamed in through the arched windows, catching on motes of dust that shimmered like flecks of gold. Yet beneath the warmth, there was an undercurrent—a hush that wasn't silence, but listening.

Amara sat at the heavy wooden table, her fingers brushing the edges of the ancient book. Its cover still glowed faintly, as though its brilliance had not fully dimmed. Every time she looked at it, her chest tightened with a strange mix of fear and recognition.

Sebastiano paced near the hearth, his movements taut, restless. He had killed men in the shadows of the farmhouse, defended her with a precision born of necessity—but the quiet presence of the book unnerved him more than bullets ever had.

And though Elias was gone, his words remained like a current moving through the house: The guardians will test you. The book does not yield its truth because you demand it. It yields when you become the truth it guards.

Amara swallowed, her voice low. "Do you feel it? Like the house itself is watching?"

Sebastiano stopped pacing, his gaze drifting over the glowing symbols faintly flickering across the stone walls. He gave a single, sharp nod. "I feel it. I see it, look at the walls."

She placed her palm flat on the cover of the book, its glow brightening beneath her touch. She looked at him, her voice trembling but sure. "We can't run from this. We have to see it through."

He moved to her side, his hand covering hers on the book. The glow deepened, threads of light weaving between their fingers as if binding them together.

The air shifted—cooler now, edged with a strange vibration that prickled across their skin.

Amara's pulse quickened. "It's beginning."

Sebastiano's dark eyes locked on hers. "Then we face it together."

The book flared, and the farmhouse groaned as though opening its lungs. Symbols shimmered across the walls, spilling light that twisted into shapes—archways, constellations, the faint outlines of figures stirring in the glow.

The guardians' test had begun.

Chapter Forty-Three
The Guardians Awaken

The farmhouse pulsed with light, each stone seeming to breathe as symbols cascaded down the walls in rivers of gold. The air grew dense, thick with the hum of unseen voices resonating through the beams and floorboards, echoing like chants carried across centuries.

Amara clutched Sebastiano's hand, her breath caught in her throat. The glow from the book spilled across the table, expanding outward until it touched the floor, the walls, and finally the ceiling, wrapping the room in a shimmering sphere of light.

And then—figures began to emerge.

They did not step through doors or windows, but from the light itself, as though the farmhouse walls had thinned to reveal another reality. Cloaked forms wove into existence, their features hidden, their presence towering though they did not move. Each radiated an aura of immense gravity—neither hostile nor kind, but absolute, like laws written before time itself.

Amara's knees trembled. She felt their gaze not on her face, but inside her, as though the guardians were peeling back every layer of her being, searching for truth beneath flesh and thought.

Sebastiano stood straighter, but she felt his hand tighten on hers. For once, his steady composure wavered.

One of the figures raised a hand, and the room fell utterly still. When it spoke, its voice was not sound but vibration, sinking straight into their bones.

"You who have opened the seal, you are seen. You are weighed. You are not yet proven."

The words reverberated through Amara, each syllable striking like a bell rung in the chambers of her heart. She wanted to speak, to say she did not understand, but her tongue felt heavy, as if words were forbidden unless invited.

Another figure leaned forward, its cloak shimmering with faint constellations. "The key is not the book, nor the chest. The key is the bearer. Show us if the flame is in you."

Amara gasped, clutching her chest. The sensation she had felt in the attic—the stars, the symbols, the memories stirring just beyond reach—ignited within her. A warmth spread outward, filling her veins, her skin, until her entire body glowed faintly in answer.

The guardians' cloaks rippled, as though stirred by an unseen wind.

Sebastiano turned toward her, his eyes wide. "Amara…"

Her glow brightened, threads of light weaving upward from her heart, streaming like golden smoke toward the guardians. They reached out, their hands hovering as if measuring the purity of her light.

And then one voice, deeper than the rest, rolled through the chamber:

"She carries it. But the shadow clings. Both must be tested. Both must stand."

The guardians' gazes fell upon Sebastiano.

His breath caught, and for the first time in years, fear flashed across his face.

Chapter Forty-Four
Marchetti's Calculus

The storm had gathered above his estate like a crown of iron. Black clouds rolled across the horizon, thunder muttering low and constant as though the heavens themselves were restless. Marchetti stood at the heart of his command room, the great hall he had transformed into a war chamber of light and glass. Dozens of holographic panes floated in the air—maps, satellite feeds, coded transmissions—all orbiting him like planets circling their sun.

But tonight, none of them gave him ease.

On one of the feeds, the farmhouse glowed faintly in the grainy infrared of his surveillance drone. Power signatures surged and faded like a heartbeat, readings that no machine could properly quantify. Even the analysts had faltered, stammering about electromagnetic pulses and heat spikes with no rational cause. Marchetti silenced them all with a flick of his hand. He knew better than they.

"The key is stirring," he murmured, his reflection caught in the glass. "And with it, the lock begins to yield."

Leone stood in the shadowed corner, arms crossed, his bulk coiled with the stillness of a predator waiting for command. "Your faith in prophecy is becoming… impractical," he said quietly, though not without a trace of challenge. "What we saw at the farmhouse—those readings defy science. It could as easily destroy her as it could awaken her."

Marchetti turned, his blue eyes narrowing to shards of ice. "And yet she lives. That alone tells me the prophecy bends toward truth. You see chaos. I see inevitability."

He walked to the long table, laying his hand flat against a spread of old parchment—the Brotherhood's recovered fragments, fragile and yellowed, inked with symbols whose meaning had eluded scholars for centuries. His other hand rested on the glowing interface of a digital map, lines of power and ley converging upon a single point: the farmhouse.

"The convergence is not accident," Marchetti said, his voice low, deliberate. "This house was chosen, built upon the seam where worlds touch. The Brotherhood knew it. They sealed their treasure inside and bound it to bloodlines. Now she is there, in possession of the house, the chest, and the book. Every piece is falling into place."

Leone's jaw tightened, but he said nothing.

Marchetti's smile was thin, almost cruel. "You doubt me because you do not understand. But you will. Soon, the world will understand. And when the key is fully awakened, when the lock yields… I will be the one to open it. And what lies beyond will belong to me."

Lightning flared through the windows, illuminating his figure against the storm. For an instant, his shadow loomed vast and distorted across the chamber walls, more monster than man.

"Double the watch on D'Amato," he commanded suddenly, his tone hard as steel. "He wavers. His loyalty strains. If he falters, I want his body on my desk before dawn. But not before he has served his use."

Leone inclined his head slowly, though his eyes betrayed a flicker of something unspoken. "As you command."

Marchetti returned to the window, staring into the dark horizon where the storm raged. The farmhouse glowed faintly on his screen, pulsing like a beacon.

"The key awakens," he whispered, almost reverently. "And the world trembles in its sleep."

Chapter Forty-Five
The Stirring

The farmhouse breathed with a light not of this world.
Threads of pale gold still clung to the walls and beams,
fading slowly as though the house itself exhaled after
holding its breath too long. The air was heavy, vibrating
with a low hum that seemed to seep from the very stones.

Amara and Sebastiano descended the stairs and stood at
the edge of the glowing chest, Amara's hand hovering just
above its surface. The sigils carved into the lid still
shimmered faintly, their curves alive like molten fire
cooling to embers. Sebastiano was at her side, his body
tense, one hand on her arm as though he feared what would
happen if she touched it again.

"You feel it too," she whispered, her voice almost
breaking against the stillness.

Sebastiano's jaw tightened. "It's not just light. It's
watching us."

The farmhouse creaked as though in answer—timbers
settling, or perhaps something deeper stirring.

And then, the chamber shifted. The space stretched
beyond its stone walls, shadows receding as though
swallowed into a vast unseen horizon. Amara gripped
Sebastiano's hand as four figures of radiant light stepped
forward, their forms neither male nor female, ageless, their
presence heavy with eternity.

The Guardians.

Their voices rose together, woven as one:

"The Key is chosen. But the Key cannot turn without the
Hand."

Amara's breath caught, her eyes drawn to Sebastiano. The words pierced him deeper than they did her.

One Guardian extended an arm. A dagger materialized in its palm—luminous, half-real, its edges pulsing with unseen fire. It lowered toward Sebastiano.

"You have walked in shadow," the voice intoned. "Your hands have served two masters. Now you must choose, before us, who you are."

Sebastiano stared at the dagger, the weight of years pressing on him—Marchetti's commands, the lives taken, the loyalty demanded. His hand trembled as he reached for the hilt.

A second Guardian stepped forward, its voice like fire breaking stone.

"To serve the Key, you must cut away the chain of your old master. If you cannot, the hidden knowledge will remain sealed."

Sebastiano's breath came hard, shallow. His gaze flicked to Amara, her eyes shining with fear and faith. She touched his arm, not guiding, but reminding him he was not alone.

He closed his eyes, then opened them, fierce and resolute. His fingers wrapped around the dagger's hilt.

The third Guardian spoke, its voice softer, yet crushing as stone:

"One cut severs your past. Another binds your future. Choose."

The dagger pulsed in his hand, alive, waiting.

Sebastiano lifted the dagger. Its weight was unlike any blade he had ever held—heavier than steel, yet burning with a lightness that seemed to strip away the marrow of his bones. The hilt thrummed in his palm, alive, demanding.

The Guardians closed in, their light forming a circle around him and Amara. The air thickened, trembling with the resonance of something vast, unseen.

Sebastiano's mind reeled. Marchetti's voice echoed in the back of his skull, commanding, cold. Loyalty is everything. Obedience is survival. Years of service, of killing without hesitation, surged against the tide of something new, something he had not allowed himself in decades—hope.

Amara's hand brushed against his arm, steady, anchoring him in the present. Her eyes locked with his, wide and unblinking, filled not with fear but with belief.

"Sebastiano," she whispered, her voice almost lost in the hum of the Guardians. "You already know who you are."

The dagger pulsed, flaring so brightly it lit every shadow in the farmhouse.

His hand trembled. One cut would end the life he'd built, the chains of Marchetti, the blood-soaked path behind him. Another would bind him irrevocably to Amara—to the Key, to a destiny larger than his own.

His chest heaved as the Guardians' united voice pressed like thunder:

"Choose. For hesitation is death. The Key cannot turn without the Hand."

Sweat beaded along his brow. The dagger hovered inches above his own forearm—where the mark of Marchetti's Brotherhood still lingered faintly beneath his skin like a brand burned long ago.

Sebastiano exhaled, the sound raw and ragged. His knuckles whitened around the hilt.

The farmhouse held its breath.

Chapter Forty-Six
The Fracture

Duke Antonio Marchetti stood at the window of his study, but he wasn't watching the gardens. His reflection glared back at him in the glass—silver hair combed to precision, jaw set like carved stone. Yet beneath that polished exterior, fury coiled.

The latest report lay on the desk behind him, its words like acid. D'Amato was no longer simply watching the woman. He was… with her. Protecting her. Choosing her.

"Traitor," Marchetti muttered, his breath fogging the glass.

The door creaked open. Leone entered without knocking, as he often did. A cigarette smoldered between his fingers, its smoke curling toward the gilded ceiling. "Your instincts were right," Leone said flatly. "D'Amato is slipping. The woman has turned his head."

Marchetti turned slowly, his expression unreadable. "And what would you have me do, Leone?"

Leone took a drag, his dark eyes narrowing. "Strip him of choice. Remind him of what loyalty costs. If he resists, I'll cut him down myself."

For the first time in years, Marchetti felt a tremor of unease. Leone had always been brutal, but now there was something in his tone—an edge of independence that went beyond mere obedience. "Careful," Marchetti said, his voice low, deliberate. "You exist because I allow it. Don't mistake your zeal for authority."

Leone smiled faintly, though it never touched his eyes. "Authority? No, Duke. Efficiency. I see cracks before they spread. And this—" he flicked ash into a crystal tray "—

this is spreading. You've coddled D'Amato for too long. I won't."

Marchetti's jaw clenched. He hated the truth in Leone's words. Sebastiano had always been reliable, his loyalty a weapon sharpened by years of blood. The woman had become his weakness—and the game was tilting out of Marchetti's control.

He turned back to the window, speaking more to himself than to Leone. "The prophecy bends toward her. If D'Amato falters, it bends through him as well. That makes him dangerous... but also necessary."

Leone crushed the cigarette into the tray, his smile twisting cruelly. "Then let me be the knife that decides which he is."

Marchetti finally looked at him, his eyes cold as winter steel. "Do what needs to be done," he said softly. "But if you fail me, Leone... remember this: I do not forgive twice."

Leone inclined his head, but as he left, the faint smirk on his lips told a different story.

For the first time in decades, Marchetti felt it—that subtle, shifting scent of betrayal in his own house.

And outside, unseen from his study, a hawk circled the estate—its shadow gliding over the marble fountains like an omen.

Chapter Forty-Seven
The Hound Unleashed

Leone's boots echoed through the marble corridor as he left
Marchetti's study, each step heavy with intent. The guards
stationed at the far end stiffened as he passed, their gazes
flicking toward him with unease. Everyone in this house
knew—Leone was not a man to cross.

He descended into the sublevels of the estate, where
light gave way to stone and silence. The old wine cellars
had long since been repurposed into something darker:
interrogation rooms, weapon stores, cells meant for men
who never saw daylight again. Here, Marchetti's empire
wasn't refined opulence—it was bone and blood, power
enforced by fear.

At the end of the hall, Leone pushed open a heavy iron
door. Inside, a single bulb buzzed overhead, swinging
slightly on its cord. A man sat slumped in a chair, wrists
bound, face swollen from hours of beatings and questions.
His breath came in ragged wheezes.

"Bring him up," Leone barked to the two men standing
guard. They straightened immediately, hauling the prisoner
upright.

The man groaned. His accent marked him as local—
Capri, perhaps Naples. A petty informant caught feeding
crumbs to the wrong side. Leone didn't care who he was.
What mattered was the message.

Leone stepped forward, towering over him. "Tell me
again," he growled. "Who sent you to sniff around the
farmhouse?"

The prisoner's eyes, bloodshot and wild, flicked upward.
He licked bleeding cracked lips, trembling. "I—I told you.

A man. Foreign. Paid me to watch the cliffs, to report if anyone… if anyone touched the house."

Leone crouched, his scarred hand gripping the prisoner's jaw. "Foreign. Which man? What name?"

The prisoner whimpered. "He never gave it. Only—only that the key would awaken soon."

Leone's smile was slow, wolfish. He released the man with a shove.

He turned to the guards. "Dispose of him. He's useless. Leave nothing to find."

The guards obeyed without hesitation, dragging the man out into the corridor. His muffled cries faded, swallowed by the stone.

Alone again, Leone lit another cigarette, the flame catching in his cold eyes. Marchetti still thought he was in command, but Leone had already decided. The prophecy was not Marchetti's to claim—it was his.

He drew a knife from his coat pocket and pressed the blade against his palm until a bead of blood welled up, red and vivid in the dim light. He whispered into the shadows, the words a vow older than the Duke's empire:

"When the key awakens, it will answer to me. Not to the Duke. Not to anyone else. Me."

The bulb above flickered once, then steadied, as though the room itself had heard.

Chapter Forty-Eight
The Hand and the Key

The dagger burned like a living flame in his grip, its golden light licking across the scar of his old allegiance. Sebastiano's breath came sharp and ragged, each inhale a war between fear and defiance. The Guardians' voices pressed like thunder:

"One cut severs your past. Another binds your future. Choose."

His knuckles whitened on the hilt. For a heartbeat, the weight of Marchetti's shadow pressed heavy against his back, chains that had dragged him through a life of blood and silence. Then Amara's voice cut through, trembling but steady:

"Sebastiano... look at me. You already know."

His eyes locked with hers, and in that instant, he knew. With a hoarse cry, he slashed the blade across the faint mark burned into his forearm. The brand hissed, black smoke curling as it sizzled away, consumed by the dagger's golden fire. The farmhouse shook, beams creaking as though exhaling after years of pressure.

The Guardians' tone softened, a bell across water: "The past is severed. The chain is broken."

Sebastiano's chest heaved, but the dagger still pulsed in his grasp, demanding more. His gaze dropped to Amara. Her presence was the only anchor in the storm, the only truth he had left.

Slowly, with trembling hands, he turned the blade inward—not to his flesh, but toward the space above his heart. He pressed the edge against his skin, just enough for the light to pierce him. Amara gasped, reaching for him, but he shook his head.

"This," he whispered hoarsely, eyes never leaving hers, "is for you."

He dragged the blade across his chest—not deep, but enough for blood to mingle with light. The wound flared golden, the glow racing outward like a living seal. Symbols bloomed across his skin, spiraling outward from the cut until they converged over his heart in a sigil not of Marchetti, but of the Brotherhood's ancient vow—restored, reborn.

The farmhouse blazed as if a sun had ignited within its walls. Amara staggered back, shielding her eyes, but the warmth wrapped her like an embrace.

The Guardians' voices rang like a thousand chimes: "The past is cut. The future bound. The Hand and the Key are joined."

Sebastiano dropped the dagger to the floor, its light dimming to embers. He swayed, nearly collapsing, but Amara caught him, holding him against her as the glow slowly receded.

When his eyes opened, the old shadows were gone. What remained was fire.

Amara pressed her forehead to his, her tears hot against his cheek. "You chose me," she whispered.

"I chose us," he breathed, voice raw but steady.

The chest pulsed once—slow, deliberate—its sigils alive as though it had felt the vow sealed.

But far away, beyond the cliffs and sea, a ripple spread outward. And in Marchetti's study, a glass of wine quivered, its surface disturbed by something only he could sense.

Chapter Forty-Nine
The Echo

In the stillness of his study, Duke Antonio Marchetti lifted a crystal glass of Barolo to his lips, savoring the richness of it, when the vibration came. Subtle at first, then sharp—his hand trembled, the wine rippling against the rim. He stilled, his sharp blue eyes narrowing on the surface of the liquid.

Something had shifted.

He rose, the heavy leather chair groaning behind him, and crossed to the center of the room where a circular table was inlaid with brass channels and crystal nodes. At his touch, the table flared to life—holographic streams spiraling upward, ancient glyphs entwined with digital code. The prophecy matrix.

The center crystal pulsed once.

Marchetti's breath caught in his throat, his heart thundering with a mixture of triumph and rage.

The Key had turned.

"Impossible," he muttered. "Not without me."

Footsteps clicked against marble, and Leone entered, a predator in black, his expression unreadable. He paused at the sight of the pulsing projection, his dark eyes flicking from the light to Marchetti.

"It has begun," Leone said flatly, his voice like stone breaking.

Marchetti whirled on him. "I should have been warned! How could this happen without my command?"

Leone's lips curled into the barest shadow of a smile. "Because the Key does not answer to you, Duke. It never has."

For a breath, silence stretched razor-thin.

Then Marchetti's voice cut like a blade. "Careful, Leone."

But Leone didn't flinch. He stepped closer, his massive frame looming. "The chest stirs. The prophecy awakens. And if the Hand has chosen, then your role is not master... but beggar."

Marchetti's glass shattered in his grip, blood mingling with wine as shards cut into his palm. He didn't so much as blink. His eyes burned with cold fire.

"I built this empire," he hissed. "I bought every stone of this hunt with blood, gold, and time. Do not forget who holds the leash."

Leone leaned in, his breath hot and acrid. "Perhaps the leash was never yours."

The words hung in the air like smoke, dangerous and heavy.

At last, Marchetti stepped back, crimson dripping from his hand onto the Persian rug. He turned toward the glowing matrix, his jaw clenched. "No matter. If the Key awakens, then the convergence comes sooner. And when it does—" His lips curled into a grim smile. "—whoever holds her, holds the world."

Leone said nothing, but his silence was a weight of its own, thick with menace.

Outside the estate, thunder cracked across a clear sky, though no storm had been forecast.

The net was tightening.

Chapter Fifty
The Gathering Storm

The underground war room beneath Marchetti's estate was a cathedral of steel and glass. The vaulted ceiling glowed with cold light, maps projected in shifting layers—Capri at the center, its cliffs and roads rendered in crimson detail. Rows of operatives in black suits stood at attention along the perimeter, their faces hard, their silence absolute.

Marchetti entered with a bandaged hand, the blood seeping faintly through white linen, but his stride was unbroken. The wound had not weakened him; it had sharpened him. Leone's words still echoed like poison in his veins, but they would be answered—in blood or obedience.

He raised a hand, and the room stilled.

"The Key has turned," he said, his voice carrying the weight of thunder. "The prophecy has stirred. And with it—our moment."

A ripple moved through the room, restrained but electric.

Marchetti gestured, and the map of Capri expanded, glowing with heat signatures, drone flight paths, hidden tunnels beneath the island. Red markers swarmed around one pinpoint of light—the farmhouse.

"There," he continued, "is the fulcrum of history. Within those walls lies what generations of fools failed to uncover. And now it begins to open. It is ours. It will be mine."

He turned, his sharp gaze sweeping across his men. "Leone believes himself untouchable, that the prophecy bends to his will. Let him. He forgets I command armies, not shadows. He forgets who owns the world's silence."

At his nod, screens lit with faces across continents—generals, financiers, operatives embedded in governments. They bowed their heads slightly, awaiting his word.

"Deploy the advance unit to Capri," Marchetti ordered, his voice like steel snapping. "Seal every exit. Tighten every road. No one enters or leaves that island without my knowledge."

One of his commanders spoke, his tone cautious. "And D'Amato, sir?"

For a long moment, Marchetti was silent. Then his lips curved into a smile that chilled the room.

"Bring him in alive if possible. Dead if necessary. The prophecy names her, not him. But if he resists..." Marchetti's eyes gleamed cold and merciless. "Then let his blood water the roots of my empire."

The room echoed with a crisp unison: "Yes, Duke."

Marchetti stepped back, his hands clasped behind him, gaze fixed on the glowing farmhouse on the map. His voice dropped, almost reverent, but filled with venom.

"The Key awakens. The Hand bleeds. And soon, the world will kneel."

Above the estate, the first true storm clouds gathered, rolling across the horizon toward Capri.

Chapter Fifty-One
Encircled

The farmhouse lay quiet in the pale hush of dawn, its stones still warm from the night of fire and visions. Amara stood at the terrace doors, staring toward the sea, her shawl wrapped tightly around her shoulders. The horizon shimmered with light, yet unease crept into her chest like a gathering fog.

Behind her, Sebastiano moved through the kitchen, every sense sharpened. He had slept little, haunted not by dreams but by the memory of the blade, the mark it left, the vow it sealed. His life had split into before and after, and now he felt every shadow outside the farmhouse pressing closer.

Amara turned when she heard his steps. Her eyes searched his face, finding in it both the man she had come to love and something new—etched deeper, harder, forged by fire.

"You feel it too," she said softly.

Sebastiano stopped at the threshold, his gaze locking with hers. "Yes. They're coming. Marchetti won't wait now. He'll throw everything he has at this place."

Amara's fingers tightened on the shawl. "And Leone?"

His jaw clenched. "Leone doesn't follow. He hunts. And he'll want me broken before he ever reaches for you."

The farmhouse seemed to shudder at his words, a faint hum threading through the beams as though the house itself was aware of the tightening noose.

Amara crossed the room, placing her hand on Sebastiano's marked arm. "Then we don't wait for them to close in. We decide what happens next."

He looked down at her hand, then back into her steady eyes. The truth of her words struck him with force. For the first time, he was not merely shielding her from Marchetti's empire or Leone's cruelty—he was standing with her, side by side, bound by something that had begun long before either of them remembered.

From outside, the faint thrum of rotors whispered across the cliffs—distant but closing.

Amara lifted her chin, resolve hardening her voice. "The farmhouse isn't just stone, Sebastiano. It's alive. The chest, the Guardians—they want us to fight, but not with fear. With what they've given us."

Sebastiano drew her closer, his lips brushing her hair. "Then we fight together."

The hum of the farmhouse deepened, as though answering their vow. Light shimmered faintly along the stairwell, a pulse that promised the house was no longer theirs alone.

Outside, the first dark specks of drones cut across the Capri sky.

Chapter Fifty-Two
The Descent

The low thrum of approaching rotors rattled the windowpanes. Amara's breath caught as she glanced to the sky, but Sebastiano's hand closed firmly around hers.

"Downstairs," he said, his voice steady though his jaw was tight. "The Guardians didn't give us the chest to let it sit idle."

Together they moved quickly through the farmhouse, the air thick with anticipation. The glow from the chest still pulsed faintly in the chamber, a heartbeat in the dark. When they reached it, the sigils etched into the lid brightened, responding to their presence.

Amara stepped closer, her palm brushing the wood. The chest shifted, the lid rising slowly without a touch. Inside lay not treasure but tools: relics bound in cloth, gleaming fragments of metal, scrolls sealed with wax so old it looked brittle as bone.

Sebastiano reached first. His hand brushed over a pair of blades, slim and curved, forged of some alloy that shimmered with a faint golden sheen. When he gripped one, the weapon seemed to recognize him—the hilt warming, the weight balancing as though it had been crafted for his hand.

Amara leaned over the chest, her eyes widening at the soft glow surrounding one object: a circlet of interwoven silver and gold, delicate yet radiant, its band carved with constellations. As she lifted it, the room itself seemed to breathe—dust stirring, beams groaning, a whisper filling the chamber: The Key awakens; the Hand is bound. Together you stand, or together you fall.

Amara pressed the circlet against her chest, trembling. "This… it's not just an ornament."

"No," Sebastiano said, tightening his grip on the blade. "It's a mark. A shield. Whatever this prophecy means—it starts with us."

Above them, the farmhouse shook. A drone swept low, its shadow cutting across the terrace. Then came the distant grind of wheels on gravel—the convoy arriving.

Amara turned toward Sebastiano, the circlet glowing faintly in her hands. "We don't have much time."

He nodded, his eyes blazing with resolve. "Then we use what we've been given. We turn this farmhouse into the line they cannot cross."

The chest closed on its own, the sigils locking once more. The hum in the air thickened, as though the farmhouse itself braced for the storm descending upon it.

Chapter Fifty-Three
The First Strike

The night split open with fire.

A shudder ran through the farmhouse walls as the first rocket struck the outer stone terrace, spraying shards of rock into the garden. The olive trees swayed violently under the blast, their branches snapping like brittle bones.

Sebastiano dragged Amara down just as the second explosion roared overhead, shattering one of the upstairs windows. Glass rained through the hall in glittering shards, catching the moonlight like falling stars.

"They're here!" Sebastiano's voice was sharp, his blade already in hand.

Amara's pulse thundered in her ears as shouts echoed from beyond the walls—Marchetti's men, dozens of them, their boots pounding against the earth. She could see them through the broken window: black-clad figures flooding the cliffs, rifles glinting under floodlights mounted on armored trucks.

"The Chamber" Sebastiano barked, his grip closing around her arm. But even as he moved to pull her toward the stairs, the chest pulsed again—its glow spilling up through the cracks in the floorboards, flooding the room in waves of gold.

Amara staggered, clutching the circlet to her chest. The hum rose, vibrating through her bones until she could barely breathe.

And then she heard it—clearer than the chaos outside. A whisper, not in her ears but in her blood:

Wear it.

Hands trembling, she lifted the circlet and placed it on her head.

The world convulsed.

Light surged outward from her body, a blinding wave that threw shadows across every wall. The farmhouse itself responded, its ancient beams groaning, the sigils carved into its stones flaring alive as if the house had been waiting centuries for this moment.

Outside, Marchetti's men halted mid-charge. Their rifles wavered, their helmets gleaming as the golden light washed over them. Some stumbled back, blinded, others dropped to their knees as though crushed beneath invisible weight.

Sebastiano turned, his eyes widening as he looked at her. "Amara…"

The circlet burned against her brow, but she didn't remove it. She raised her hand instinctively, and the golden wave flared again—this time striking the lead truck. The vehicle screeched, lifted from the ground as though seized by unseen hands, and slammed into the cliffside with a force that shook the earth.

Amara gasped, reeling, the circlet's glow dimming slightly. "I—I don't know how I did that."

Sebastiano caught her before she fell, steadying her. His blade gleamed as he pulled her close. "Then we'll learn in the fight," he said fiercely. "Whatever this is—it's ours now. And we'll use it."

Another rocket streaked toward the farmhouse. But before it struck, the walls themselves shimmered, a translucent barrier flaring into place. The rocket exploded against it, the impact swallowed by golden fire.

The farmhouse had become a fortress.

And the battle for the Key had begun.

Chapter Fifty-Four
The Unmasking

Far from the cliffs of Capri, in the heart of his fortified estate, Duke Antonio Marchetti stood in silence before a wall of holographic screens.

On them: chaos. The farmhouse glowing like a beacon, his men faltering, trucks overturned by unseen force, rockets swallowed by walls of golden light. And at the center of it all—her.

Amara Savard.

Her figure radiated with a brilliance the lenses could barely capture, the circlet blazing like a star fallen to earth. Every gesture she made bent the field of battle, turning his precision-trained operatives into children lost in a storm.

Marchetti's jaw clenched, his reflection ghosting across the glass as he leaned closer. "So it's true," he whispered, voice like a blade dragged over stone. "The Key has turned."

Behind him, Leone shifted in the shadows, arms folded across his massive chest. His expression carried no awe—only hunger. "She carries it," Leone said. "The light bends to her. You see now why I said the time was near."

Marchetti didn't turn. His eyes drank in the vision of Amara, her power unfurling with terrifying ease. "Yes. But power is nothing without a hand to shape it. And she is untested. Raw."

Leone's lips curved into a thin, humorless smile. "Raw can be broken. Bent."

Marchetti exhaled slowly, then finally faced him. His gaze was glacial, but there was a flicker of something else beneath it—fear, buried deep. "Prepare the second wave. If she has awakened, then we no longer fight for stone and prophecy. We fight for the world."

Leone's grin widened, cruel and eager. "At last."

The screens flickered again, showing Sebastiano cutting down a pair of soldiers at Amara's side, his blade moving like liquid steel. He was no longer Marchetti's man—that much was clear.

Marchetti's voice dropped to a whisper, but the venom carried across the room:

"Then D'Amato dies first."

Chapter Fifty-Five
The Shadow Approaches

The farmhouse still trembled with the aftershocks of Amara's awakening. Golden fire clung to the beams like veins of living light, pulsing in time with her breath. Outside, the night swirled with smoke, and the faint cries of retreating soldiers dissolved into the sea wind.

Sebastiano stood at the broken threshold, his dagger slick, his chest heaving. His ears rang with silence too complete, too unnatural. Not victory. Not yet.

He looked back into the farmhouse. Amara's skin aglow with threads of power that moved like rivers beneath her flesh. She was radiant, unearthly—and utterly unaware of how brightly she burned.

Sebastiano's grip tightened on the dagger. A prickle crawled over his skin, sharp and invasive. Not the Guardians. Not Leone. This was colder. Older.

Marchetti.

The sensation pressed against his chest like a hand, invisible but undeniable. For years he had lived under that shadow, obeying, bleeding, killing at the Duke's command. And now, though miles of sea and stone separated them, Sebastiano felt him. Marchetti's will—a storm gathering.

He moved quickly to Amara, crouching beside her. His voice was low, urgent. "Amara. Listen to me."

Her eyes lifted, wide and shimmering, as though she'd just surfaced from deep water. "I felt it," she whispered. "Something vast, reaching for us. It knows I've awakened."

Sebastiano cupped her face, forcing her to meet his gaze. "That was Marchetti. He will come himself now, not just send men. He's watched me bleed for him, watched me kill, watched me survive when others did not. And I tell you this—when Marchetti steps onto the field, it is not to fight. It is to consume."

Her breath caught. "Then what chance do we have?"

Sebastiano's jaw clenched, torn between fear and resolve. He pressed the dagger flat against his chest, feeling its strange warmth. "We don't fight him as soldiers. Not me. Not you. We fight him as what the prophecy says we are. The Key. The Hand."

The farmhouse groaned, timbers bowing as if under invisible weight. Outside, the sea roared louder, waves crashing against the cliff in unnatural rhythm.

Sebastiano pulled Amara to her feet. His eyes burned with a fire she had not seen before—something between love and defiance. "He's coming. And when he does, I'll meet his shadow with steel. But you…" He touched her chest, just above the glow of the circlet. "…you must meet it with light."

The air split—three sharp cracks, like whips lashing across stone. Outside, the first of Marchetti's machines stirred the night sky, black silhouettes against the moon.

The net was closing.

Chapter Fifty-Six
The Storm Breaks

The farmhouse shuddered as the first strike fell. Glass shattered in the upper windows, raining down in glittering shards. The ground shook under Amara's feet, dust sifting from the rafters.

Sebastiano shoved her back from the door just as a blast tore through the garden wall, stone and ivy exploding outward. The night filled with smoke and the hiss of fire, the once-quiet cliffside now a battlefield.

Shapes emerged from the haze—men in black tactical gear, their faces hidden, weapons gleaming with the cold sheen of Marchetti's arsenal. They moved with precision, a tide of shadows sweeping toward the farmhouse.

Sebastiano was already moving, the dagger in his hand blazing faint gold as if answering the chest's light. He met the first intruder with brutal efficiency, steel clashing against steel, sparks scattering into the night.

"Inside!" he barked over his shoulder, his voice rough. "Amara—go downstairs and stay with the chest!"

But Amara couldn't move. Her body shook, her palms burning as though the fire within her begged release. The farmhouse itself seemed to cry out, beams groaning, the floorboards humming beneath her feet. The chest in the chamber below glowed brighter, answering her unspoken terror.

Through the smoke, a new figure appeared. Tall. Unhurried. A presence that made the air itself recoil.

Marchetti.

He stepped onto the broken terrace as though entering a ballroom, his silver hair gleaming, his tailored coat untouched by the chaos. His eyes—icy blue, merciless—swept over the scene until they found her.

"Amara Savard," he said, his voice carrying effortlessly over the din. "So, the Key has turned at last."

Her heart hammered. Sebastiano staggered back, blood streaking his temple, his dagger still alight in his grip. He spat into the dirt; his gaze locked on Marchetti.

"You'll have to kill me to touch her."

Marchetti's smile was faint, cruel. "Oh, Sebastiano. That was always the plan."

The soldiers tightened their circle. The farmhouse walls flared with golden light, fighting to repel them. The chest pulsed violently, its sigils sparking like lightning across its lid.

And Amara—her hands lifted without thought, light pooling in her palms.

The storm had broken.

Chapter Fifty-Seven
Words of Iron

The smoke curled around Marchetti like a cloak, the shattered terrace framing him in jagged ruin. Yet he moved as though none of it touched him, his polished shoes silent on broken stone. Soldiers held their line behind him, rifles steady, the night alive with the click of metal and the hiss of flames licking the garden wall.

Amara's breath caught in her throat. She had expected a monster—but Marchetti radiated something colder, something worse: certainty. His presence was iron bent into human form, unshakable and deliberate.

"You think this farmhouse protects you," he said, his voice cutting through the roar of the fire, steady and smooth. "You think the Guardians care for you? You are mistaken. They do not love—they use."

The words pierced her, heavy with a rhythm that seemed almost rehearsed, as though he had spoken them countless times before to break others.

Sebastiano spat blood into the dirt, his dagger raised, its golden light flickering against the soldiers' rifles. "You'll not touch her."

Marchetti's eyes slid to him, faint amusement flickering across his face. "And yet, here you stand, blade in hand, pretending at loyalty. You've always been mine, Sebastiano. Bound by blood, by debt, by fear. Do you think one woman's touch undoes decades of my claim?"

Sebastiano's grip trembled. His chest heaved with rage, but deep inside, the brand on his forearm burned as if to remind him—Marchetti was not lying.

Amara stepped forward, the chest glowing in the chamber below them like a heart torn open. Her voice wavered but did not break. "You don't control me. And you don't control him."

Marchetti's smile curved like a blade. "Oh, child… control is an illusion. Influence, pressure, timing—that is the true art. And you—" his gaze burned into her, cold and merciless, "—you are the Key. The prophecy was clear. You were never chosen for freedom. You were bred for purpose. To open what no man can. And when it opens fully, when the convergence crowns, you will not wield it. I will."

The soldiers tightened, rifles aimed at her chest. Sebastiano stepped in front of her, dagger blazing, though his knees buckled under the weight of Marchetti's words.

Amara's palms burned with light, but her voice steadied. "You're wrong. This power doesn't answer to you. It never will."

Marchetti tilted his head, regarding her almost tenderly. "Then prove it. Open the chest before me. Show me you are more than a frightened girl playing at destiny."

The farmhouse groaned. The sigils on the chest blazed as if ready to answer the challenge.

And Sebastiano—his hand faltered, caught between fear of Marchetti's hold and the unshakable pull of Amara's light.

Chapter Fifty-Eight
Breaking the Chain

The words hung heavy in the farmhouse, Marchetti's voice wrapping around Sebastiano like coils of iron. You've always been mine. The truth of it burned like fire in the scar beneath his skin.

Sebastiano staggered, his dagger flickering in his grip as though even the light wavered. The soldiers saw it, rifles shifting eagerly, fingers brushing triggers. Marchetti's smile widened, patient and cruel.

"You see?" the Duke murmured. "He knows. He remembers. Every order followed. Every life taken. You cannot carve that away with a knife."

Sebastiano's vision blurred, the smoke and fire bending into memories: blood-stained missions in faraway cities, the cold satisfaction in Marchetti's voice when he obeyed without hesitation. He heard the screams of those who had begged him to stop—and his silence as he carried out the orders.

His chest heaved. The dagger shook. For one raw instant, he almost believed Marchetti.

Then—Amara's hand touched his.

"Sebastiano," she whispered, her voice steady against the storm. "You're not his. Not anymore. Look at me."

He turned. Her eyes blazed with conviction; with something he had long forgotten he could deserve—forgiveness. She saw him, all of him, and did not turn away.

The brand on his arm burned hotter, as though resisting her pull. Sebastiano snarled through clenched teeth, ripping the sleeve back. The faint sigil, dark as ash beneath the skin, pulsed in time with his heartbeat. Marchetti's claim.

With a cry torn from his soul, Sebastiano raised the dagger high—and drove it into his own flesh.

The farmhouse erupted in light. Golden fire consumed the sigil, devouring the brand until nothing but clean skin remained. Sebastiano gasped, falling to one knee, his arm blazing with freedom. The weight he had carried for decades—the chains, the silence, the blood—fell away like dust in the wind.

Marchetti's smile shattered. "No." His voice cracked like thunder. "NO!"

Sebastiano rose slowly, the dagger steady once more, its light brighter than before. His eyes burned with a clarity Amara had never seen in him.

"I am not yours," he said, voice low, trembling with fury and release. "Not now. Not ever again."

The soldiers hesitated. Even the walls seemed to lean toward him, as though the farmhouse itself bore witness.

Amara's chest tightened, her own power stirring in response. She could feel it building inside her, a tide she could no longer contain.

But Marchetti—Marchetti only smiled again, colder, sharper. "Break your chain if you wish," he said softly. "The Key still belongs to me."

And with those words, the chest roared—its sigils blazing, its lid trembling as if ready to answer the clash of will.

Chapter Fifty-Nine
Golden Fire

The silence after Sebastiano's declaration was razor-thin, a breath before the storm. Marchetti's eyes glittered, cold and venomous, and his hand flicked with the smallest gesture.

The farmhouse shattered into chaos.

Gunfire cracked, deafening in the confined stone walls. Muzzle flashes stuttered like lightning as soldiers surged forward, their boots pounding the ancient floorboards. Splinters rained, shards of plaster burst from the walls, and the acrid sting of smoke filled the air.

Sebastiano lunged, pulling Amara behind the stone hearth as bullets tore across the kitchen. The dagger pulsed in his grip, flaring with every heartbeat, almost eager for the fight. He rose into the fray, blade slashing a golden arc through the smoke. The first soldier fell, his rifle clattering against the tiles.

"Stay down!" Sebastiano barked, his voice hoarse, his body moving with lethal precision. Every strike was a vow, every deflection a denial of Marchetti's chains.

But the soldiers kept coming. Their shadows swarmed like wolves, driving him back step by step. His blade sang, parrying, slashing, but he could not hold them all.

Amara pressed her back against the cold stone, her breath sharp and uneven. She could feel it again—that hum, that pressure in her chest. The chest below them throbbed in answer, its sigils blazing brighter with every shot fired, every cry torn from Sebastiano's throat.

Her hands trembled. Not from fear—no, something else. A rising heat, a current she could not contain. She could hear it whispering, almost singing, in a language she knew but had never learned.

Sebastiano staggered, a rifle butt crashing against his ribs. He grunted, twisting, but another soldier caught him from behind, locking his arm. The dagger nearly fell from his grasp.

"Sebastiano!" Amara's voice broke across the gunfire.

And then—the pressure inside her shattered.

Light erupted from her hands, a torrent of golden fire searing across the farmhouse. It wasn't heat but force, a wave that hurled the soldiers backward as though they were leaves in a storm. Rifles flew from their hands, crashing against the walls. The very stones of the house seemed to sing, vibrating with the release.

Sebastiano fell free, the dagger steady once more in his grip, his wide eyes snapping toward her.

Amara stood, her body glowing with threads of light pouring through her skin, her hair lifting as though caught in a current no one else could see. Her eyes—no longer only hers—burned with the same sigils carved into the chest.

The farmhouse fell into stunned silence. The soldiers who could still move scrambled back, terrified.

Marchetti's voice, carried through the open door, was not anger but awe.

"At last," he whispered. "The Key awakens."

Chapter Sixty
The Flame Bursts

The farmhouse walls shook as the soldiers pressed in, boots hammering across the stones, rifles raised. Their shouts echoed, sharp and guttural, a tide of violence pouring toward the heart of the house.

Amara's chest burned. The hum she had felt for days now roared into a deafening crescendo. Her hand, trembling, lifted of its own accord.

And then the world broke open.

Light erupted from her, a torrent of gold-white fire that seared the air. The nearest soldiers were thrown back, their weapons clattering uselessly to the ground, metal warped, barrels twisted. Shouts turned to screams as the farmhouse floor itself pulsed with the shockwave, knocking them off their feet.

Sebastiano shielded his face against the brilliance, his dagger alive with the same flame, the sigils along its edge glowing like molten script. He staggered forward through the blast, his voice low and steady, meant only for her:

"Amara—listen to me. Breathe. Anchor yourself. Do not fight the light. Guide it."

Her eyes, wide with terror and wonder, found his through the blaze. The force pouring out of her threatened to consume everything—it felt infinite, wild, uncontainable. But his voice cut through, a tether in the storm.

She gasped, forcing air into her lungs. Her fingers curled inward, as if grasping invisible reins. The flood slowed, narrowed, focused. The soldiers scrambling at the threshold were pinned by beams of light instead of consumed by fire, their rifles snapping apart like brittle twigs.

Sebastiano reached her, his hand closing over hers, the dagger pressed between their palms. The farmhouse shook again, but this time with rhythm, like the beating of a giant heart. Together, they pushed back—just enough.

The last soldier dropped to his knees, weapon shattered, before stumbling out into the night. Silence returned, fractured only by the echo of groans and the hiss of smoldering wood.

Amara fell against Sebastiano, her body trembling, her pulse racing. The glow dimmed around her, settling back into the chest, leaving only faint golden veins across the stones.

"I—I didn't mean to—" she stammered, her voice raw.

He pressed his forehead to hers, his chest heaving. "You did what you were meant to do. But it was only the beginning."

A sound carried in from beyond the broken doors— slow, deliberate applause.

Marchetti's voice followed, smooth and cold, rolling through the night like smoke:

"Magnificent. The Key awakens indeed."

He had not fled. He had not even drawn a weapon. He stood beyond the shattered gates with his men, untouched, his pale eyes gleaming with triumph.

Sebastiano tightened his grip on the dagger, pulling Amara closer behind him. His voice dropped to a growl.

"This isn't over."

Marchetti's smile was thin, his silhouette framed by torchlight. "Oh, I should hope not. Leone is coming. And when he arrives… the real test begins."

Chapter Sixty-One
The Second Wave

The echo of Marchetti's applause lingered in the night, carried on the salt wind rolling up from the cliffs. His soldiers, broken and scattered, had limped back to regroup, but the Duke stood untouched—untouchable in his own mind. His eyes glinted with the cold satisfaction of a predator who believed the hunt had only just begun.

And then the ground trembled.

From the darkened road below, a deeper rhythm rose—a cadence of boots, of something heavier than flesh and bone. The air grew dense, thick with a suffocating weight that seemed to press against the lungs. Even the torches wavered, their flames bending away as though in fear.

Marchetti's smile faltered.

Leone had arrived.

The figure that emerged from the shadows was not like the men Marchetti commanded. Leone moved with the inevitability of an avalanche, his massive frame swathed in a cloak that caught no light. At his back came a cadre of his own—a handful of fanatics, eyes hollow, faces painted with symbols that twisted the old sigil of the Brotherhood into something grotesque.

Where Marchetti's men had carried rifles and tactical gear, Leone's bore relic weapons—curved blades blackened with ash, staves etched with runes that pulsed faintly in the night. The air around them rippled, disturbed by currents of power too old and dark to be called human.

Marchetti's jaw tightened, though he masked it quickly. "You bring your own dogs into my hunt?" His voice was calm, but each word rang with venom.

Leone didn't stop until he stood just beyond the broken gates of the farmhouse, his hulking silhouette towering even against the ruined doors. His eyes, black as pitch, scanned the scene—the scorched soldiers, the fractured stone, the faint glow still bleeding from the chest within.

And then he smiled, slow and merciless.

"The Key awakens," Leone said, his voice carrying like a curse. "And she will not be yours, Duke. She will be tested. She will burn. And if she fails—she will be mine."

Inside the farmhouse, Amara shivered, though no wind touched her. Sebastiano felt it too—the oppressive weight of a predator far worse than Marchetti, worse than any army. His grip on the dagger tightened, his other arm circling Amara instinctively.

The farmhouse itself groaned, its beams vibrating as if in protest. The sigils along the chest flickered, answering the threat that now stood at its threshold.

Two powers had come for them—one clothed in wealth and calculation, the other in raw, unrestrained violence. And Amara knew, as surely as the blood thrumming in her ears, that the true battle was only beginning.

Leone raised one hand, massive and scarred, his fingers curling as though to crush the farmhouse from afar. His voice boomed, guttural, final:

"Let the second wave begin."

Chapter Sixty-Two
The Relics of Blood

Leone's hand fell in a silent command, and his followers surged forward.

They did not move like soldiers. They moved like predators.

One raised a staff carved from bone, its length inscribed with twisting runes that glowed a sickly green. With a guttural chant, he drove it into the earth. The ground buckled, cracks spiderwebbing outward, exhaling a foul vapor that made the air sting the lungs. The farmhouse shuddered, its timbers groaning in protest as if the soil beneath it had been poisoned.

Another swung a blade curved like a crescent moon, its edge blackened with centuries of blood. He slashed the air, and the arc of his strike didn't stop at the edge of the steel—shadow itself followed, a scythe of darkness ripping toward the farmhouse like a physical wound in the night.

A third carried chains, each link engraved with symbols that writhed like serpents. He spun them with a force that should have broken bone, and when they snapped against the ground, sparks of crimson fire burst forth, searing marks into the stone like brands from hell itself.

The night erupted with their fury. They were not simply armed—they were instruments of something older, darker, twisted from the Brotherhood's forgotten rituals into weapons of terror.

Inside the farmhouse, glass shattered as the wave of power slammed against the walls. Amara stumbled, clutching Sebastiano's arm. Her chest burned, the resonance of the chest vibrating through her as though answering the dark assault.

Sebastiano's dagger pulsed, the light along its blade flaring brighter each time one of the relics struck. He felt its will as clearly as his own heartbeat: Fight. Protect. Do not falter.

"Sebastiano—" Amara's voice trembled as another blast of shadow energy raked across the shutters, splintering wood. "They're not like Marchetti's men. They're—"

"Something worse," he finished grimly, pulling her back from the window as shards of glass rained across the floor.

Outside, Leone threw his head back and laughed, the sound booming, echoing off the cliffs like thunder.

"Do you feel it, Key?" he roared, his massive arms spreading as if to embrace the chaos. "This is the second wave—the storm that tests your light! Show yourself, or be broken!"

The farmhouse trembled again. The chest pulsed harder, its sigils glowing as if awakened by the challenge. Amara felt it calling—not just to her, but through her, stirring something deep within that she could no longer deny.

Sebastiano caught her gaze. Her eyes were wide, alive with fear—but beneath it, there was fire.

And he realized: if the farmhouse survived this night, it would not be because he wielded the dagger.

It would be because Amara finally embraced the power that had chosen her.

Chapter Sixty-Three
The Glimpse of the Key

The relic-born assault battered the farmhouse with unrelenting force. Flames of unnatural color licked the shutters, chains of crimson light rattled across the walls, and each pulse of darkness pressed like a hand trying to crush the roof into the earth.

Amara staggered back as a beam of shadow burst through the window, slicing across the kitchen table and splitting it clean in half. Sebastiano lunged, pulling her close, the dagger flashing as he deflected another arc of corruption that hissed against its light. Sparks scattered across the floor like dying stars.

But even the dagger trembled now, its glow straining against the weight of the onslaught. Sebastiano's jaw was set hard, his muscles taut with the effort, sweat beading across his brow.

"Amara—get back!" he shouted. "The dagger will hold—"

"No."

Her voice was quiet but resolute, cutting through the chaos.

Amara stepped forward, her bare feet crunching across glass. She raised her hand, her palm facing outward. Below the floorboards in the chamber the chest burst to life, its golden sigils pulsing as if waiting for her command. The farmhouse roared with the clash of relics outside, but inside, she felt only a profound stillness, a silence that pressed against her ribs like the pause before a storm.

She closed her eyes.

And the chest answered.

A hum rose—not from wood or stone, but from her own chest. A vibration so deep it filled her bones, her blood, her breath. Her hair lifted in the unseen current, her skin glowing faintly as if lit from within. The farmhouse itself seemed to inhale.

Then she opened her eyes.

They shone like twin suns.

The next strike from outside—a whip of shadow meant to cleave the house in two—hit an invisible barrier and shattered like glass against stone. The shards of darkness dissolved into nothingness, scattering harmlessly into the night.

Golden light began spilling from Amara's fingertips and surged outward, weaving into a shield that expanded from the farmhouse like the dome of a cathedral. Every relic-born strike slammed into it with a deafening thunder, but the light absorbed them, bending their fury into silence.

Outside, Leone froze mid-laugh. His men stumbled, their relics buckling, their chains snapping like twigs.

Sebastiano stood behind her, chest heaving, his dagger blazing in resonance with the shield she had created. He couldn't look away.

Amara Savard—the woman he had once thought a target to be guarded—was revealed now in her truest form. The prophecy was no longer rumor. The Key had fully awakened.

Her voice carried across the field, strong and unyielding, though she herself trembled at its force.

"You cannot break what was sealed in light."

The ground shook as the shield pulsed, sending a wave of golden radiance outward that knocked Leone's men off their feet. Their relics sputtered, dimmed, then fell silent in their hands.

Leone himself staggered a step, his grin vanishing into a snarl. His eyes, wild with fury, locked on the farmhouse as the golden dome glowed brighter still.

For the first time, the butcher of Naples did not laugh.

Chapter Sixty-Four
Leone's Challenge

The battlefield had fallen into a stunned silence. Leone's men sprawled across the rocky ground, their relics sparking faintly, smoke curling from shattered chains and broken talismans. The golden dome of Amara's shield still shimmered, humming with the resonance of something older than time.

And then Leone stepped forward.

He did not hurry. His stride was measured, deliberate, like a predator closing the final distance before the kill. His massive frame seemed even larger beneath the sickly moonlight, his shadow stretching long across the scorched earth.

Sebastiano shifted closer to Amara, the dagger blazing white-hot in his grip. "Stay behind me," he growled.

But Amara didn't move. Her gaze was fixed on Leone, steady and unwavering.

Leone stopped just beyond the dome of light. His lips curled into a sneer, though his eyes burned with something harder, hungrier. He lifted his hand, revealing a blade unlike the crude relics his men had carried. This weapon pulsed with a crimson glow so deep it seemed to bleed darkness, its edge whispering with smoke that hissed against the air.

"The Key has awoken," he rumbled, his voice echoing like rolling thunder. "And the Hand has chosen." His gaze flicked briefly to Sebastiano, then back to Amara. "But light without trial is nothing. Let us see if the fire burns when pressed to iron."

Without warning, he struck.

The crimson blade cut into the dome with a shriek like tearing metal. Sparks exploded outward, golden and red colliding, twisting into violent streams that scorched the earth. The shield held, but cracks spiderwebbed across its surface, light splintering as though tested by the weight of a thousand storms.

Amara staggered, clutching her chest as the strain surged through her body. Sebastiano caught her, holding her upright with one arm while raising the dagger with the other. The blade responded instantly, flaring with golden fire, its radiance pushing back against Leone's strike.

Leone snarled, driving his weapon harder. The dome shrieked louder, splinters of light raining like falling stars.

Amara's eyes flared again. "No," she whispered, voice trembling with pain yet steady with conviction. She pushed Sebastiano's arm down gently. "This isn't yours to fight. It's mine."

Before Sebastiano could protest, she stepped forward, placing her palm against the cracking dome. Her hand glowed brilliantly, the golden light surging through the fractures like molten gold filling broken stone.

The cracks sealed. The dome blazed brighter than before. Leone's crimson blade quivered, its edge hissing as though recoiling from the touch of her power.

For the first time, Leone's sneer faltered.

Amara raised her other hand, her voice ringing with clarity, not shouted but carried with the weight of command:

"You cannot cage light. And you will not take me."

The dome didn't just hold—it expanded. The force of it struck Leone like a tidal wave, driving him back across the field. His blade sputtered, crimson flames licking at the edge before guttering out. He dropped to one knee, his laugh gone, his breath ragged.

Yet even on his knees, Leone's eyes burned with defiance. He spat blood, then wiped it from his mouth with the back of his hand, his grin returning in a broken, feral shape.

"Good," he rasped. "Good. The flame is real. The prophecy lives." He rose slowly, staggering but unbroken. "And that means you are worth killing myself to claim."

His words were not bravado. They were truth. Leone had no fear of death—only hunger for the kill.

He raised his blade once more, its crimson glow flickering back to life.

The real test was only beginning.

Chapter Sixty-Five
The Unveiling

The air quaked as Leone surged forward, his crimson blade screaming with malice, cutting jagged arcs through the night. The ground itself trembled beneath his charge, the sheer weight of his will pressing against the farmhouse like a storm pressing against glass.

Sebastiano tensed, dagger raised, every instinct screaming to protect Amara—but the moment he stepped forward, the light stopped him.

A golden force, soft as silk and strong as iron, pressed him gently back.

"No, Sebastiano," Amara whispered, her voice layered now—hers and another, deeper, ancient. "This is not your burden. It is mine."

Her hair lifted as though caught in a current of unseen wind. The glow in her eyes ignited fully, no longer a shimmer but a blazing fire, golden-white with threads of sapphire. The sigils carved into the farmhouse walls lit in answer, one by one, cascading like constellations come alive. The chest below shuddered, its lid vibrating as if singing in resonance with her.

Leone's blade came down with all his monstrous strength, crimson fire shrieking as it met her outstretched hand.

And stopped.

The impact sent ripples of raw energy through the field—windows shattered, trees bowed, stones split. Sebastiano shielded his face, the dagger in his grip glowing in sympathy, but Amara stood unmoved. The crimson blade hovered inches from her palm, its dark fire sputtering as if starved for air.

Leone roared, muscles straining, veins bulging as he tried to force it down. "You are a girl—nothing more! You cannot—"

Amara's voice cut him off, calm and absolute:

"I am not just the Key. I am the Light you fear."

Her palm pulsed, and the dome that had been a shield became something else entirely—no longer defense, but release.

The farmhouse exploded with radiance. Golden fire poured from Amara in a wave that seemed to come from every direction at once, searing through the night. The crimson blade dissolved like wax in a furnace, its shards melting into nothing. Leone was hurled back, his massive body lifted from the ground and slammed into the earth with the force of a falling star.

The wave rolled outward, erasing shadows, burning Leone's men into vaporized echoes of themselves, their relics shattered into dust. The sky itself seemed to split open, stars flaring brighter overhead as though bowing to the surge of power below.

Sebastiano fell to his knees, awe flooding him as the brilliance surrounded him but did not burn. He could feel it in his bones, in his blood—her power was not of destruction, but of revelation.

When at last the light subsided, the battlefield lay silent. The farmhouse still stood, but its stones glowed faintly, as though remade by the energy that had passed through them. The chest no longer shook—it lay still, its lid now half-open, a faint golden mist curling from within.

And Leone—Leone lay broken on the ground, his once-monstrous presence reduced, his blade gone, his body scorched by light. Yet his eyes remained open, still burning, still alive, though barely.

Amara lowered her hand, her body trembling from the release. She turned slowly toward Sebastiano, her eyes dimming back to human warmth.

He rose unsteadily, reaching her just as her knees gave way. Catching her in his arms, he whispered against her hair, voice thick with awe and fear alike:

"You are more than the prophecy, Amara. You are everything."

Behind them, Leone's ragged voice rasped from the dust:

"This… is not the end."

Chapter Sixty-Six
The Hand of the Duke

The farmhouse shook with the residue of Amara's power, golden threads still vibrating through the rafters. The air was acrid with smoke, singed stone, and the guttural retreat of Leone's laughter as it faded into the distance. He was gone—for now. But the echo of his vow clung to the walls like soot.

Sebastiano pulled himself to his feet, blood streaking his jaw, his eyes fixed on Amara with awe and fear intermingled. She stood radiant in the aftermath, the chest's light still pouring through her veins, her eyes like molten stars.

Silence pressed in—then broke.

From the blackened edge of the vineyard, headlights bloomed in the night. Engines growled low, deliberate, like predators circling their prey. More than a dozen vehicles drew into position, their beams fanning across the cliffside. The crunch of boots on gravel followed, crisp, disciplined, not the chaos of Leone's brutes but the precision of soldiers.

And then he came.

Duke Antonio Marchetti stepped from the lead car, his presence immaculate, his white silk scarf catching the sea breeze, his silver hair gleaming under the floodlights. He walked forward as if he owned the earth beneath his shoes, his cane tapping against the stones though he did not need its support. Soldiers parted for him, forming a corridor that funneled toward the battered farmhouse.

Amara stiffened, Sebastiano instinctively shifting to stand at her side. Marchetti's cold blue eyes swept over the scene—the ruined bodies of Leone's fallen, the scorched earth, the farmhouse glowing faintly with otherworldly light. His lips curved into a smile that was more knife than warmth.

"Well," he said, his voice carrying with a refined ease. "So the prophecy does not lie. The Key has awoken."

He removed his gloves with precision, tucking them into his pocket as if the devastation around him were no more than a parlor game. His gaze lingered on Amara, sharp and unyielding, before sliding to Sebastiano.

"And you," Marchetti murmured, his voice silk laced with steel. "The loyal hound who has slipped his chain. I wondered how long before you forgot who fed you, who clothed you, who gave you purpose. And now I see…" He tilted his head. "You've traded loyalty for lust."

Sebastiano's jaw clenched, his knuckles whitening as his hand brushed the dagger hidden beneath his shirt.

Marchetti's smile deepened, cruel and unhurried. "Do you think love will shield you, ragazzo? Do you think this… flame beside you will keep you warm when the world is burning?"

The soldiers tightened their circle, weapons gleaming in the artificial light. Marchetti raised a hand, halting them with a single gesture.

"No," he said softly, his eyes never leaving Amara's. "This is not a night for bullets. This is a night for choices."

His cane struck the stones once, a sharp report that echoed like a gavel. "Amara Savard—Key of the Brotherhood—come to me. Step forward, and I will give you the world. Stand against me, and I will grind everything you love to dust."

The sea below crashed against the cliffs, as though the earth itself waited for her answer.

Chapter Sixty-Seven
The Key Speaks

The air grew heavy, the sea's roar below a muted hush against the weight of Marchetti's words. Soldiers stood like statues, their rifles lowered but ready, the circle tightening around the farmhouse as though fate itself had closed its grip.

Amara stepped forward.

Sebastiano's hand darted to her arm, his grip desperate. "Don't," he hissed under his breath.

She glanced at him, her gaze steady, her voice quiet but unwavering. "I must."

She pulled free, her steps deliberate, and the golden threads still pulsing in her skin caught the floodlights, setting her aglow. Every soldier's eyes followed her, every breath seemed to falter as she came to stand in the open, face-to-face with the Duke.

Marchetti's smile widened. "Ah. At last."

The world narrowed to the two of them—his cold blue gaze, her molten fire.

"You speak of giving me the world," Amara said, her voice carrying in the still night. "But the world you offer is rot dressed in silk. You build your empire on blood, on chains, on the silence of those too broken to resist." She raised her chin, her voice gathering strength. "That is not power. That is fear."

The Duke's eyes glittered, the smile never leaving his lips. "And yet fear rules better than love. Ask history."

"Then history has waited for me," she answered, the words spilling from her as though something greater spoke through her. "I am not your Key, Antonio Marchetti. I am the flame that will burn your locks to ash."

Gasps rippled through the soldiers' line. Sebastiano's chest swelled with a fierce, unspoken pride, though his muscles tensed, ready for the strike he knew would follow.

Marchetti's smile faltered, just slightly, like glass spiderwebbing with the first fracture. His cane struck the ground once, sharp, final.

"So be it."

He lifted his hand. The soldiers raised their weapons as one.

And yet—none fired.

The rifles trembled in their hands, barrels quivering as if pulled by unseen currents. A soft hum rose, low and resonant, vibrating from the farmhouse itself. The chest glowed again, brighter this time, its sigils alive as though Amara's words had called it forth.

Marchetti's eyes narrowed. "Ah… so it has begun."

Chapter Sixty-Eight
The Breaking Point

Marchetti's hand dropped.

The crack of rifles split the night. Muzzle flashes strobed across the cliffs, the air filling with the acrid bite of gunpowder. Bullets screamed toward the farmhouse, shredding the silence that had held so taut.

Sebastiano lunged, dragging Amara toward cover, his body twisting to shield hers. Stone splintered above their heads as rounds slammed into the walls, sparks and dust raining down.

But then—

The chest roared.

A sound, deeper than thunder and older than the earth, burst from within. Its sigils flared, blinding, threads of molten gold shooting across the farmhouse beams. The bullets slowed midair, their copper casings spinning like insects caught in amber.

Amara straightened.

Her fear melted, replaced by something vast, luminous, eternal. Golden fire raced through her veins, pulsing in rhythm with the chest. The farmhouse itself seemed to bow to her, every stone and timber humming in recognition.

Her eyes burned with light as she lifted her hand.

The bullets dissolved into motes of brilliance, scattering like dying stars. The soldiers staggered, shouting in confusion, weapons ripped from their grip and hurled into the sea by unseen force.

Amara's voice rang out—not hers alone, but layered, as if a chorus spoke through her: "The Key has turned. The chains are broken."

The ground shuddered, the very cliff trembling underfoot. Sebastiano could only stare, his heart pounding with awe and terror in equal measure.

Marchetti did not flinch. He raised his cane, tapping it once against the stone. His smile returned, cruel and thin.

"So," he murmured, voice carrying over the chaos, "the Key has chosen. Then let us see if your flame burns brighter than the darkness I command." He stepped back into the shadows.

The soldiers, scattered and stunned, drew back— Marchetti's shadow stretching long across the firelit farmhouse.

Chapter Sixty-Nine
The Shattered Triumph

For a heartbeat, silence.

Then Marchetti's soldiers fell where they stood, their black armor cracked open like shells. The farmhouse glowed, its walls alive with sigils that pulsed in rhythm with Amara's breath. Sebastiano stood at her side, chest heaving, dagger still in his hand. The air reeked of iron and smoke, but it was still—eerily still.

Sebastiano turned to her, his eyes wide, awe and disbelief mingling in equal measure. "Amara..." His voice broke, the words catching in his throat. "You—you did this."

Amara's chest rose and fell in rapid rhythm, the golden light that had poured from her still clinging to her skin like a mantle. She swallowed hard, her voice trembling with both fear and wonder. "No... we did this."

Their hands met, trembling but firm. For a fleeting instant, the farmhouse felt like a sanctuary again—light beating back shadow, the impossible weight lifted.

And then the laugh came.

Low at first, curling up from the ruined threshold. A sound that scraped bone and rattled memory. Not Marchetti's cold calculation—no. This was darker, primal, a growl forged into mockery.

Both Amara and Sebastiano turned toward the doorway.

Through the smoke stepped Leone.

He was bloodied but unbowed, his massive frame filling the broken arch of the farmhouse door like a beast returning to its lair. His coat was torn, one arm streaked with ash and crimson, yet his eyes burned with a fire more dangerous than any wound. In one hand, he carried a weapon that seemed half-forged, half-grown—a blade whose edge shimmered like molten glass, veins of black fire crawling across its surface.

"You thought this was victory," Leone said, his voice a guttural thunder. He dragged the weapon against the stone as he entered, sparks leaping with every step. "But this?" He gestured at the fallen soldiers, the still-glowing farmhouse. "This is nothing. A prelude. A whisper before the scream."

Sebastiano stepped in front of Amara, dagger raised, his stance iron despite the exhaustion in his limbs. "You should have stayed in the shadows, Leone."

Leone grinned, teeth flashing white through the blood on his lips. "The shadows are where I was born, boy. But tonight—" His eyes cut to Amara, dark and gleaming. "—tonight, the light itself will kneel."

The farmhouse shook as he slammed the butt of his weapon into the floor. A pulse of black fire erupted outward, snuffing candles, dimming sigils, choking the golden glow until only a few threads of light clung desperately to the walls.

Amara staggered, gasping as if the air had been punched from her lungs. The chest on the table rattled violently, its sigils flickering as though caught between two warring tides.

Leone advanced, every step deliberate, savoring their faltering strength.

"Now," he whispered, his voice curling around them like smoke. "Now, little key, let me see if your light burns bright enough to survive me."

Chapter Seventy
The Clash of Shadows and Light

Leone lunged.

The black-flame blade cleaved the air, its heat so intense the wood of the farmhouse hissed and cracked where it passed. Sebastiano moved instinctively, dagger raised, catching the strike—but the force of it hurled him backward, slamming him into the stone hearth. The dagger shone brightly for an instant, then sputtered as if struggling against the weapon's corruption.

"Sebastiano!" Amara's cry rang out, raw and terrified.

Leone turned his full attention on her. His grin widened, savage, blood dripping from his temple. "There you are. The Key. I can feel it—your power, humming like a storm about to break. Show me, girl. Show me if you're worthy."

Amara's chest heaved as the farmhouse dimmed under Leone's aura. She could feel the weight of him pressing on her, not just his presence but the shadow of every life he had extinguished. Her knees nearly buckled beneath the tide of despair he carried with him.

But beneath the despair was something else—something that answered back.

The chest burst completely open with a thunderclap, its lid slamming against the stone pedestal. From within, a torrent of golden fire erupted, threads of light spiraling outward like living veins of sun. They coiled around Amara, lifting her hair, searing her vision with sigils older than speech.

Her eyes blazed white-gold.

The farmhouse floor thrummed, every sigil carved into its beams now blazing in unison. Sebastiano staggered upright, awe freezing him in place as Amara lifted her hand.

Leone sneered, bracing himself. "Yes. Yes, that's it. Give me your best. Let me taste the fire."

Amara's voice was no longer hers alone—it was layered, countless voices speaking through her. "I am not yours to test."

Her outstretched hand erupted with light, a beam of pure brilliance crashing into Leone's chest. He roared, his black blade raised against it, the clash deafening as dark fire collided with golden radiance. Sparks and embers sprayed across the room, burning into wood and stone alike.

The force shook the farmhouse to its foundations.

Leone staggered, his boots grinding against the floor, his blade quivering under the onslaught. His laughter broke through the roar of power—mad, defiant. "More! If this is all you are, you'll never stop me!"

Amara's light surged brighter, pouring through her veins until the air shimmered. Images flickered across the farmhouse walls—visions of temples, stars, battles fought long before their time. The weight of countless lives pulsed through her, and in that moment, she understood: she was the Key, but also the lock. The light was hers to command.

With a cry that echoed beyond the farmhouse, Amara thrust both hands forward.

The golden blaze expanded into a sphere, engulfing Leone in its center. His laughter turned to a guttural roar as the black fire of his blade shattered, shards sizzling into smoke. His massive frame convulsed, light searing across his flesh like brands.

And yet, as the brilliance reached its peak, Leone hurled his voice above the storm. "This is not my end, girl! I will crawl from the ashes of your light—and when I return, the world itself will bleed!"

With a final, earth-shaking pulse, the light hurled him backward, through the farmhouse wall. Stone and timber exploded outward as Leone's body was cast into the night, swallowed by shadow and flame.

The silence that followed was deafening.

Amara collapsed to her knees, the glow fading from her eyes, her body trembling with the force of what she had unleashed. Sebastiano was at her side in an instant, catching her before she fell.

He whispered, his voice hoarse but steady, "You've done it, Amara. You've driven him back."

But Amara, her breath shallow, shook her head. "No... he's not gone. He'll return. Stronger. Darker. And when he does—"

Her gaze lifted to Sebastiano's, fierce even through her exhaustion. "—we'll have to be ready."

Chapter Seventy-One
The Duke's Resolve

Far from the battered farmhouse, in the cold brilliance of his estate's war room, Duke Antonio Marchetti stood before a wall of living glass. Holographic maps hovered across its surface—Capri, Naples, Rome—lines of red and gold flaring like arteries across the Italian peninsula. His eyes, ice-pale and merciless, fixed on the pulsing beacon that marked the farmhouse.

The signal had spiked and flared only moments ago. His analysts had stammered reports, their voices cracking: a surge of unknown energy, readings off the charts, satellites momentarily disrupted.

Marchetti had not raised his voice. He had leaned closer, studying the pulsing wave. A wave that told him everything he needed to know.

"The Key was completely awake."

Behind him, Leone's absence hung heavy. Word of his retreat had not yet reached the Duke, but the silence spoke louder than any message. Leone was a brute, a beast given to theatrics—but he had never failed to report. That silence meant only one thing: he had been tested... and found wanting.

Marchetti's lips curled, though not in anger. It was a cold, calculating smile. "So. She is stronger than I thought. All the better. A weak Key is worthless."

A man in a dark suit approached, bowing his head. "Signore, shall we mobilize the next wave? The teams in Rome await your orders."

Marchetti clasped his hands behind his back, pacing slowly before the glowing maps. "Not yet. Leone has softened the walls, shaken her. If she believes she has triumphed, she will relax. And when she does—" He snapped his fingers, the sound echoing sharply in the room. "—we strike. Not with shadows. Not with brute force. With precision. With inevitability."

His eyes narrowed, voice dropping to a whisper that carried across the room like the hiss of a blade unsheathed. "We will not simply capture her. We will harness her."

The aide hesitated. "And if D'Amato resists?"

Marchetti paused, staring at the glowing farmhouse icon. For a moment, silence reigned. Then his answer came, soft and lethal:

"Then he dies. The prophecy names her, not him. He is replaceable."

The room grew colder as the Duke turned, his coat sweeping like a shadow around him.

"Prepare the net. Leone's failure only proves the game has entered its final stage. The Key is awake—and soon enough, she will kneel. Willingly, or broken."

He strode from the chamber, leaving the screens flickering with silent maps and the ghostly glow of war yet to come.

Chapter Seventy-Two
Leone's Oath

The storm had passed over Capri, but in the hollow where shadows gathered, Leone walked unshaken. His massive frame moved with a predator's grace, blood still spattered across his black coat like battle paint. His men—what few remained—limped behind him, silent, broken things with eyes cast low. Even the fiercest of them dared not meet his gaze.

They reached the edge of a crumbling chapel, its bell long fallen, its nave open to the sea. Leone entered alone. The air smelled of salt and rot, old incense long since burned away. He set his weapon—a curved blade still slick with dark ichor—on the altar, then braced his hands against the cold stone, bowing his head.

For a long while he said nothing. Only the wind through broken arches carried sound. Then a laugh, low and guttural, rolled from deep in his chest.

"She burns with fire," he growled, eyes glinting beneath the dim light. "The Key. The chosen. I have seen her light, and it seared my flesh but not my spirit." He lifted his hand, showing the blackened scars where Amara's power had struck. Instead of shame, there was reverence in the gesture. "I am marked. And because I am marked, I cannot fall until the marking is answered in full."

His voice rose, echoing off the chapel's broken walls, a sound between prayer and curse. "Marchetti believes he owns fate. That he bends prophecy to his will. But he is blind. It is not wealth nor armies that will rule when the Convergence arrives—it is will, and mine is forged in fire."

He drew a dagger and carved a single sigil into the altar, the twisted seal of his blood oath. The blade bit deep, stone screaming beneath his hand. "I swear it. I will rise again. I will shatter Marchetti, I will break D'Amato, and I will possess the Key until the light bends or burns out."

The last word thundered through the ruined chapel, carrying into the night like the toll of a funeral bell.

Behind him, his men shifted uneasily. They had seen him vow before. But this time, there was something different in his tone—an inevitability that chilled even the most hardened.

Leone turned at last, his scarred hand closing over the hilt of his weapon. His smile was jagged, more beast than man.

"Prepare yourselves," he said, his voice low but cutting through the air like a blade. "This is not defeat. This is beginning."

The waves crashed below, and the chapel seemed to tremble with his vow.

Chapter Seventy-Three
The Duke's Fury

The chandeliers in Marchetti's villa blazed with gold, but the light did nothing to soften the storm raging in his study. Reports lay scattered across his desk—drone footage, intercepted transmissions, fragments of the farmhouse battle—and every sheet bore the same insult: failure.

He stood at the window, fists clenched behind his back, the garden below immaculate as always, yet he saw only fire and ruin in his mind. The words whispered from his men haunted him still: Leone lives.

"Impossible," he muttered, his breath fogging faintly against the cold pane. "He should be ash. Broken. Gone."

But Leone was not gone. Leone had made his oath.

The door creaked, and one of his advisors slipped inside, pale with fear. "Duke... Leone has sent word." He placed a folded scrap of parchment on the desk, as out of place among Marchetti's sleek holographic devices as a snake in a nest of wires.

Marchetti unfolded it slowly. The ink was jagged, the message brief:

Your net is cut. The Key will be mine.

Marchetti's jaw clenched. His knuckles whitened until the parchment tore in his hands. "Mine," he hissed, voice low, vibrating with fury. "She is mine. Not his."

The advisor took a trembling step back, but Marchetti spun, his blue eyes blazing cold fire. "Gather every asset. Every soldier, every watcher, every whisperer in the cities. Double the surveillance. I want to know everything. Leone thinks himself untouchable? Then we will show him that empires are not built by oaths. They are built by power."

He strode to the table, where a holographic display bloomed to life—maps of Capri and Naples, tactical overlays pulsing with bright red nodes. Marchetti stabbed a finger toward the farmhouse. "This is the axis of it all. The Key, the prophecy, the Convergence. Everything converges here. And I will not let it slip into Leone's filthy hands."

His voice dropped lower, almost reverent with obsession. "Amara Savard was drawn to that house because fate demanded it. But fate is a servant, not a master. And I will make it serve me."

The advisor bowed, too terrified to speak, and fled the room.

Left alone, Marchetti poured himself a glass of deep red wine, his reflection flickering in the glass. He raised it like a toast to the night beyond the window.

"To destiny," he murmured. Then, with a thin, humorless smile: "And to the ruin of all who stand against me."

Chapter Seventy-Four
The Stillness After Fire

The farmhouse was quiet again, but not in the way of
before. Quiet like the air after a storm, heavy and taut,
carrying the scent of scorched stone and the echo of power
unleashed.

Amara stood in the center of the great room, her hands
trembling at her sides. The light that had poured from her
moments ago still shimmered faintly across the walls, as if
the stones themselves remembered it. She drew a slow
breath, her body aching in places she didn't know could
ache—not from battle, but from the sheer weight of
something vast flowing through her.

Sebastiano moved closer, his dark eyes never leaving
her. He looked at her not as a soldier measuring an ally, nor
as a man guarding the woman he loved, but as one who had
just witnessed the impossible. His hand hovered at her arm,
not touching yet, as though he feared even the brush of his
skin might unravel her.

"You…" His voice cracked, then steadied. "You were
the prophecy. Every word of it."

Amara shook her head, her breath shaky. "No. Not me.
Something… through me. I couldn't stop it if I wanted to.
It's like the farmhouse, the chest, the Guardians—they all
opened me like a door I didn't even know I had."

Sebastiano finally touched her, his fingers closing gently
over her wrist, grounding her. "Then you cannot walk back
through it now. The Key has turned. And once turned, it
cannot unturn."

The farmhouse groaned faintly, its timbers creaking as if in agreement. A thread of golden light traced itself along the beams before fading again.

Then came a sound—low, resonant, not from outside, not even from the chest, but from the stones themselves. The walls seemed to shiver, their very grain speaking in a chorus that filled the air.

"Guardians awakened. The Key has turned. The Hand is bound. But the Convergence draws near."

The voices overlapped, neither male nor female, neither young nor old—timeless, layered with the memory of centuries.

Amara froze, her breath catching in her throat. Sebastiano's grip tightened on her wrist.

"What does it mean?" she whispered.

The farmhouse moaned again, beams quaking under unseen weight. The words came slower this time, like a warning etched in thunder:

"Two shadows walk. One craves dominion, one craves ruin. But only the Light remembers the true path. Choose well, Key and Hand, for the earth itself will tremble when the sky aligns."

Then the house fell silent, the golden threads flickering once more before fading entirely.

Sebastiano's face was pale, his eyes shadowed with a gravity Amara had never seen before. He pulled her against him, not out of passion but out of fear he could not name.

"They're telling us," he murmured, his voice rough, "that the worst has not yet come."

The silence stretched, then the farmhouse spoke once more, its words deeper, heavier, as though the very stones carried the weight of the cosmos:

"The Convergence approaches. When seven lights weave as one across the heavens, the vault of the world shall open. Satellites will bow, oceans will shift, and the hand that holds the code will command the earth itself."

Amara staggered back, her breath caught. The air shimmered faintly, a vision blooming against the walls—stars wheeling, planets aligning in impossible symmetry. A river of light threaded through them, pulsing downward toward the Earth.

She saw it: a surge like a tidal wave of energy crashing into the world's fragile web of machines. Screens flickering. Satellites falling from orbit. Whole nations silenced in an instant.

Sebastiano saw it too and he reached for her, steadying her shoulders as her knees nearly gave. His face was pale, but his voice held steady. "That is what Marchetti wants. To seize that power. To bend it all to his will."

Amara shook her head slowly, her eyes wide with terror and awe. "If he controls it... there won't be nations anymore. Just him. Just his voice, everywhere."

The farmhouse pulsed once more, its voice dropping to a final, ominous whisper:

"The Key awakens to guard, or the Key awakens to enslave. No middle path. No second chance."

And then, silence—thick, suffocating, final. The glow faded from the walls, leaving them alone with the echo of destiny that had just been laid bare.

Sebastiano pulled Amara into his arms. She did not resist. Her face pressed to his chest, her breath shallow, his heart thundering against her cheek.

Neither spoke. There were no words left—only the knowledge that the world itself now hinged on their next choices.

Chapter Seventy-Five
The First Breath After Silence

The farmhouse was still. Too still. Dust hung in the beams
of afternoon light like frozen motes, caught between
movement and eternity. Every sound had retreated—the
cicadas, the distant sea, even the ticking of the old clock in
the kitchen.

Amara and Sebastiano had settled for the night in the
chamber below, where the chest rested on its pedestal,
glowing softly in the dim light. From its keyhole, a beam of
light cast a sigil upon the stone wall—an ever-shifting mark
of mystery and power. They had dragged a mattress and a
few blankets down from above, making a small bed beside
the chest, their temporary haven in the depths.

Amara clung to Sebastiano's chest, her cheek pressed
against him as if his heartbeat alone tethered her to the
world. But the echo of the farmhouse's final words gnawed
at her, circling in her mind like a vulture: No middle path.
No second chance.

At last she pulled back, her eyes searching his face. His
jaw was rigid, his gaze shadowed, yet when he looked at
her there was no hesitation. Only resolve.

"They've given us the choice," she whispered, her voice
trembling. "Guard or enslave. But what does that mean for
us? For me?"

Sebastiano cupped her face in his hands, his thumbs
brushing against her skin. "It means you cannot run from
what you are anymore. And I cannot run from what I've
been." His eyes flicked downward, to the faint cut along his
forearm where he had severed the brand of Marchetti's

Brotherhood. "We stand together now—or we don't stand at all."

The chest pulsed faintly, its glow subdued but alive, as though waiting. Amara's felt it, her breath catching. "The chest hasn't finished with us. I can feel it. Whatever it holds, it hasn't fully revealed itself yet. We need to open it and look inside"

Sebastiano followed her gaze, then shook his head grimly. "Not yet. Not while Marchetti and Leone circle us like wolves. When we open it again, it should be on our terms, not theirs."

She nodded, but her fingers still itched to touch the lid. It was as if the symbols sang to her blood, pulling her toward them with every passing moment. She tore her eyes away, grounding herself in Sebastiano's steady presence.

"We don't have time," he said finally, breaking the silence. His voice was steady, clipped, all soldier now. "Marchetti will come back. And Leone..." He trailed off, jaw tightening. "Leone won't stop until he's tasted blood."

Amara drew in a breath, the farmhouse air suddenly heavy again. "Then we prepare," she said, surprising herself with the steel in her own voice. "If they want to come, let them. This house chose us. Maybe it can protect us."

For a moment, Sebastiano's lips curved into the faintest smile. "Now you sound like the woman the Brotherhood feared," he said softly, almost reverently.

The farmhouse gave no reply this time—only silence, as if it, too, waited.

And outside, beyond the stone walls and vineyards, the first dark clouds of an approaching storm gathered over the horizon.

Chapter Seventy-Six
The Shadow Moves

The Tyrrhenian Sea rolled dark and heavy beneath a leaden sky. Far from Capri's glittering harbors, where tourists sipped Aperol spritz in careless ease, three sleek black vessels cut across the waves in formation. Their hulls bore no markings, their wakes swallowed swiftly by the sea. Inside, armed men waited in silence, weapons checked and re-checked, faces set with the grim focus of those long accustomed to blood.

At the head of the lead vessel stood Duke Antonio Marchetti. His tailored coat did nothing to blunt the bite of the salt wind, yet he looked every inch the sovereign surveying his domain. His silver hair was slicked back, his sharp eyes fixed on the dark smudge of land rising ahead: Capri.

He clasped his hands behind his back, his jaw tightening. The farmhouse was there. The Key was there. And with each hour that passed, the prophecy drew closer to its apex. He could feel it, the way a hunter feels the heartbeat of prey thrumming through the forest floor.

"Report," he said, his voice carrying easily over the roar of the engines.

A man in combat gear stepped forward, bowing his head slightly. "Our forward scouts confirm that Amara and Sebastiano are both at the farmhouse. Leone's forces have not yet moved on the property. But they are in position on the far side of the island. Watching. Waiting."

Marchetti's lips thinned. "Leone." He spat the name like venom. "He fancies himself a predator, but he has forgotten who holds the leash."

The man hesitated. "Sir, Leone no longer answers to—"

"Enough." Marchetti's voice cut like a blade, silencing the soldier instantly. "Leone is nothing without my networks, my money, my reach. If he chooses to play the wolf, he will learn what it is to starve."

He turned back toward Capri, his eyes narrowing. The sea spray caught the light, flecking his face, but he remained utterly composed.

"This ends tonight," he said, his voice low, deadly. "Bring the island to its knees if you must. Burn the vineyards. Tear down the walls. But bring me Amara Savard alive."

The soldier nodded once and retreated. Orders spread through the ranks with efficient quiet, weapons primed, radios alive with clipped confirmations.

Above them, the first roll of thunder cracked across the sky. Storm and steel would strike together.

Marchetti raised his glass of Barolo—steady even on the rocking deck—and took a measured sip. His eyes glinted with cold certainty.

"The Key is mine," he murmured to himself. "And I will be the hand that turns it."

Chapter Seventy-Seven
Leone's Vigil

Deep in the bowels of a crumbling monastery carved into the cliffs of Capri's far side, firelight danced against stone walls blackened by centuries of smoke. The place stank of damp limestone, sweat, and something older—something that clung like mildew but carried the tang of blood.

Leone knelt bare-chested before the altar, his massive shoulders gleaming with oil, his skin tattooed in jagged sigils that twisted across his torso like coiled serpents. Before him, an ancient reliquary lay open, its contents nothing more than rusted chains and a cracked fragment of bone. Yet he bowed to it with the reverence of a priest before relics of a forgotten god.

Around him, his men—hulking shapes draped in dark leather, faces masked in iron half-helms—chanted low, the rhythm guttural, more growl than prayer. They were not soldiers in Marchetti's sense. They were beasts caged in flesh, men broken and reforged under Leone's will.

One of them stepped forward, dropping to a knee. "Duke Marchetti moves. His ships cut the sea. They'll strike the farmhouse by nightfall."

Leone's head rose, his eyes burning like coals in the flicker of the torches. A smile tore slowly across his face, too wide, too sharp.

"Good," he said, his voice gravel, his teeth catching the firelight. "Let the Duke play the lord, with his glass of wine and his polished boots. Let him think the Key is his to hold. When his men bleed on that soil, when the farmhouse burns, only then will he understand whose hunt this truly is."

He stood, towering, the chant of his men rising with him. He seized the fragment of bone from the reliquary and ground it into dust in his palm. The ash sifted down, smearing across his chest like war paint.

"I will not take her alive for his leash," Leone snarled, the cavern vibrating with the force of his voice. "Amara Savard awakens, and her power will answer me. The Key belongs to the hand strong enough to hold it—and mine is the only hand that does not tremble."

His men roared in answer, a sound more beast than human, shaking loose flecks of stone from the ceiling.

Leone lifted his great blade, its edge nicked and blackened from years of blood. He pressed it to his tongue, the iron sharp enough to draw a bead of red. He let the taste linger before he spoke again, voice guttural with promise.

"Tonight, Marchetti learns he is no master. Tonight, the Key learns fear. And if she dares unleash her light against me—" he spread his arms wide, head thrown back in a laugh that echoed like thunder—"then the heavens themselves will see what it is to break."

The chant swelled, the torches guttered, and Leone's oath etched itself into the dark.

Chapter Seventy-Eight
The Landing

The sea lay black and restless beneath a moon veiled in cloud. From the cliffs above, the farmhouse slept in silence, its windows dark, its stones holding the last whispers of golden light. But out beyond the rocky curve of the coastline, shadows stirred.

A convoy of sleek vessels slid across the water, their hulls painted in muted gray, their engines whisper-quiet against the tide. No flags flew. These were not naval ships bound by country or creed—they were Marchetti's fleet, crewed by men whose loyalty had been purchased with blood and gold.

On the lead vessel, General Rinaldi stood at the prow, his uniform immaculate, his face a mask of cold discipline. The man had spent three decades in the Duke's service, a soldier who had long ago traded conscience for command. He watched as the dark outline of Capri swelled larger, the jagged cliffs looming like teeth ready to bite.

"Hold formation," he barked into the comm at his collar. "No signal. No lights. We strike the cliffs beneath Anacapri as planned. The farmhouse will not see us coming."

At his back, lines of armored soldiers stood silent, helmets concealing their faces, rifles gleaming faintly in the dim moonlight. But it was not their weapons that drew unease—it was the cargo crates lashed to the decks, each one stenciled with the Duke's crest. Inside lay tools far more terrible than steel and powder: devices scavenged from forgotten vaults, mechanisms infused with fragments of the prophecy itself. Machines that bent light, that unraveled sound, that could disorient and disable a mind without spilling a drop of blood.

Weapons meant not merely to kill, but to subdue the Key.

A younger officer at Rinaldi's side shifted uneasily. "Sir… what if Leone's men are already on the island? Reports suggest he's moving without the Duke's sanction."

Rinaldi's jaw tightened. He kept his gaze fixed on the cliffs, his tone sharp. "Then we cut through them as well. The Duke commands. Leone is a dog who will learn his place, or be put down like one."

The boats slid into the narrow cove beneath the cliffs, hidden from sight of the farmhouse above. Soldiers leapt into the surf, water churning around their armored legs, as they dragged ramps into place and rolled the first of the Duke's crates onto the stony beach.

Rinaldi lifted his hand. His voice cut the night like steel.

"By dawn, the Key will kneel. And should she resist— her light will burn for the Duke's crown alone."

Above, the farmhouse windows flickered faintly, as though the stones themselves shivered at the coming storm.

Chapter Seventy-Nine
The Duke's Hand

Far from the farmhouse, where the cliffs of Capri met the restless sea, Duke Antonio Marchetti stood in a chamber that felt more like the sanctum of a king than the command post of a general. The room was paneled in dark walnut, lined with shelves of leather-bound volumes whose spines gleamed with gilt. At the chamber's center stood a semicircle of holographic displays, their cold light painting his aristocratic face in sharp relief.

On the screens, the operation unfolded with precision. Grey boats knifed through the indigo waters, their engines silent to anyone listening on shore. Men clad in tactical gear crouched low, weapons ready, their movements as disciplined as a single body. Overhead, silent drones skimmed the wind, their lenses transmitting every detail back to Marchetti's command chamber.

The Duke clasped his hands behind his back, his posture as immaculate as the tailoring of his suit. He had dressed for war as though for the opera—midnight jacket, silk tie, shoes polished to a sheen. Regal, composed, a man who believed he was born not only to witness history but to bend it.

"Landing in five minutes," reported his aide, a man in a dark headset whose voice carried none of the awe that flickered across his eyes when he glanced at Marchetti.

The Duke inclined his head, his gaze fixed on the glowing screens. One vessel had surged ahead—a spearpoint slicing through the dark water. Inside it crouched Leone's chosen men, hulking silhouettes whose strange weapons caught the light with an ominous gleam.

Even across the distance of the feed, Marchetti could sense their feral edge. He did not flinch; he had made use of monsters before—and this time, he would again.

Even the Duke had been forced to admit that only Leone's ruthless precision could lead the assault now. To seize control of the key, this final confrontation demanded a brutality equal to the power it sought to contain. Leone had taken command of the attack on the farmhouse, fully aware of the force awakening in Amara—the Brotherhood's ancient energy stirring through her, a strength that had waited centuries for the right vessel to release it.

"Leone," Marchetti murmured, tasting the name like bitter wine. "Let us see if your ambition outpaces your loyalty this time."

His eyes shifted to another feed—thermal images of the farmhouse perched above the cliffs. The old walls glowed faintly with residual heat signatures, not from fire, but from something the machines could not fully interpret. A pulse that did not belong to any known spectrum. His jaw tightened, though his expression otherwise remained serene.

The prophecy was not myth. The farmhouse lived. The Key had turned.

He leaned closer, his reflection ghosting across the glass. "Bring me the Key," he whispered, voice like a prayer and a command in one. "Alive if possible. Broken if necessary. The world bends tonight."

Behind him, the aide shifted uneasily but said nothing. He had seen the Duke's gaze—piercing, glacial, unshakable. There was no room for doubt in a man who believed he already owned tomorrow.

Marchetti lifted a crystal glass from the table beside him, the Barolo within catching the glow of the screens. He raised it in a toast to no one.

"To destiny," he said softly. "And to those strong enough to claim it."

He drank, his eyes never leaving the farmhouse that flickered on the screen like a beacon.

Chapter Eighty
The Calm Before the Storm

The morning unfolded with a deceptive gentleness.
Sunlight slanted across the farmhouse terrace, washing the
stone walls in a golden hue that made them seem timeless,
inviolate. The sea below was impossibly calm, its surface
like liquid glass, the only movement the slow drift of gulls
wheeling lazily against the horizon.

Amara stood by the open window, a cup of coffee
warming her hands. The scent of roasted beans mixed with
salt air and the faint perfume of jasmine carried in from the
garden. For a fleeting moment, she allowed herself to
believe in the illusion—that they were safe, that the night
of fire and visions had burned itself out, leaving only quiet
in its wake.

Behind her, Sebastiano moved through the kitchen with
quiet purpose, rolling his sleeves as though the simple act
of preparing food might anchor him in normalcy. He sliced
bread, drizzled it with oil, and set it to toast in the pan. To
anyone else, it might have looked like the morning after an
ordinary night.

But both of them knew better.

The farmhouse still hummed faintly beneath their feet,
its stones thrumming with a rhythm neither of them could
name. Every so often, Amara felt the pulse in her chest
answer it—like two heartbeats aligning. And every so
often, Sebastiano's eyes flicked to the windows, his
movements too sharp, too deliberate, betraying the
vigilance gnawing at him.

"It's too quiet," he muttered finally, breaking the fragile
spell.

Amara turned, her gaze steady. "You feel it too."

He nodded, setting the knife down with care. "This isn't peace. It's waiting."

As if to prove him right, the air shifted—so subtly it could have been missed. The gulls scattered, their wings flashing white as they veered inland. A faint vibration trembled through the glass panes of the window, so slight Amara wondered if she had imagined it.

She set her cup down, her breath shallow. "They're coming."

Sebastiano's jaw tightened. He crossed to her side, his hand brushing hers—not by chance, but as a deliberate anchor. "Then we prepare. No more running from what this house demands."

The farmhouse itself seemed to creak in assent, a low groan through its beams, as though it too sensed the tightening of the net around them.

And far below, hidden in the mist that curled along the cliffside road, black vehicles were already winding their way upward, their engines hushed, their intent anything but gentle.

The storm was moving in.

Chapter Eighty-One
The Last Quiet

The farmhouse seemed to hold its breath with them that morning. A fragile calm settled over the air as they gathered what they would need for what lay ahead—the stillness before the storm waiting just beyond the horizon.

His gaze locked with Amara's, and the love shining in her eyes stole the breath from his chest, holding him in a silence that spoke more than words ever could. She stood across from him, the morning light weaving through her hairlike threads of fire.

"We're going to need your strength and power to get through this," Sebastiano said softly, his hand resting over her heart. "Your strength is in here. You carry the full power of the Brotherhood now."

Then he drew her into his arms, holding her close, savoring the fragile stillness between them—the quiet before the storm that was already gathering beyond the shore.

Her breath caught, not just at his touch, but at the truth of his words. She could still feel the farmhouse's pulse echoing in her bones, a rhythm that was no longer just her own. She nodded slowly.

Leaving Sebastiano at the table, Amara went downstairs to the chamber. At the center the stone pedestal stood holding the chest. Its sigils dark for now but never truly dormant. She knelt before it, her hand hovering an inch above the carved lid. Closing her eyes, she let her breathing steady, reaching inward for the connection that had frightened her at first but now felt like the only path forward.

The air stirred. Faint motes of light rose from the chest, like dust illuminated by the sun, swirling gently in the stillness. They didn't flare, didn't burn—only shimmered, waiting.

Sebastiano stepped in behind Amara, watching her with his quiet love. The steel in his expression lost as he watched from the arched doorway.

Silence hung in the air. In that moment, they both knew: this farmhouse was no longer just a shelter. It was a fortress, and perhaps even a temple. But whether it would continue to stand or fall depended on their choices—and their unity.

Outside, the vehicles climbed higher, their black paint glinting once as the sun broke fully over the horizon. Still hidden, still minutes away.

Inside, the farmhouse braced itself with them.

Chapter Eighty-Two
The Thread Between

The farmhouse kitchen smelled faintly of espresso and woodsmoke, though neither had touched their cups. The coffee sat cooling on the table, forgotten, as if both knew the simple rituals of morning had already slipped out of reach.

Amara leaned against the old stone counter, her arms folded, eyes following Sebastiano as he checked and rechecked the pistol, sliding the magazine in, sliding it out again, as though control could be wrestled from repetition.

"You don't have to prove anything to me," she said softly.

His hands stilled. He lifted his gaze to hers, dark eyes shadowed by something deeper than fear. "This isn't about proof. It's about keeping you alive."

Her heart twisted at the weight in his voice. She crossed the room and placed her hand over his, forcing the pistol down onto the table. "You've already done that," she whispered. "Every moment since we met, you've been guarding me—even when you weren't sure why. Even when it nearly broke you."

The silence between them deepened, charged with truths neither had spoken aloud. Slowly, Sebastiano lifted his free hand to her face, his thumb brushing across her cheek.

"You don't know what it's like to carry blood on your hands," he murmured. "Men I've killed for Marchetti, women I've betrayed, lives I ended because I didn't have the strength to choose differently. And yet—" His voice broke, husky, as though the words themselves fought to stay buried. "Yet you look at me as if none of it matters. As if I can be something else."

Amara pressed her forehead against his, closing her eyes. "Because you can. Because you are. The man in front of me now is not the man who served him. You cut that tie when you chose me. When you chose this."

Her fingers found his, threading together, and for a heartbeat the farmhouse seemed to hum with approval, the low vibration rising faintly in the floorboards like a sigh of recognition.

Sebastiano kissed her then—not with the urgency of the night before, but with a quiet intensity that was somehow fiercer. A vow made not in words, but in the press of lips and the thrum of heartbeats shared. It was a kiss that acknowledged what waited outside their walls and yet refused to let it steal the moment from them.

When they parted, their foreheads lingered together, breath mingling. Amara whispered, "Whatever happens, we face it together."

His eyes burned, not with fear, but with conviction. "Together."

The farmhouse seemed to settle into silence once more, as though it too had taken the vow.

And outside, hidden by the curve of the hills, the convoy crept closer—black metal glinting like the edge of a blade poised to fall.

Chapter Eighty-Three
The Serpent at the Door

Amara felt it before she heard it—the farmhouse seemed to lean into the silence, as though every stone braced itself for what the air already knew. Sebastiano stiffened at her side, his head lifting sharply. His hand went to the small pistol at his hip, though both of them understood it was nothing against what was coming.

Then it came.

The low, rolling growl of engines, not one but many, climbing the narrow road that wound like a snake through the cliffs below. The sound grew into a roar, tires crushing gravel, gears grinding under the weight of armored vehicles. In the distance, lights flared—a constellation of headlights sweeping up the hillside in perfect formation.

Amara's breath caught. "They're here."

Sebastiano pulled her back from the window, his jaw set, eyes burning with grim resolve. "Marchetti doesn't waste time once he makes a move. This is his full force."

The farmhouse groaned faintly, timbers shivering as though the earth itself echoed the approach. Amara felt the chest's quiet hum beneath the floorboards—a pulse in rhythm with her own heart. The prophecy whispered again in her mind: The Key awakens to guard, or the Key awakens to enslave.

She reached for Sebastiano's hand, their fingers tangling tightly. For a brief moment, the world narrowed to their locked gaze. His eyes held no fear—only defiance, and a vow stronger than any he had spoken aloud.

Outside, engines cut to silence. The night pressed in, thick and breathless. Then the first shot split the air. Glass shattered inward, spraying across the farmhouse floor like falling stars.

The assault had begun.

The echo of the first gunshot rolled across the cliffs, then silence reclaimed the afternoon as though the world itself held its breath. The broken window gaped like a wound, moonlight spilling through jagged shards.

No voices. No footsteps. Just the stillness of men waiting, unseen but everywhere.

Sebastiano pulled Amara lower, pressing her gently behind the thick stone wall. His hand lingered against her cheek for one heartbeat longer than necessary. "They're probing us," he whispered. "Testing for movement. The next volley won't miss."

Amara's pulse thundered in her ears. She could feel the farmhouse vibrating faintly, as if its ancient stones recognized what was coming. Somewhere deep within, the chest stirred, its hum climbing like a chord tightening on a bowstring.

Then—out in the night—a sound.

Boots crunching gravel. Dozens. No, more. The muted signal of hands raised in unison, and the slick metallic slide of rifles primed.

Sebastiano's lips brushed her ear, his voice a vow wrapped in steel. "Stay with me. Whatever happens—we hold until the farmhouse itself chooses."

And then the day erupted.

A rain of bullets tore into the walls, the farmhouse shuddering under the onslaught.

Chapter Eighty-Four
The Breach

The farmhouse walls shook under the assault, centuries-old stone coughing dust with every impact. Windows shattered one by one, raining glass like hail onto the floors. The air filled with acrid smoke and the sulfur sting of gunfire.

Amara crouched low, her arms wrapped around herself, the sound vibrating in her bones. But beneath the chaos she felt it—the farmhouse's pulse. The chest downstairs thrummed like a heart in overdrive, its rhythm echoing inside her ribcage.

Sebastiano was already moving. His body was a blur of trained precision as he seized one of the rifles left by Marchetti's fallen scouts. He cracked open a window shutter just enough, sighted through the smoke, and returned fire. A scream split the night—one of the soldiers falling in the courtyard. Another followed, then another.

But still they came. Black-clad figures fanned out, pressing closer, their boots pounding against the stone paths, their rifles spitting fire. Flares streaked overhead, painting the farmhouse in a hellish red glow.

"Sebastiano!" Amara cried, fear slicing through her.

He turned, his eyes burning with both resolve and something far deeper. "The walls will hold only so long," he shouted over the barrage. "But the house—it's with us. Do you feel it?"

Amara nodded, trembling. "Yes... it's alive."

As if answering her words, the floor beneath them quaked. Symbols hidden in the flagstones flared to life, blazing with golden fire. The bullets striking the walls slowed mid-air, dropping harmlessly to the floor as if the house itself refused to let them through.

A soldier hurled a grenade. It sailed toward the farmhouse door—then froze, suspended in mid-air before dissolving into dust, erased by an unseen hand.

The soldiers faltered, their formation breaking, panic rippling through their ranks.

Sebastiano reached for Amara, his voice fierce. "Now, amore mio. Call it. The farmhouse is waiting—for you."

Amara rose, her hair whipping in the rising wind that now howled through the rooms. The glow climbed the walls, traced the beams, gathered at her feet like a tide rushing toward its shore. She lifted her hands, and the air itself seemed to bend.

Outside, the storm of gunfire sputtered. The soldiers, once fearless, felt the ground shift beneath them. The farmhouse had awakened—and Amara stood at its heart.

Chapter Eighty-Five
The Shield Under Fire

The courtyard was a storm of smoke and fire. Marchetti's soldiers pressed hard, their rifles barking, their shouts cutting through the night. But the farmhouse held—their bullets fell to dust, their grenades dissolved in the air, their bodies thrown back by unseen force.

Still, they kept coming, like waves breaking against a cliff, relentless, certain that sheer numbers would prevail.

Then the ground shuddered.

Not from the farmhouse this time—but from the road beyond. A deeper rumble, heavy and deliberate, like beasts loosed from their chains. The soldiers in the courtyard faltered, some turning toward the sound, confusion shadowing their faces.

Out of the smoke they came.

Leone led them—taller than all, his scarred face carved in firelight, his coat dark as spilled blood. Behind him marched a phalanx of horrors—men in armor painted with sigils twisted from the old Brotherhood's seal, their eyes gleaming with unnatural light. Their weapons were cruel things, shaped like jagged bone and steel, humming with a resonance that made the farmhouse walls groan.

Marchetti's soldiers instinctively parted, a ripple of fear passing through their hardened ranks. Even they recognized this was no ordinary ally—these were predators loosed into the night.

Leone stopped at the shattered gate, his massive frame outlined in the fire's glow. His lips split into a grin that held no warmth, only hunger.

"Savard!" he roared, his voice carrying like thunder across the stone. "Key of the Brotherhood—let us see what you are."

His men surged forward, a tide of darkness, their weapons cutting arcs of light that made the very air scream.

Inside, Sebastiano pulled Amara back from the door, his breath ragged, his eyes hard. "This is the moment. They've come together—Marchetti's pawns and Leone's beasts. If the farmhouse is with you, then it's now or never."

Amara's heart pounded, but the fear that had knotted her chest began to unravel. The farmhouse pulsed around her, the chest downstairs thrumming in time with her blood. She felt it—every stone, every beam, every sigil was alive, waiting, listening.

The guardians' whisper pressed into her mind: "The Key awakens through fire. When darkness unites, the flame must answer."

Amara lifted her hands, and the farmhouse answered with her.

The walls blazed, the roof-beams glowed, and the ground itself trembled as the power surged toward her, gathering, building. Leone's laughter rolled like thunder as he raised his weapon high, striding forward even as the air turned molten with light.

Chapter Eighty-Six
The Breaking Point

Leone's stride was unhurried, almost leisurely, as though the chaos of the courtyard belonged to him alone. His men fanned out, their jagged weapons shrieking with unearthly resonance, cleaving the night with arcs of sickly light. Marchetti's soldiers recoiled from the wave, falling back instinctively, leaving Leone the stage he craved.

Sebastiano stepped forward.

His blade caught the glow of the farmhouse, the dagger of the Guardians still humming faintly from the cuts that had severed his past. He planted himself in the breach of the doorway, his body shielding Amara.

"Back inside!" he growled over his shoulder.

But Amara didn't move. Her eyes locked on him, her chest tight, her breath ragged. She saw the mark of Marchetti's Brotherhood still faint on his arm, saw the set of his jaw, the calm readiness in his eyes. He was prepared to die here, to hold Leone back with his own blood if it meant buying her a heartbeat more.

"No," she whispered, her voice breaking. "Not like this. Not you."

Leone laughed, low and rumbling. "D'Amato. Always the loyal dog. But now you guard her? Do you think your blade will stop me?" He lifted his monstrous weapon, its edge humming like a hive of hornets, the air itself buckling around it.

Sebastiano raised the dagger, steady though his pulse thundered. "Then try me."

The two men locked eyes—predator and protector, shadow and flame. For an instant the world narrowed to this alone: the inevitability of the clash.

And in that instant, Amara's fear became fire.

Her vision blurred with tears as she reached for Sebastiano—but what answered wasn't her hands. It was the farmhouse, the chest, the Guardians, the Convergence itself.

A roar split the night as light erupted from her body, cascading outward in spirals of gold and white. The walls of the farmhouse blazed like a star, the courtyard flooded in brilliance so fierce that Leone's men shrieked as their weapons cracked, splintered, and fell apart in their hands.

Sebastiano staggered back as the wave passed through him, not burning, not breaking—but filling him, lifting him as though every wound, every chain had been stripped away.

Leone stood his ground, the force hammering into him. His grin faltered, his weapon shattering in his hands. His massive frame buckled, yet he refused to fall, his roar a mix of rage and awe.

"KEY!" he bellowed over the storm. "This is only the beginning!"

The light flung him and his surviving men into the smoke, their forms tumbling into shadow. But even as they vanished, his laughter lingered, twisted and terrible, echoing across the stones.

When the brilliance finally dimmed, the courtyard lay silent. Smoke curled from shattered weapons. Marchetti's soldiers were gone—scattered like ash. Only Sebastiano and Amara remained standing in the threshold, the farmhouse behind them glowing faintly, as though sighing after the storm.

Amara swayed, her body trembling with the aftershock. Sebastiano caught her, pulling her against his chest. Her hands clutched his shirt, her face pressed to him, tears streaking her cheeks.

"You nearly died," she whispered.

His arms tightened around her. "But I didn't. Because of you."

And for the first time, he understood—the Key was not just power. It was her.

Chapter Eighty-Seven
The Duke Enters

Out of the smoke he came.

Duke Antonio Marchetti walked as though the carnage were nothing more than theater staged for his arrival. His black coat was immaculate despite the ruin around him, his silver hair gleaming under the fractured light. His polished shoes clicked softly on the stone, a rhythm steady and unhurried, in sharp contrast to the chaos still smoldering in the courtyard.

He clapped once—slow, deliberate, the sound cutting through the silence like a blade.

"Magnificent," he said, his voice smooth as silk, echoing against the farmhouse walls. "Truly magnificent."

Sebastiano stiffened, pulling Amara closer behind him. His dagger glowed faintly, still alive with the Guardians' fire, but his hand trembled. This was not Leone's brute force—it was something colder, sharper, a mind that had played the game far longer.

"Stay back," Sebastiano warned, his voice taut.

Marchetti's smile deepened, though his eyes remained ice. "My dear boy," he said softly, "you stand there like a lion, ready to tear me apart, yet you and I both know where your loyalties were forged. My blood flows through the oath on your skin. You were mine long before she ever touched your heart."

Amara's pulse quickened. She stepped forward before Sebastiano could stop her, her voice steady despite the tremor in her chest. "You don't own him. Not anymore."

Marchetti's gaze slid to her, lingering, appraising. His smile thinned. "Ah. The Key speaks." He let the words hang in the air, savoring them. "You burned away Leone's toys, shattered his men as though they were made of glass. But tell me…" His head tilted, his eyes narrowing. "Do you even know what you are holding inside yourself? Do you know what you've just unleashed into the world?"

Amara said nothing, though the farmhouse behind her pulsed faintly in answer, its voice waiting.

Marchetti stepped closer, unflinching as Sebastiano held the dagger between them. "You think this was power?" he asked, his voice dropping to a hiss. "This was a spark. When the Convergence comes, when the satellites bend and the seas obey, only one hand will command the code." His eyes flashed, blue fire in the smoke. "And that hand will be mine."

Sebastiano moved, placing himself squarely in Marchetti's path. His voice was steel. "Not while I draw breath."

Marchetti's gaze softened almost affectionately, though venom laced his words. "And that, Sebastiano, is exactly what I'm counting on."

Chapter Eighty-Eight
The Gathering Fire

For a breath, time stilled. Smoke curled between them like phantom veils, the air too thick, too charged to draw easily.

Amara's chest rose and fell, her heartbeat a drum against her ribs. She could feel Sebastiano's stance beside her—solid, unyielding—but it was the farmhouse itself that answered, its stones thrumming beneath her bare feet, as though the earth wanted to rise through her.

Marchetti's eyes never left hers. Cold, piercing, serpentine. "You don't even understand the fire in your veins," he said softly, almost coaxing. "You think it's yours. But it is older. Wiser. Hungrier. Do you truly believe you can hold it without breaking?"

The words cut, but Amara didn't flinch. She felt the heat building inside, that strange light surging in waves that pushed against her skin as though demanding release. Sebastiano's hand brushed her back, grounding her, yet it only stoked the fire more—love entwined with fury until they were indistinguishable.

Her lips parted, breath trembling. "I am not afraid of you."

The farmhouse pulsed in agreement, its beams creaking, its unseen heart glowing faintly once more. Dust rained from the ceiling like falling stars.

Marchetti's smile thinned. "Then you are already lost."

He lifted one hand.

The ground shook as if the island itself bent to his command. Hidden charges planted deep beneath the soil roared to life. With a deafening crack, the outer walls of the vineyard exploded, earth and stone erupting skyward.

Black-clad soldiers poured in through the breach, their weapons bristling with unnatural energy, their eyes masked and cold.

Sebastiano lunged forward, dagger blazing. Amara staggered back, the wave of dust and sound threatening to crush her lungs. But the fire in her chest—no, in her very soul—ignited fully now. It demanded release.

The storm had begun.

Chapter Eighty-Nine
The Wound and the Flame

Steel clashed in the farmhouse yard, a storm of bodies
pressed against stone walls and splintered beams.
Marchetti's soldiers swarmed like a black tide, their rifles
barking, their blades flashing. Sebastiano moved among
them with lethal precision, each strike of his dagger a blur,
each step placed with the instinct of a man who had
survived battlefields most never lived to tell of.

But numbers pressed him back. Three at once lunged,
and he spun, cutting two down, yet the third slipped past
his guard. A flash of steel arced low.

Amara's cry split the night.

Sebastiano staggered, his blade still clutched tight, but
blood bloomed dark across his side where the knife had
found him. He gritted his teeth, refusing to fall, forcing his
body to stand between Amara and the soldiers pouring in.

"Stay back!" he growled, his voice rough but
unyielding, cutting down the man who had struck him even
as his knees threatened to give.

Amara froze, her heart lurching violently. The sight of
his blood, the smell of iron filling the air—it shattered
something inside her. The man who had guarded her life
with his own now swayed, wounded, his breath harsh and
ragged.

"Sebastiano!" she screamed, rushing forward, but he
turned his head just enough, eyes blazing.

"Don't—don't lose focus. You are the Key."

Those words, cracked with pain but fierce with
conviction, pierced her deeper than any blade. The soldiers

closed in again, boots pounding, rifles raised, voices shouting.

And then the world broke.

A sound tore from Amara's chest, not entirely human— a cry threaded with grief, fury, and love so fierce it bent the air itself. Light erupted from her skin, golden at first, then white-hot, a torrent spilling outward like a tidal wave. The sigils etched into the farmhouse walls ignited, flaring as though the house itself answered her.

Soldiers were hurled backward, their weapons ripped from their hands. Some screamed, others fell silent as the surge struck them like a hurricane of light and thunder. The very ground trembled beneath their boots.

Sebastiano, half-kneeling, raised his arm against the brilliance, his heart pounding—not with fear, but awe. She stood in the center of the storm, hair whipping like flame, her eyes no longer simply human but burning with the fire of the convergence itself.

The Key had awakened.

And every man who dared to step closer felt the weight of it, the raw judgment of power born from love.

Chapter Ninety
The Duke Steps Through Fire

The courtyard lay in ruins—rifles shattered, bodies strewn across the stones. Smoke curled in the air, streaked with the golden glow that still clung to Amara's skin. Sebastiano, bloodied but standing, held himself steady at her side, though every breath burned like fire.

And then came the sound that cut through it all—slow, deliberate clapping.

From the outer gate, framed by shadows and torchlight, Marchetti walked forward. His immaculate suit bore no speck of dust, his silver hair combed back as though untouched by battle. Around him, his personal guard parted the wreckage, their black uniforms unbroken lines of discipline.

"Well," he said, voice carrying like steel struck on stone. "The legends spoke of a Key that would awaken with fire and storm. And here you are, burning my men to ash." His smile was thin, almost amused. "Impressive. But power without direction is nothing more than chaos."

Amara's chest heaved, light still flaring behind her eyes. "You think you can control this?" she said, her voice low, shaking with fury and disbelief.

Marchetti stepped closer, unfazed by the scorch marks on the stones, by the tremor that still rippled through the farmhouse walls. He looked her over not as a threat, but as an asset. A priceless artifact that had just proved real.

"I don't think," he said smoothly. "I know. You are the culmination of centuries of work—knowledge buried, protected, hunted. And I have spent a lifetime gathering the fragments of that prophecy so that when you awakened, you would awaken for me."

Sebastiano moved half a step forward, his blade trembling in his bloodstained hand. "You'll never touch her," he spat, his voice rough with both pain and rage.

Marchetti's eyes flicked toward him, cool, disdainful. "Sebastiano. My faithful hound. Still barking at his master even as he bleeds." He let the words hang, then added softly, "I raised you from the mud of your family's servitude. Don't pretend loyalty was ever a choice."

Sebastiano's jaw clenched, but he held his ground.

Marchetti's gaze returned to Amara, steady, piercing. "The Convergence draws near. Satellites, oceans, the vault of the earth—all of it answers to the Key. Do you really think you can stand against the weight of history alone? No, my dear. You will break. They all do. Better to bend now—to me—and rule beside me, than to shatter when the world crushes you."

For the first time since the storm of light had erupted, Amara faltered—not in strength, but in certainty. His words pressed like cold iron, tempting, invasive. She felt Sebastiano's hand brush against hers, weak but steady, anchoring her.

Her voice trembled, yet it carried: "You mistake me, Duke. I was never awakened to serve you."

The farmhouse groaned, a deep, resonant sound, as though it too rose against Marchetti's claim.

Chapter Ninety-One
The Duke's Gambit

The silence stretched, taut as wire. Smoke curled in ghostly ribbons between them, catching the moonlight. The night seemed to hold its breath, every shadow leaning toward the farmhouse.

Marchetti did not flinch under Amara's defiance. Instead, he smiled, the kind of smile that spoke of decades spent bending empires to his will. Slowly, deliberately, he extended a gloved hand toward her—not in threat, but in invitation.

"Power is not for the righteous," he said softly, his tone coaxing, almost paternal. "It belongs to those with vision. And I alone have the clarity to wield it. Join me, Amara Savard. Walk away from this ruin. Leave the boy bleeding at your side. Together, we will not just survive the Convergence—we will command it."

The farmhouse groaned again, timbers shifting like an old beast stirring in protest. The light in the chest at the center pulsed faintly, its glow syncing with Amara's racing heartbeat.

Sebastiano leaned close, his whisper frayed with pain. "Don't listen… it's poison." His bloodied fingers squeezed hers, anchoring her even as his body trembled.

Marchetti's gaze flicked to the gesture, his smile tightening, sharpening. "You would throw away the fate of nations for a soldier's touch?" His hand stayed outstretched, gloved fingers gleaming in the firelight. "Choose wisely, girl. The Convergence waits for no one."

For a heartbeat, Amara stood frozen—Sebastiano's touch grounding her, Marchetti's voice digging like a blade into her mind, and the farmhouse itself thrumming with a power that seemed to demand an answer.

And then, from the darkness behind Marchetti, came the faintest sound. A boot scraping stone. Another figure stepped forward, slow and deliberate, breaking the charged stillness.

Leone.

His monstrous frame caught the light, his scarred mouth curving into a smile devoid of warmth. His men fanned out behind him, their weapons glinting with cruel invention.

Marchetti did not turn, though his jaw tightened. "You're late," he said coldly.

Leone's laugh rumbled low, like thunder rolling in a cavern. "Not too late." His gaze fixed on Amara, his eyes gleaming with hunger. "Just in time."

Chapter Ninety-Two
The Shattered Balance

Night came in heavy as though the island itself was crouched in dread. Between Marchetti's gloved hand and Leone's looming shadow, the farmhouse stood like a heart about to rupture.

Amara's pulse thundered in her ears. Sebastiano swayed at her side, his body trembling, his hand sticky with blood where it pressed against his wound. He refused to fall, though every breath came ragged, shallow.

Marchetti's voice slid into the silence, silken and poisonous. "One does not squander destiny on sentiment. Step into history with me, Amara. Or be buried beneath it."

Leone laughed—a sound jagged as broken glass. "History?" His scarred lips curled, his eyes fixed on Amara with a predator's hunger. "She's not your history, old man. She's my fire to cage."

The words tore through Sebastiano like a blade. His hand slipped from hers as his knees buckled, his strength at last faltering. His body struck the farmhouse floor with a dull thud, the sound echoing like a gunshot in the charged stillness.

"Sebastiano!" Amara dropped to her knees, her hands frantic against his chest, feeling the faltering rise and fall of his breath. He had lost a lot of blood.

His lips moved, broken words escaping in a whisper meant only for her. "Don't... let them... take you..."

Her tears burned hot, falling onto his bloodied shirt. And then—something deeper than grief stirred. A soundless scream building in her chest, pressing against bone and skin until the farmhouse itself seemed to tremble in sympathy.

The chest flared, its sigils igniting as though her anguish were the key it had waited for all along. Light speared upward through the floor, striking the beams, crawling the walls, flooding the air until it was impossible to tell where the farmhouse ended and Amara began.

Both men—Marchetti with his poised control, Leone with his brutal hunger—fell into shadow against the blaze awakening in her.

And Amara rose.

Chapter Ninety-Three
The Breaking of Kings

The farmhouse shook as though the stones themselves recoiled from the violence. Smoke curled through shattered windows, mixing with the metallic sting of blood in the air.

Leone stepped into the ruined courtyard like a storm made flesh, his monstrous men flanking him, their weapons dripping with otherworldly light. His presence bent the air, his grin cruel and certain.

And behind him—emerging from the haze like a figure untouched by fire—came Marchetti. Immaculate even amidst the ruin, his silver hair gleamed in the moonlight, his tailored coat unblemished by ash. He carried no weapon. He needed none. His voice was sharper than steel.

"It ends tonight," Marchetti declared, his gaze sweeping over Amara—lingering with cold hunger on the chest that still pulsed faintly behind them.

Leone's laugh rumbled low. "Yes… it ends. But not as you imagine, old wolf."

Marchetti's eyes narrowed. "Careful, Leone."

Too late. Leone moved with terrifying speed, faster than his massive frame should allow. A blade, black and serrated, flashed in his hand. Before Marchetti could turn, Leone drove it into his side.

The sound was sickening—a crack of ribs, the wet gasp of breath stolen. Marchetti staggered, his hand flying to the wound, blood blooming dark against the pale silk of his shirt. For the first time in decades, his mask of untouchable control fractured. His eyes widened, not in fear, but in fury.

Gasps rose from his men. Amara's heart lurched in her chest.

"You dare?" Marchetti rasped, voice thick with pain. "Strike me?"

Leone leaned close, his teeth bared, his voice like gravel dragged across stone. "I don't bow, Antonio. Not to you. Not to anyone. The Key is mine."

Marchetti's knees buckled, but he did not fall. Even wounded, even bleeding, he stood with the poise of a king who refused to kneel. His gaze burned with hatred, fixed on Leone, and then shifted—slow, inevitable—toward Amara.

"She... will never... choose you," he spat.

Leone only grinned wider. "Then she will be broken until she has no choice."

Amara's stomach twisted. Sebastiano was barely conscious and had no strength before the immensity of the two forces now colliding over her. Her breath came ragged, fear clawing at her chest.

Amara looked at Sebastiano and saw him flinch—his hand slick with blood where the blade had cut deep across his side. The sight broke something in her.

The farmhouse pulsed.

Light coiled up Amara's spine, tearing free of her skin in ribbons of gold. Her hair lifted as if caught in a celestial wind, her eyes blazing like molten suns. The ground trembled beneath her feet.

Leone stepped back, his grin faltering for the first time. Even Marchetti, pale with blood loss, straightened, his eyes widening.

Amara's voice carried, layered with the resonance of something not human:

"You sought the Key. Now face what it unlocks."

The heavens split with light.

Chapter Ninety-Four
The Wrath of the Key

The air itself seemed to rip apart as Amara lifted her arms. Golden fire roared from her chest, ribbons of light weaving outward like living serpents. The farmhouse, once dim and scarred, became a beacon—its stones glowing, its timbers thrumming as though joining her cry.

Leone snarled, raising his monstrous blade. His men surged forward, their twisted weapons humming with unnatural energy. But the first wave never reached her. A sweep of Amara's hand sent a wall of light crashing outward, bodies flung like rag dolls into the shattered courtyard walls. Weapons dissolved in midair, warped into harmless shards of dust.

Sebastiano staggered back, shielding his face from the brilliance, his side dripping blood. Yet even through the blaze, he could not look away. She was incandescent, divine, terrifying and beautiful all at once.

Leone roared and lunged, his bulk a storm of fury. Amara did not retreat. She opened her palms, and a column of light shot skyward, wrapping around him. The glow seared against his skin, etching sigils of fire into his flesh. He howled, his monstrous strength straining against her radiance, but for the first time, fear shadowed his eyes.

"Submit," her voice thundered—not hers alone, but layered with the chorus of the Guardians, deep and resonant. "Or be unmade."

Leone spat blood, defiant even as his knees buckled. "I do not bend!" he bellowed, his teeth gritted. "I will return! I will tear your light to pieces!"

With a final surge, he slashed his blade downward. The light shattered around him like glass, sparks spraying into the night. Broken, wounded, but not destroyed, Leone stumbled back into the shadows. His monstrous men dragged him away, retreating into the smoke. His vow lingered in the air, sharp as steel:

"This is not the end, Key! It has only begun!"

Silence followed his retreat, broken only by Marchetti's ragged cough.

Amara turned slowly. The Duke still stood, blood soaking his side, his once-impeccable poise dimmed but not extinguished. He straightened, forcing dignity into his trembling frame.

"You think yourself chosen," he said, voice low, venomous. "But power without control… destroys. And you will destroy everything you love."

His eyes flicked toward Sebastiano, and his lips curled into a faint, bloodied smile. "Especially him."

Amara's power flared hotter, her light blazing high, ready to obliterate him where he stood.

The farmhouse shuddered, the Guardians' chorus swelling in her ears: "Guard or enslave. Choose."

Her hand trembled, fire coiling at her fingertips. The choice burned before her: end Marchetti now—or hold the blade of her wrath.

Chapter Ninety-Five
The Retreat

The battlefield fell to a stunned, ringing silence. Smoke
coiled through the shattered olive grove, the earth still
trembling faintly from the force of Amara's release.
Bodies—some groaning, some stilled forever—lay strewn
across the stone terrace where the farmhouse had once
stood proud.

Marchetti staggered back, his face ghost-pale, one hand
pressed to his side where blood seeped through the fine
weave of his suit. His sharp blue eyes burned with fury, but
the arrogance had cracked. He no longer looked
untouchable. He looked mortal.

Leone was already gone, vanished into the trees with his
surviving men, but his laughter still lingered like smoke in
Amara's ears.

Sebastiano swayed to his feet beside her, his shirt
clinging to him, dark with blood. He tried to put his hand
on her arm, but his knees buckled and Amara felt terror
unlike any she had known.

Marchetti's voice rasped across the ruin, carrying the
weight of his vow: "This is not finished. You will not keep
what is mine."

Then, with a curt gesture, his men rallied around him.
They pulled him toward the waiting convoy at the edge of
the grove. Engines roared, black smoke rose, and the Duke
of shadows retreated into the night, leaving only his
promise behind.

Amara dropped to her knees as Sebastiano collapsed
against her, his weight heavy, his breath ragged. She

gathered him to her chest, her trembling hands trying to staunch the blood at his side.

"Stay with me," she whispered, her voice breaking. "Please, stay with me."

The farmhouse door hung broken on its hinges, but its presence still pulsed faintly, as though urging them inward. With all the strength she had left, Amara dragged Sebastiano across the threshold.

Inside was ruin—splintered beams, shattered glass, the echo of the Guardians' voices long faded. Yet the hidden chamber beneath the farmhouse—the one that had long safeguarded the chest—still stood, half-buried beneath the rubble. With trembling urgency, Amara wrenched the door open and half-carried, half-dragged Sebastiano down into the dim passage below.

The air was cool, damp, filled with the scent of stone and salt. Candles guttered faintly in their sconces, lit by no human hand. Here, beneath the storm, was stillness.

She laid Sebastiano down on the cold floor, her palms pressed to his chest, his breath shallow. His dark eyes fluttered open, struggling to focus on her.

"Amara…" he rasped, his lips bloodied. "If I fall—"

"Don't," she choked, her tears spilling freely. "Don't you dare leave me. Not now. Not ever."

The farmhouse seemed to hum in answer, a vibration rising through the stones beneath her knees, pressing against her palms. For the first time, she felt her power stir not in fury, but in love.

And she realized: it could destroy. Or it could heal.

Her hands glowed faintly, golden threads seeping from her fingers into Sebastiano's wounds. His body arched, a strangled groan escaping him as the light sank deeper, searching, knitting.

Above, in the distance, far beyond their knowing— Marchetti straightened in the back of his armored car. His breath hitched as torn flesh mended, pain dissolving. His lips curved into a slow, terrible smile.

Amara did not know it yet. But the act of saving Sebastiano had awakened Marchetti as well.

Chapter Ninety-Six
The Healing

The chamber below the farmhouse glowed as though dawn itself had seeped into the stone. Amara knelt over Sebastiano, her hands pressed firm against his chest, her tears dripping onto his skin. Every beat of his faltering heart echoed through her, each ragged breath a knife tearing her apart.

"Don't leave me," she whispered again, her voice trembling but fierce. "Not when I've just found you again. I love you with all of me. I don't ever want to live a life without you."

The glow around her hands flared brighter, golden threads weaving into the wound, knitting torn flesh, sealing blood. The power surged through her like fire and ice all at once, flooding veins she didn't know could carry such force. She gave every heartbeat to him. Her vision blurred, her strength draining with every pulse of light she gave. Her body shook, her lips whispering broken prayers, not to gods, but to the universe itself—pleas that he live, that he stay.

Sebastiano convulsed, his body arching against the stone, a strangled cry escaping him. Amara felt the power of the Brotherhood surging through her as the wound healed. She nearly pulled away, afraid she was hurting him, but the farmhouse itself seemed to whisper through the walls: Do not falter. Love is stronger than fear.

And then—his hand found hers. Weak, trembling, but real. His dark eyes opened, hazy but alive.

"Amara..." His voice was a rasp, a thread of sound, but it was enough.

Her sob broke free as she collapsed against him, her forehead pressing to his. Relief poured through her so strong it left her trembling. "You're here," she whispered, clinging to him as though the earth itself might tear them apart. "You're still here."

The light dimmed, retreating back into her chest like embers cooling, though its warmth lingered. She could feel his heartbeat now—stronger, steadier—beneath her palm. The wound that had threatened to claim him was almost gone, replaced by a new scar that gleamed faintly in the candlelight. The Brotherhood had brought Sebastiano back to her.

Exhaustion hit her in a crushing wave. Her arms trembled, her body near-collapse, but Sebastiano caught her, gathering her into his arms despite his weakness. He held her close, pressing his lips to her hair, his breath ragged but steadying.

"I've got you, rest against me," he murmured, awe threading through his voice.

She pulled back enough to meet his gaze, her tears shimmering in the golden light. "I couldn't lose you," she whispered. "Not now. Not ever again."

His hand lifted to her cheek, his thumb brushing away a tear. His eyes burned with something deeper than gratitude—something fierce and unyielding. "Then I am yours," he said softly, the vow carrying the weight of truth. "In this life and every life after."

They clung to each other in the quiet, the chamber holding them like a sanctuary while the world above reeled from war.

But neither of them knew—miles away, in the depths of his estate, Duke Antonio Marchetti straightened, the gash in his side gone, his body whole. He touched the place where death had nearly claimed him, his sharp eyes gleaming with realization.

"The Key heals as well as destroys," he murmured, a slow smile curling his lips. "And her gift binds us all."

Amara's lips parted, her breath trembling, but steady enough to answer him. "Then in this life, and every life after, I am yours." Her words came with a strength that surprised even her, a vow rising from somewhere deeper than time.

Their foreheads pressed together, hearts beating in sync, the farmhouse silent except for the whisper of their breath. For one suspended instant, the world was only them, bound not by fear or prophecy, but by love.

Then her body gave way. The exhaustion she had held back through sheer will swept over her in a crashing wave. Her eyes fluttered shut, her weight sagging into him.

Sebastiano's caught her and pulled her close, lowering her gently against his chest, his arms encircling her as though he could shield her from the world.

Her breathing was shallow, but steady. He pressed a desperate kiss to her temple, his tears mixing with her damp hair. Relief battled fear, but the vow she had spoken lingered in him like fire, burning away the shadows.

He held her, rocking gently in the golden glow that still lingered faintly in the chamber, whispering against her hair: "Rest, my love. I'll hold the line. Whatever comes, I'll stand."

The farmhouse answered with a low hum through its timbers, like an unseen guardian keeping watch.

Chapter Ninety-Seven
The Duke's Sustenance

Dawn was breaking across Marchetti's estate, painting the marble fountains in pale rose and gold. Yet inside his sanctum, no light of the natural world was permitted. The shutters were drawn, the great windows sealed, and the chamber glowed instead with the sterile brilliance of machines.

Antonio Marchetti reclined in a chair of polished steel and leather, its arms bristling with slender tubes and glass vials. A physician in white gloves moved with rehearsed precision, inserting a line into the vein at his wrist. Dark crimson blood flowed out, filling the chamber with the faint metallic tang of iron, before being drawn through a filtration system and returned to his body, cool and enhanced.

Marchetti closed his eyes, exhaling slowly as the infusion began. The serum was his own creation, perfected through decades of theft, bribery, and research carried out in hidden laboratories. It carried the essence of youth harvested from the unwilling—stem cells, genetic grafts, rare compounds stolen from every corner of the globe. Where others aged, he grew sharper. Where others weakened, he grew unyielding.

The physician adjusted the flow with practiced care, his movements precise beneath the Duke's silent, watchful gaze. Marchetti lay still, the soft hum of his treatment filling the sterile air. The serum coursed through his veins like liquid fire, and behind his closed eyes, his mind turned to Leone.

Leone overreaches, he thought, the words sliding through the silence like smoke. *He forgets his place.* Yet there was method in the monster's use. *For this final taking of the Key, I need his brutality—his unrestrained hunger. Let him strike first, let him drain some of the power she holds. Then, when her strength wanes, my forces will move in and finish what he began.*

A faint smile ghosted across the Duke's lips. *He imagines himself the hand of destiny, but he is only a beast. Dangerous, yes—but beasts can be harnessed. Or put down.* His pulse slowed, the serum's power settling deep into his body. *He will not take the Key,* he thought, a cold certainty blooming within him. *She belongs to me.*

The Duke's blue eyes snapped open, cold and piercing after the last of the treatment went into his veins. He gestured sharply, and the physician removed the IV from the Duke's arm and left the room quietly closing the door behind him. Rising from the chair, Marchetti rolled his sleeve down. The faint puncture in his arm was already sealing, the skin flawless, unmarred by time.

He walked to his satellite projection of the island. Capri glowed at its center, the farmhouse marked with a crimson sigil. Around it, threads of movement tracked his men, his drones, his ships. A tightening web.

"The Convergence approaches," he whispered, his fingers brushing the map as though caressing a lover's skin. "Seven lights weaving. Oceans bending. And when the vault opens I will be the one who commands the code. It will be me."

He stood before the map in silence, the hum of machines steady at his back. His body was fed by stolen life, his will sharpened by obsession. The Key had awakened—but the Duke would be the hand to turn it.

And in his mind, the world was already his.

Chapter Ninety- Eight
The Duke's Command

"The Key—Amara Savard—is fully awake," he said, his voice low but ringing with the weight of iron. "The prophecy is no longer a whisper. It breathes."

A shiver of unease moved through the room. He felt it, the subtle tightening of shoulders, the caught breaths, but paid it no mind. His gaze swept the ring of commanders, sharp and unyielding, until silence gathered around him like smoke.

"Amara Savard has awakened to the truth of what she is—and to the power she was born to command," Marchetti said, each word honed to precision. "She knows now how to summon it, to shape it, to bend it to her will. And soon she will stand before the choice that will decide the fate of this world: to claim dominion and crown herself its sovereign… or to let the Earth rise along its destined path."

He drew a steady breath, the fire in his eyes banked but not hidden. "For us, it means the ascension of power—true, unrestrained power. The age of waiting is over. The Brotherhood will no longer serve in the shadows. We will rule."

He spread his hands then, the movement deliberate, almost ceremonial. "I was destined to be her counterpart—to guide her, to shape her, to rule beside her. She will see it soon enough. She is mine. Together, we will reign."

His gaze lifted toward the vaulted ceiling, voice rising like thunder breaking across stone. "The Convergence nears. Seven lights will cross the heavens, and the vault will open. The one who claims it will hold the pulse of the world in their hands—the tides, the satellites, the breath of the Earth itself."

Chapter Ninety-Nine
The Blood Oath Deepens

Beneath the ruined monastery outside Naples, Leone stood shirtless in the circle of his men. The lamplight made the scars across his body gleam like runes carved in flesh, each one earned in violence, each one worn as a mark of devotion. His eyes burned with a feverish light as he lifted the obsidian-bladed knife.

Before him, a basin brimming with dark liquid quivered—wine thickened with ash and blood. The smell of iron and smoke filled the air, choking those who knelt closest.

"They think me broken," Leone said, his voice booming off the stone vaults. "They think the Key's fire has wounded me, that I will limp away and nurse my scars like some whipped cur."

He raised his arms, muscles coiled, knife catching the flame. "But I tell you, brothers—what burned me has only fed me! Her power is not a weapon to fear. It is a chalice. And I will drink it dry."

A guttural cheer rolled through the chamber, savage and raw.

Leone's grin split wide, a jagged thing. "Marchetti gathers his ships, his soldiers, his drones. He believes the Key will kneel to him. But what are machines before blood? What is steel before the oath we bear?"

He dragged the knife across his palm, blood dripping into the basin. "I vow before the old gods and the dead ones—I will have the Key. I will chain her light to the darkness where it belongs."

One by one, his men came forward, slicing their hands, letting their blood fall into the basin. The surface writhed, black and red, as if alive. When the last had bled, Leone plunged both hands into the basin and smeared the mixture across his chest, painting sigils of war.

His voice sank to a growl. "Tonight we are the storm that precedes the Convergence. We will feast on light and shadow alike. Let Marchetti think he's winning as we siphon Amara's strength, leaving her a candle guttering before the Duke arrives at the farmhouse. After that, I will carve Marchetti's name into the ledger of the dead, seize my Key, and let her lead my dark legions — to twist the planet itself to my command."

The men howled, pounding their fists against the stone until dust rained down from the ceiling.

Leone stood unmoving, eyes closed, breathing the frenzy like incense. When he opened them again, they gleamed like a beast staring from the mouth of a cave.

"Capri will bleed," he whispered. "The Key will scream. And the world will learn the taste of my vengeance."

Chapter One-Hundred
The Duke's Gambit

The study was dim, its only light the pale gleam of moon through high windows and the cold shimmer of holographic maps spread across Marchetti's desk. The Duke stood tall before them, hands clasped behind his back, his profile etched like a statue in the faint glow. Every red dot pulsing on the map represented a unit of his men closing the net tighter around Anacapri.

He had shed his jacket, rolled his sleeves. The marble floor beneath him reflected a man composed, but his reflection in the glass above his desk betrayed the truth—eyes burning, jaw clenched, hunger and fury warring beneath the mask.

He pressed a control, and the maps shifted. Overlays of satellite feeds flickered: thermal scans of the farmhouse, infrared sweeps of the cliffs, intercepted drone footage. Marchetti leaned closer, his eyes narrowing.

"The Key," he murmured, almost to himself. "And the hand that dares guard it."

His aide, a wiry man with a voice that carried no inflection, cleared his throat softly. "Your orders, sir?"

Marchetti straightened. "We strike in waves. Leone will rush in first, as always. He will break his teeth on her light. That will weaken her—drain her. Then we move. Precision, not chaos. While she spends her strength fending off the beast, we slip the chain around her throat."

The aide nodded, tapping commands into his wrist console. Units shifted on the maps, concentric arcs tightening around the farmhouse like a serpent coiling to strike.

Marchetti turned away from the desk and walked to the tall windows, gazing out where the gardens lay serene, unaware of the violence plotted above them. His reflection in the glass stared back: a man who had waited decades for this hour.

"She has the full power of the Brotherhood behind her now," he whispered, voice dark silk. "The prophecy ensures it. But awakening is not enough. Power must be guided, contained. And when the world trembles, it will not tremble for her. It will tremble for me."

He lifted a crystal glass of Barolo from the sill, swirling the wine until it caught the moonlight.

"Begin," he said simply.

Behind him, the aide transmitted the signal. Across the island, men moved silently into position. In the air, unmarked drones turned their lenses to the farmhouse. And beneath it all, satellites far above shifted orbit at Marchetti's command, preparing to harness the first threads of the coming Convergence.

The Duke drank deeply, his eyes still fixed on his own reflection.

"Let Leone tear at the gates," he murmured, lips curving in the ghost of a smile. "I will be the one who walks through them."

Chapter One Hundred-One
The Beast Unleashed

The cliffs shook before dawn.

It began as a low vibration, so faint it might have been mistaken for thunder rolling far out at sea. But the sound grew, deepened, became a guttural roar that seemed to crawl up from the earth itself. Amara stirred, her hand tightening instinctively around Sebastiano's. He had felt it too—the air pressing heavy, a primal warning.

Above, the farmhouse walls trembled. Dust sifted from the beams. The sigils carved into the old stones flared for a heartbeat, as if bracing against something vast and violent approaching.

And then came the howl.

It tore through the dawn like a blade of iron dragged across the sky—inhuman, shuddering, filled with rage and hunger. The cry of Leone's war-beasts, men twisted beyond recognition, surged across the hills.

From the olive groves and jagged gullies they came, shapes half-shrouded in shadow, their movements wrong, too fast, too heavy. Muscles corded with ritual scarring, faces masked with iron fangs, weapons that glowed faintly with stolen fire. Their laughter was a jagged thing, broken and wild, a sound that made the night itself recoil.

At their head, Leone advanced. His cloak was black as ash, his chest bare despite the cold, his flesh carved with sigils that writhed when the torchlight struck them. He carried no gun, no blade of steel—only a staff of bone bound in bronze, its tip glowing faintly like an ember stolen from some infernal forge.

He raised it high, and the air split.

The ground buckled, stones cracked, and the beasts with him roared as one, their cries merging with the hum of unnatural energy. Leone's grin was a wound cut across his face.

"The Key is awake, and so is the storm," he bellowed, voice carrying across the cliffs to the farmhouse. "Amara Savard! The world belongs to those willing to seize it!"

The war-beasts surged forward, their weapons shrieking as they lit the air with arcs of jagged fire. The first wave crashed against the invisible boundary of the farmhouse—the shield left by the Guardians. Sparks exploded, the barrier flickering under the assault.

Inside, Amara gasped as she felt the strike ripple through her bones. Sebastiano steadied her, his jaw clenched, eyes fixed toward the stairs.

"They've come," he said, his voice low, taut as a bowstring.

The farmhouse groaned, beams straining as if to hold back the tide. The chest pulsed once, its light answering the storm outside.

Amara lifted her head, her dark eyes fierce even through the fear. "Then it's time."

Chapter One Hundred Two
The Falcon's Vigil

From the terrace of his Amalfi stronghold, Duke Antonio Marchetti watched the chaos unfold through the eyes of his machines.

Dozens of holographic screens hovered in the cold air before him, each one a live feed from drones circling Anacapri like steel-winged falcons. Their lenses caught everything—the war-beasts thundering across the olive groves, the arcs of stolen fire striking the farmhouse shield, the flash of Leone's staff splitting the dawn.

Marchetti stood unmoving, hands clasped lightly behind his back, the posture of a man at prayer. But there was nothing pious in his gaze. His eyes, glacial and calculating, traced each image with surgical precision.

Leone's madness had broken from its leash. His oath of rivalry was no longer veiled but declared with every strike against the farmhouse. Marchetti's lips curved into the faintest smile.

"So," he murmured, his voice a low purr. "The beast bares its teeth."

Behind him, his advisors stood silent, unwilling to break his reverie. They knew better. Marchetti's temper was not loud—it was razor-sharp, honed by decades of power and the certainty of command.

On the central feed, the farmhouse flared. For a heartbeat, the shield glowed bright enough to blind the drones, and Marchetti's eyes narrowed. When the light cleared, he saw her—Amara Savard, standing in a window like a figure carved from flame and night.

Even through the grain of the transmission, her presence struck him. Calm. Defiant. A resonance that unsettled even him.

"The Key is awake," he said softly, repeating the prophecy's line as though savoring the taste of it. "But will it guard... or enslave?"

Leone's beasts struck again, hammering the barrier until sparks fell like meteors across the stones. Marchetti studied the moment, measured it, and then turned slightly toward his waiting men.

"Deploy our first wave," he ordered. "But not to strike— yet. Hold them at the perimeter. Let Leone bleed himself on her defenses. Let him weaken what I intend to claim."

His gaze sharpened, his voice dropping lower, colder.

"When he falters—and he will—we move. And when we move, it will not be to contest, but to claim."

The screens flickered, Leone's roar carrying even through the drone's distant microphones. Marchetti tilted his head, almost amused.

"Shout all you wish, Leone," he murmured. "In the end, even your fury will serve me."

Chapter One Hundred Three
The Shield Under Fire

The farmhouse shook.

The first impact cracked through its walls like thunder, rattling the beams, sending dust spiraling from the rafters. Amara staggered, her hand shooting out to brace against the stone as the floor seemed to buck beneath her. Sebastiano was at her side instantly, his arm tightening around her waist.

From beyond the windows, the world was a storm. Leone's war-beasts—hulking shadows stitched with steel and sorcery—hurled themselves against the shimmering barrier that still wrapped the farmhouse. Each strike made the shield flare with golden light, then dim dangerously, as though each heartbeat cost it more strength than the last.

"Sebastiano," Amara whispered, her voice trembling. "It won't hold."

He steadied her, his own jaw set with grim resolve. "It will hold," he said. "As long as you're here. The shield is tied to you, Amara. Not the stone. Not the mortar. You."

Her throat tightened. "But if I falter—"

"Then I will not let you falter." His words were raw, cut from the very center of him. "If this place falls, then I fall first."

The farmhouse shuddered again, beams groaning, glass shivering in the windows. From the courtyard came the roar of something not-quite-human, its cry splitting the dawn like iron dragged across stone.

Sebastiano pulled her closer, his body between hers and the sound. "They're probing the shield," he muttered. "Looking for its weakest point."

"Leone," Amara said, her voice low. She could feel him out there—his presence like a shadow pressed against the edges of her mind, hungry and relentless. He wasn't just striking the barrier with force. He was pressing his will into it, trying to bend it, to crack her resolve from within.

Her chest tightened, her hands trembling as she pressed them against the farmhouse wall. The shield pulsed faintly beneath her palms.

"They're going to break through," she whispered. "And when they do—"

Sebastiano caught her face in his hands, forcing her to meet his eyes. His gaze burned with steadiness, a flame against her rising fear.

"When they do," he said fiercely, "we stand. Together. As we always were meant to."

Outside, another strike came—a war-beast's massive claws raking the shield, leaving trails of sizzling sparks. The barrier rippled, thinning.

And in that moment, Leone's voice rose above the storm, carried on a guttural roar that seemed to split the sky:

"Key! You will open—or you will break!"

The farmhouse walls glowed faintly in response, as if bracing for the next blow.

Chapter One Hundred Four
The Beast in Flesh

The ground itself seemed to recoil as Leone stepped into view.

From the courtyard's haze of dust and sparks, his massive form emerged, towering above even the beasts he commanded. The war-things fell back at his arrival, as if they too knew the hierarchy written in blood and fear.

He wore no armor—his body was its own. Muscles knotted like cables under scarred skin, his frame marked by ritual brands that glowed faintly with ember-red light. His eyes, black as obsidian, locked on the farmhouse with a hunger that was almost holy in its savagery.

"Savard!" His voice thundered, striking the shield like a weapon of its own. The barrier shivered under the force, the light dimming dangerously. "You cradle power you cannot hold. Come with me and rule by my side or watch this sanctuary crumble into ash."

Amara pressed her palms harder against the wall, her pulse racing as the shield trembled beneath her. She could feel him—his will, sharp and invasive, probing for cracks not in stone but in her.

Sebastiano stepped forward, placing himself between Amara and the door. His hand tightened on the dagger the Guardians had given him, its faint glow a defiance against the shadow looming outside.

"You'll never have her, Leone, she's not moving to the dark side" he growled, his voice low but steady.

Leone's laugh was a brutal thing, a sound like chains snapping. He spread his arms wide, welcoming the clash. "Then bleed for her. She'll bend or die.

With that, he strode closer, each step shaking the earth, until he stood directly before the farmhouse door. The war-beasts howled, their claws scraping the barrier, but Leone raised one massive hand. They froze at his command, leaving silence that pressed like a blade.

He leaned close, his breath fogging the barrier between them, and his black eyes seemed to pierce straight through Amara's soul.

"You are the Key," he whispered, and though his tone softened, it was more terrifying than his roar. "And Keys are not meant to guard. They are meant to open."

The barrier flickered, a golden shimmer barely holding, as if even it feared the truth in his words.

Amara gasped, her body trembling under the weight of his presence. "Sebastiano…" she whispered, her voice raw, "I can't hold it much longer."

And Leone's grin widened, savage and certain.

Chapter One Hundred Five
The Lion's Reckoning

The farmhouse walls shook as Leone's black gaze pressed harder against the shield. Amara's arms quivered, the golden barrier faltering like a candle flame in a storm.

Sebastiano's hand tightened around the dagger, ready to fight, but he could see her knees buckling, her lips pale, her body straining under a force no mortal could withstand.

And then something broke inside her—not the shield, but the fear.

Her eyes snapped open, burning with a light that was not her own. She thrust her palms outward, a cry ripping from her throat.

The barrier didn't collapse. It surged.

A wave of gold erupted from the farmhouse, laced with streaks of white fire, blasting outward in a shockwave that sent Leone staggering back. His beasts screamed and fell, thrown against the stone walls. Dust rained from the rafters, the ground split with jagged cracks, and for a moment the farmhouse itself seemed to hover in a cocoon of radiance.

Leone's laugh cut through the roar, low and guttural, even as blood trickled down his lip from the force of the blow. He wiped it away with the back of his massive hand, grinning through the crimson.

"Yes," he growled. "There it is. The fire hidden in the Key."

Amara collapsed to her knees, gasping for breath. Sebastiano was at her side in an instant, steadying her, his arm wrapping protectively around her shoulders.

"Stay with me," he whispered. "You're stronger than he knows."

But Leone was already advancing again, his footsteps heavy, unhurried, like a predator circling prey that had just bared its fangs.

"Do it again," he demanded, his voice shaking the broken stones. "Show me the storm that hides inside you. Or I will rip it out myself."

The farmhouse lights flickered, responding to Amara's racing pulse, the chest downstairs thrumming as though it, too, awaited her choice.

Sebastiano rose to meet Leone, dagger glowing faintly in his hand, but Leone's eyes never left Amara. The Key. The storm. The prize he had sworn his life to claim.

The air between them vibrated—charged, expectant, ready to break again.

Chapter One Hundred Six
The Dagger's Stand

Sebastiano moved before Amara could rise, his body shielding hers as he lifted the dagger. The golden blade pulsed, alive with the fire of his vow, its edge humming like a struck bell.

"Enough," he growled, his voice low, steady, but brimming with a dangerous resolve. "You'll not touch her."

Leone's grin widened, sharp and cruel. "So the hound bares his teeth." He spread his arms, towering, as though inviting the strike. "Prove you're more than a shadow hiding in her light."

Sebastiano lunged.

The dagger carved arcs of radiant gold through the dim air, each swing searing against Leone's blackened blade. Sparks flared, fire against ash, light against void. The clash rattled the farmhouse, sending splinters raining down.

Leone pressed forward with monstrous strength, his strikes heavy and unrelenting, each blow meant to break not just the blade but the man who wielded it. But Sebastiano held firm, muscles taut, every ounce of his being focused on one truth: Amara must be protected.

Amara, still on her knees, watched with her heart in her throat. Every time Leone's sword descended, she flinched. Every time Sebastiano countered, her chest surged with both pride and terror.

Leone sneered, forcing Sebastiano back step by step. "You fight well, D'Amato. But your strength is borrowed. You wield power you barely understand. What happens when it's gone?"

With a sudden twist, Leone slammed the flat of his blade against Sebastiano's ribs. The impact knocked the air from his lungs and drove him to one knee. Blood welled where steel had bitten flesh.

"Sebastiano!" Amara cried, scrambling forward, her hands reaching for him, her power trembling to life again in response to her fear.

Sebastiano staggered back to his feet, raising the dagger once more despite the blood soaking his shirt. His voice was hoarse but unyielding.

"I'd fight you with bare hands before I let you near her."

The dagger blazed brighter, golden fire wrapping up his arm, feeding off his defiance. Leone's grin faltered—just for a heartbeat—as the light pushed back against his darkness.

But the cost was written on Sebastiano's face: pale, drawn, his strength waning.

Amara's hands shook, her pulse thundering in her ears. She could feel it now—the farmhouse, the chest, the Guardians—all waiting, all calling her to act.

If she stayed silent, Sebastiano would bleed out before her eyes.

If she rose, the storm would break again.

The Last Strike

Sebastiano's vision blurred, but the fire in his arm did not dim. Leone bore down on him, their blades locked in a struggle of brute force against raw will. The void-steel screamed against the golden dagger, sparks flying, shadows and light tearing at each other in the air around them.

With a guttural roar, Sebastiano twisted his body, ignoring the pain shredding his ribs, and wrenched his dagger free. In a single, desperate arc, he slashed forward—gold meeting darkness in a flash so bright it blinded them both.

The blade tore across Leone's shoulder, searing flesh, leaving behind a smoking wound that hissed as though scorched by the sun itself.

Leone staggered back, eyes wide with rage and disbelief. For the first time, his grin faltered.

Sebastiano, chest heaving, swayed where he stood. The dagger slipped from his fingers, clattering to the floor. His knees buckled, and with a strangled breath, he crumpled, collapsing onto the farmhouse floor.

"Sebastiano!" Amara's scream pierced the din, raw with terror.

She fell to her knees beside him, cradling his head against her chest. His blood warmed her hands, his breath shallow against her arm.

Leone loomed above them, clutching his scorched shoulder, his laughter returning—low, guttural, cruel. "Beautiful," he rasped. "A man's last stand. Now watch as he dies, and you come with me or follow him into death. Your choice Key."

But Amara's tears fell like sparks on embers. Her grief twisted into something vast, unstoppable. The farmhouse shuddered as if bracing itself.

A low hum rose from the chest below, climbing in pitch, fusing with the wild rhythm of her heartbeat.

Her eyes lifted, burning with a light not her own. The air thickened, golden threads unfurling from her skin like rivers of flame.

Leone's grin faltered. His voice dropped to a whisper of dread. "No…"

And then, as Sebastiano's body went limp in her arms, Amara unleashed.

Chapter One Hundred Seven
The Unleashing

Sebastiano's body crumpled to the stone floor, the dagger slipping from his hand with a metallic clang that echoed through the farmhouse like the toll of a bell. Blood spread across the tiles in a widening stain, his breath shallow, his chest barely rising.

"Sebastiano!" Amara's cry tore from her throat, raw and unrestrained, as she fell to her knees beside him. Her trembling hands pressed against the wound, desperate to hold him in this world. His eyes fluttered open, meeting hers with a faint glimmer of defiance—but his strength was already bleeding away.

Behind her, Leone advanced. His monstrous silhouette filled the shattered doorway, his weapon dripping with Sebastiano's blood, his laughter low and rumbling. "You see, girl?" he snarled. "This is what happens when you stand against me. Keys and prophecies mean nothing in the face of the inevitable."

Amara's hands shook violently, not from fear, but from something vast stirring within her chest. Her vision blurred with tears, but beneath the grief a molten fury surged—one that would not be contained.

The farmhouse began to quake. Candles shattered in their holders, beams groaned, dust rained from the rafters. The chest in the chamber under them answered her grief with a pulse of golden fire, a resonance that poured through her veins.

She lifted her head slowly, her eyes no longer dark pools of sorrow but blazing spheres of light. When she spoke, her voice was not hers alone—it carried the resonance of the

Guardians, of every voice that had guarded the Key through ages untold.

"You will not take him from me."

Her body arched, and from her chest a torrent of radiance burst forth—threads of molten gold and searing white that lashed outward like living lightning. The farmhouse walls glowed, sigils burned in the air itself, and Leone stumbled back as the force struck him squarely.

He raised his weapon, but the power shredded it into shards of smoking metal. The impact hurled him against the far wall, splintering wood and stone, his growl twisted into a roar of rage and disbelief.

Amara rose to her feet, cradling Sebastiano's head against her as the light surged higher, wrapping them both in its blazing cocoon. Her hair whipped around her face as though caught in a storm, her figure lifted slightly from the ground, suspended in the brilliance of her awakening.

The farmhouse spoke, its stones trembling with a chorus like thunder: "The Key has awakened."

Leone staggered to his feet, smoke rising from his scorched clothes, his monstrous eyes wide for the first time with something close to fear. He spat blood, his voice guttural. "This is not over. You cannot hold such fire without burning yourself to ash."

Amara's gaze locked onto him, unflinching. Her power surged once more, slamming into him with a wave of blinding light that drove him through the shattered door and into the night. His oath, broken but not extinguished, echoed in the dark as he retreated into shadow.

Inside the farmhouse, the brilliance slowly dimmed, leaving Amara trembling, Sebastiano still in her arms. She bent low, her forehead pressed against his, her tears falling like drops of fire upon his skin.

"Stay with me," she whispered, her voice ragged but fierce. "I will not let you go. Not in this life, not in any life to come."

The farmhouse lay in ruins, but its heart had spoken. The world outside would never be the same. Leone staggered back, his charred blade falling from his hand with a hiss as it hit the stones. His massive frame, once so unyielding, trembled under the storm that poured from Amara. Her power blazed brighter, her hair whipping around her like fire caught in a gale, her eyes two suns burning through the veil of the world.

He tried to rise, to roar defiance as he always had, but his voice broke into a guttural rasp. His body smoked, his skin seared by the radiance that no steel, no shadow, no oath could withstand.

"Light cannot kill me," he spat, his lips curling into a bloodied sneer. "I am the dark that outlives the sun—"

His words ended in a scream.

Amara's power surged, a tidal wave of flame and resonance that struck him full on. For an instant, Leone's silhouette loomed—towering, monstrous, defiant—and then the blaze consumed him, shredding flesh and bone, leaving nothing but ash that scattered across the farmhouse floor.

The echo of his laugh hung in the air a heartbeat longer than his body, chilling and broken, before even that was swallowed by silence.

The chest pulsed once, its sigils flaring in grim acknowledgment. One shadow was gone. One oath broken forever.

Sebastiano collapsed to his knees beside Amara, wounded but alive, his hand clutching hers. Together they watched as the ashes of Leone drifted away, carried by a wind that had no source.

The farmhouse fell still, holding its breath again. Yet both of them knew it was not over.

For where one monster falls, another waits.

And Marchetti was already coming.

Chapter One Hundred Eight
The Duke Descends

The last ash of Leone had barely touched the stones when the air split with a new sound—measured footsteps, slow and deliberate, echoing against the shattered walls of the farmhouse.

Marchetti.

He emerged from the smoke like a shadow wrapped in silk. His tailored suit was immaculate despite the chaos, his silver hair gleaming under the dim glow of the chest's fading light. He walked as if the carnage were his stage, every stride regal, untouched, inevitable. Behind him, soldiers fanned out with practiced precision, rifles raised, eyes cold.

Sebastiano tried to rise, his wounds burning, but the Duke's gaze caught him and pinned him where he stood. Marchetti didn't even raise a hand—just that look, icy and absolute, was enough to strip Sebastiano of strength.

"Bravo," Marchetti said softly, his voice carrying like a blade through silk. He glanced at the ashes scattered across the floor. "Leone was a hammer—useful for breaking, useless for shaping. And now he is nothing." His eyes turned to Amara, and the faintest smile touched his lips. "But you... you are everything."

Amara's pulse thundered in her ears, her power still sparking faintly at her fingertips. "Stay back."

Marchetti chuckled, unhurried, unshaken. "Do you truly believe you can stop me? The prophecy bends toward me, Amara Savard. The Convergence is mine to command. You are not my enemy. You are my instrument."

He stepped closer, each word weighted with the confidence of a man who had orchestrated empires. "Give yourself over, and the world will kneel. Resist... and everything you love will turn to ash. I'll take out Sebastiano now as you watch."

The soldiers raised their weapons in unison.

Sebastiano forced himself to his feet, swaying but defiant, his dagger still clutched tight. "You'll have to kill me first."

Marchetti's smile thinned, and the command fell from his lips like thunder:

"Then bleed for her."

Gunfire erupted.

Chapter One Hundred Nine
The Shattering

The farmhouse exploded into chaos. Glass shattered, splinters of wood ripped free as a barrage of gunfire tore through windows and walls. The storm that had been circling them for so long had finally broken, and it was merciless.

Amara dropped to the floor, her ears ringing with the shriek of bullets chewing through plaster. Sebastiano threw himself over her, dragging her behind the heavy oak table just as another spray of gunfire stitched across the far wall, splintering beams into clouds of dust.

"Stay low!" he barked, his voice ragged but unyielding. His side still ached from the wound he had taken in the earlier battle, but he gritted his teeth and held fast.

The farmhouse groaned like a wounded beast, every shot rattling its bones. The sigils that had once pulsed with gold now flickered faintly in protest, as though the ancient walls themselves struggled to endure the assault.

Through the dust and roar of gunfire, shadows poured through the broken door—black-armored men, faceless beneath visors, moving with machine-like precision. Marchetti's soldiers.

Sebastiano rose just high enough to fire back, his gun kicking against his palm. Two soldiers dropped, their armored bodies slamming against the stone floor, but more surged forward, filling the farmhouse with the acrid stench of gunpowder and sweat.

Amara pressed her hand to her chest. It was warm beneath her fingers. Her breath came fast, her chest burning with the pull of something vast waiting inside her.

Sebastiano grunted as a round clipped the stone near his head. He shoved her deeper into the corner, eyes fierce. "Amara—listen to me. You have to call it now. Whatever is inside you, whatever that chest gave you—use it!"

Her pulse thundered in her ears. She wanted to deny it, to cling to some illusion of safety, but Sebastiano's raw courage and the ruin closing around them stripped away the last fragments of hesitation.

She rose.

The farmhouse seemed to hush in that instant, as if the very walls recognized her choice. A faint hum rippled outward, drowning the sound of gunfire for the briefest breath. Soldiers faltered, weapons half-lowered in confusion.

And then the air itself bent.

A column of light burst from her chest, golden and searing, hurling outward in a wave that sent the nearest soldiers flying against the walls. Plaster rained down. The gunfire cut off in startled cries as the wave rolled through the farmhouse like a living storm, shattering rifles, snapping blades, searing the armor from their bodies.

Sebastiano shielded his face against the brilliance, but even as the radiance blazed, he felt awe carve through him. She wasn't merely defending herself. She was becoming.

When the light dimmed to a steady, terrible glow, Amara stood in the center of the farmhouse, her eyes blazing like twin suns. The soldiers staggered, their fear palpable, and yet still they raised their weapons, driven by Marchetti's command.

Her voice rang through the smoke and ruin, calm and unshakable, no longer just Amara's but something greater speaking through her:

"This is no longer your battleground. Leave—or be broken."

The soldiers hesitated, caught between obedience and survival.

Chapter One Hundred Ten
The Serpent Inside

Dust swirled in the air, lit by shafts of light, and there—
framed in the ruins of the farmhouse stood Duke Antonio
Marchetti. He stood just inside the farmhouse door not as a
man under fire but as a sovereign standing before his court.
His black coat, tailored to perfection, hung from broad
shoulders like the cloak of a monarch. A single gloved
hand gripped an ivory-topped cane, its polished surface
gleaming though he did not need it. Every inch of him was
composed, refined—untouched by the carnage strewn
across the floor.

Around him, a few surviving soldiers straightened
instinctively, their fear momentarily subdued by the gravity
of his presence. The smell of gunpowder and blood clung
to the air, yet Marchetti moved through the farmhouse, his
shoes silent on the fractured stone.

His eyes—piercing, blue as cold steel—found Amara
first. He studied her not with shock but with recognition, as
if he had always known she would stand there glowing like
a flame, and had only been waiting for this moment.

"So," he said softly, his voice carrying the weight of
centuries. "Will you go with me Key or will you watch him
die?"

Amara's chest still burned with the light that had erupted
from within her. She stood tall, though her breath came
quick, her hair damp with sweat, her dress streaked with
dust. Yet she did not waver. Sebastiano moved to her side,
weapon raised though his body trembled with exhaustion,
blood still seeping through the bandage at his ribs.

Marchetti's gaze shifted to him, and the faintest smile touched his lips—like a lion regarding a loyal hound. "D'Amato," he murmured. "Ever the dutiful soldier. Now you die."

Sebastiano said nothing, his dark eyes steady, his silence its own defiance.

Marchetti stepped further into the farmhouse, ignoring the bodies of his fallen men. His cane tapped once against the floor, a sound that echoed like judgment. "You both stand at the edge of a choice," he said, his voice silken, persuasive. "Amara, you hold within you the power to command the Convergence itself. To bring the world to its knees with me at your side, you would wield that power without limit. You would be revered, untouchable. The world would know your name as it once knew the names of kings and empires."

He paused, letting the vision hang in the charged air. Then, colder:

"Or you can cling to weakness. To love. To illusions of freedom. And watch as the world burns for your sentiment."

The silence that followed was suffocating, every soldier's breath caught, every shadow leaning closer to hear her reply.

Amara's eyes blazed brighter, her power stirring again, though her voice was steady when she answered:

"You mistake me, Marchetti. I am not your Key. I will never be your weapon."

For the first time, a flicker of irritation crossed his regal mask. His smile returned, but it was sharper now, a blade disguised as charm.

"Then you have chosen war."

He raised his hand.

And outside, the rumble of engines and the marching of fresh battalions shook the earth.

Chapter One Hundred Eleven
The Breaking Point

The farmhouse shook as though the bones of the earth itself were rattling through its walls. Dust rained from the beams overhead, and the sigils along the stones flared with violent light, branding the air with molten glyphs. The chest pulsed in unison with the deep rumble, as though it were a heart too large for its cage.

Amara staggered back, Sebastiano pulling her against him, his arm iron around her waist though his strength was waning. Across the room, Marchetti stood tall, defiant even as the world bent to forces beyond his command. His eyes gleamed with unshakable certainty.

"This is it," he breathed, spreading his arms as if to embrace the quake. "The Convergence... mine at last."

The farmhouse answered him with a sound like tearing cloth, deep and resonant. The floor split, glowing fissures racing outward in jagged veins of fire, forcing him to step back. The walls groaned, their plaster fracturing, the very timbers straining as though the house itself sought to eject its occupants.

Amara clutched Sebastiano tighter. "It's pushing us out," she whispered, her voice breaking through the roar. "It doesn't want us here when it happens."

Marchetti snarled, refusing to yield. "No! The Key is in this place! The Brotherhood built these walls as its cradle. It ends here, with me!"

The farmhouse replied with fury. Windows shattered outward, glass like shards of light exploding into the night. Doors flung open on their own, slamming against stone.

The chest itself lifted from the floor, hovering, the glow around it so fierce that the very air burned white.

The Guardians' voices rippled through the chaos, layered and immense:

"The heavens cannot be contained. The vault will open beneath the stars. Leave, or be broken with the walls."

Sebastiano pulled Amara toward the stairs, shielding her from falling debris as beams cracked and splintered overhead. "Move!" he shouted, his voice raw but firm.

Marchetti hesitated, his face twisted with rage and disbelief, but even he was forced back as a rift split the floor beneath him, flames licking at his boots. With a growl, he followed, his pride a mask stretched over the dawning terror in his eyes.

The farmhouse itself roared, a final convulsion of stone and timber. Sigils flared so brightly they seared the retinas, driving all three—Amara, Sebastiano, Marchetti—through the buckling doorway and into the open night.

Behind them, the farmhouse pulsed once, twice, then went still—its glow collapsing inward as though holding its breath for the moment to come.

Above, the sky had begun to change.

Seven stars trembled, drawing threads of light across the firmament, weaving toward one another in a slow, inexorable spiral.

The Convergence had begun.

Chapter One Hundred and Twelve
The Heavens Divide

The night sky blazed as though painted by the hand of a god. The seven stars arced across the firmament, dragging ribbons of light behind them until the heavens themselves seemed to unravel. Threads of fire wove together, forming a vast lattice that pulsed with impossible symmetry. The Convergence was no longer a prophecy—it was alive, searing itself into the fabric of the world.

The air turned electric. Every hair on Amara's arms rose as she stared upward, her breath stolen by the immensity of it. The earth quaked beneath her bare feet, yet she could not look away. It felt as though her own soul was stretching skyward, pulled taut between flesh and light.

Beside her, Sebastiano swayed but stood firm, his face carved in equal parts awe and pain. He had fought men, war, and shadows—but this was beyond anything his hands could master. Still, he refused to falter, his hand tightening around hers. "Whatever it is," he said hoarsely, "we face it together."

Marchetti staggered forward, his fine coat torn and smeared with dust. Yet even battered, his bearing was unbowed. His eyes reflected the burning lattice above, fever-bright, consumed by obsession.

"This is mine!" he cried, spreading his arms wide. "Do you see it? The vault opening—oceans will bow, satellites will bend, and the world will kneel! I alone was destined—"

A deep hum split the night, drowning his words. The farmhouse behind them glowed once more, though it was cracked and broken. From its ruin, a column of gold shot upward, striking the lattice above. The Convergence answered with a resonant boom, a wave of force blasting outward.

Amara staggered, shielding her face, but the wave passed through her like a breath of recognition, leaving her glowing faintly, her eyes lit with starlight. Sebastiano turned to her in stunned silence—her very skin now shimmered with the same threads that laced the sky.

The Guardians' voices fell like thunder:

"The Key is awakened. The hand is chosen. The vault divides. One shall command—the rest shall fall."

Marchetti laughed wildly, staggering closer to Amara, his face contorted with desperation. "It's me!" he shouted at the heavens. "I have given my life to this! I have killed, sacrificed, bled for this moment! She is nothing without me—I am the one!"

The stars above shuddered. The lattice wove tighter, beams of light angling downward toward the earth. The moment of judgment was upon them.

Amara lifted her gaze, her chest rising and falling as though the cosmos itself breathed through her. She felt the pull inside her, the impossible weight of choice—the Key within her, ready to turn.

Sebastiano reached for her hand, his own voice breaking through the roar. "Amara—remember who you are. Don't let him twist it. The Key doesn't serve power—it serves truth."

For the first time, Marchetti faltered. His eyes snapped to Sebastiano, and in them burned pure venom. "If I don't win nobody does. Do you wish to see her die while you watch?"

He lunged.

And above them, the heavens began to break.

Chapter One Hundred and Thirteen
The Celestial Synchronization

The heavens writhed as though the stars themselves had been drawn into battle. Seven radiant lights stretched across the sky, weaving together until they blazed in unison like a crown of fire over the world. The Convergence had begun.

Amara and Sebastiano stood just beyond the farmhouse, their backs to its fractured walls, the night wind whipping around them in wild, spiraling currents. The earth vibrated underfoot—an ancient resonance awakened, humming like a living pulse through soil, stone, and bone alike.

Across the field, Duke Antonio Marchetti emerged from the shadows with the calm of a man who believed himself chosen by fate. His coat fluttered like a banner of war, his silver hair catching the starlight, his eyes burning with a hunger that bordered on madness. Behind him surged the remnants of his soldiers, a tide of steel and gunmetal pressed into service by his will.

"You see it, don't you?" Marchetti's voice carried like a blade through the storm. He raised his arms, his silhouette outlined in the light of the seven stars above. "The prophecy was mine long before you remembered yourself. I alone understood its meaning. I alone gathered the fragments, bled the world for them, and stood against time itself to reach this moment. You are the Key, but I—" his hand struck his chest—"I am the hand that will turn it."

Sebastiano stepped forward, his sword still stained with the clash against Leone's beasts, his body weakened but his will unbroken. "You mistake your destiny, Duke. The Convergence won't bend to greed. It answers only truth."

Marchetti's laugh split the air, low at first, then swelling into a chilling crescendo. "Truth is written by those strong enough to seize it!"

With a sudden gesture, he thrust his hand skyward. The satellites orbiting high above flickered—lights winking out, screens across the globe going black, power grids stuttering like dying flames. For a heartbeat, the world trembled at his command.

Amara gasped, the vision of it pressing into her mind: planes grounded, banks frozen, entire nations plunged into silence. Marchetti's reach was not illusion—it was real, a hand tightening around the throat of civilization.

Her fear sharpened into fury. Power rose from her chest, blazing brighter than ever before, her body trembling with the force of it. The Guardians' voices echoed within her, steady as a vow:

"The Key awakens to guard, or the Key awakens to enslave."

Marchetti's soldiers surged forward, Sebastiano raised his blade high above them. His warning bought Amara another breath, another heartbeat to channel the storm within her.

Then Marchetti advanced. His presence was suffocating, the sheer weight of his will pressing against hers like chains of iron. His voice boomed over the chaos:

"Choose, Amara! Open to me, and I will raise you above all others—queen of a new order! Resist, and you condemn yourself, and him—" he flicked his gaze toward Sebastiano, who staggered against another wave—"to death."

Amara's breath caught, her chest heaving. Sebastiano fell to one knee, his blade still raised, blood dripping into the soil. The sight tore through her like fire through parchment.

She stepped forward, the air bending around her, her hair streaming in the light of the stars. Her voice rang out, steady, unyielding:

"No, Marchetti. You will not write the world in chains. The Key was never meant for tyranny."

Her palms ignited in golden flame. The farmhouse behind her pulsed in answer. The stars above flared as though leaning closer. And then—her power surged, a river breaking its dam, the storm within her no longer restrained.

Marchetti's smile faltered.

The final clash had begun.

Chapter One Hundred and Fourteen
The Fall of Marchetti

The ground itself seemed to recoil as Amara's power surged outward. Golden fire swept from her hands in a torrent, meeting Marchetti's dark will mid-air. The collision was a storm of light and shadow, the earth cracking beneath their feet, the farmhouse trembling as though it, too, awaited judgment.

Marchetti staggered, his coat whipping violently in the shockwave, but his eyes gleamed with feverish resolve. He forced his hands skyward, drawing on the satellites, on every tethered line of code he had woven into the world's systems. Lights across the horizon flickered again as though the very sky answered him.

"Do you see?" he roared above the clash. "The world bends! It listens to me!"

Amara's voice rose to meet his, fierce and unshakable: "No, Marchetti—the world resists you!"

The seven stars of the Convergence pulsed brighter, their light spilling across the land. For an instant, their beams lanced downward, striking both Marchetti and Amara, binding them in a contest of will so absolute that the night itself held its breath.

Sebastiano, battered and bleeding, forced himself to his feet. His hand closed around his blade, though his strength was nearly gone. He knew he could not reach Marchetti in time—but Amara could. His voice, hoarse but steady, rang out to her:

"Amara! Don't fight him as he fights—answer him as you are!"

Her gaze flicked toward him—her anchor, her flame. In that moment, her power shifted. The fire was no longer rage or fear; it was love, fierce and protective, rooted in every lifetime she and Sebastiano had shared.

The golden torrent expanded, its light no longer a weapon but a tide of truth. It crashed through Marchetti's defenses, searing through the dark threads of control he had woven. One by one, the satellites slipped from his grasp, blinking back to neutral orbit. His eyes widened in horror.

"No! I built this! I am destiny!"

The Convergence flared, the seven stars aligning into a perfect crown above the battlefield. Their united light struck him full force, illuminating every shadow he had hidden behind. For the first time in decades, Marchetti's polished mask cracked.

He dropped to his knees, hands clawing at the soil as though he could anchor himself against the inevitable. The farmhouse groaned with the weight of the moment, its walls shining faintly in witness.

Amara stepped forward, her voice clear, ringing like a bell across the night:

"Your destiny ends here, Antonio Marchetti. The Brotherhood guarded this power so it could never fall to men like you. Tonight, it is returned to what it was always meant to be."

Marchetti raised his face to her, his blue eyes blazing with defiance even as the light consumed him. "No key... no prophecy... no Convergence without me!"

The stars blazed, the light broke, and his scream tore across the island before silence swallowed it whole.

When the brilliance faded, only scorched earth remained where Marchetti had knelt. No body. No shadow. Nothing but the echo of a man who had thought himself greater than the truth.

The farmhouse exhaled, its walls dimming, its glow softening. Sebastiano fell to one knee, his sword slipping from his hand. Amara rushed to him, catching him against her chest, her arms trembling.

The Convergence still burned above, steady and radiant, waiting.

Chapter One Hundred and Fifteen
The Quiet Between Stars

The battlefield lay hushed, the last echoes of violence fading into the hills. Smoke curled from shattered earth, drifting lazily across the broken stones of the farmhouse walls. Above them, the heavens burned with strange beauty—the Convergence just beginning its weave, threads of starlight crossing in patterns older than memory.

Amara sat on the ground, her back pressed against a half-toppled column. Her breath came ragged, her hair damp with sweat, strands clinging to her cheeks. Her hands still trembled, though the glow within them had dimmed. It was not gone—it never would be—but for now it had receded, leaving her exhausted, hollowed by the weight of what she had unleashed.

Beside her, Sebastiano lowered himself slowly, wincing at the wound along his ribs. The cut was shallow compared to the battles he had fought before, but the sight of blood seeping through his shirt drew a sharp pang of worry in Amara's chest.

"You should lie back," she whispered, brushing his arm. "You've lost too much blood already."

He gave a faint, weary smile, his eyes lingering on her face. "I'll sit right by your side my love."

Her lips curved, though tears stung her eyes. She reached to steady him, her palm warm against his cheek as she looked right into his eyes. She was breaking with love for him.

Sebastiano caught her hand and pressed it to his lips. "I'll always stay with you," he said softly. "In this life, and every life after."

The vow fell between them like a seal, unshakable, binding. Amara leaned into him, their foreheads touching, her heart thundering against the quiet night. For a moment, all the weight of prophecy and war melted away, leaving only two souls who had found each other again, against impossible odds.

Amara slipped into his arms, collapsing against his chest. Sebastiano pulled her close to him, his protection fierce. He held her as though the act alone could shield her from the world.

Above them, the stars pulsed brighter, weaving toward alignment.

And unseen in the quiet edges of the farmhouse ruins, the air stirred—subtle at first, then stronger, as if the house itself was preparing to speak again.

Chapter One Hundred and Sixteen
The Breath Before Revelation

The farmhouse lay in silence, its ruins draped in the silver wash of the Convergence. The light above continued to braid across the heavens, slow and inexorable, but within the fractured walls time seemed to pause.

Amara stirred faintly, her cheek resting over Sebastiano's heart. His hand brushed through her tangled hair, tender, rhythmic, as if by touch alone he could anchor her to this fragile calm. Her breath was steady now, the fire inside her quieted to embers.

Sebastiano leaned back against the cool stone, eyes lifted to the stars as their silver threads wove across the night. Each shimmer seemed to burn brighter, mirroring the certainty in his heart. He had found his home in Amara—and he knew he would never live a life apart from her.

"She's waking up," he murmured to himself, though a part of him whispered it upward, as if to the stars. "And when she does, I'll be right here."

Amara shifted, her hand curling lightly against his chest. Even in sleep, she reached for him, as if some deeper part of her remembered every promise they had spoken across lifetimes. He kissed her forehead softly, a vow sealed without words.

The air thickened then—subtle at first, like the stillness before rain. The ruins trembled faintly, a hush settling over the night. Sebastiano's eyes narrowed, his hand tightening protectively around Amara's shoulder.

From the shadows at the edge of the broken hall, a figure stepped forward, his cloak catching the starlight. Elias. His presence carried the calm gravity of centuries, the weight of a man who had walked through endless veils of history.

He did not speak yet. He merely watched—the lovers entwined, the farmhouse pulsing with latent power, the heavens threading themselves into destiny. His gaze softened, as though even he, guardian and witness, was moved by what he saw.

And then, as if the house itself exhaled, Elias's voice filled the air, solemn and low:

"The hour has come. The Convergence no longer waits in shadow. You must understand what you hold, or the world will not survive what follows."

Chapter One Hundred and Seventeen
The Guardian's Measure

Elias's eyes lingered on them both—Sebastiano with his arm around Amara's still-resting form, Amara stirring faintly as though she already felt his presence in her dreams. His voice carried the gravity of stone and flame.

"You have walked through fire," he said, "but fire alone does not make one worthy. The Convergence is not a gift. It is a burden—one that has broken greater souls than yours. Before you are told what it truly is, you must prove you can bear its weight."

Sebastiano straightened, jaw taut. "We've already fought your wars, bled on your soil. What more do you demand?"

Elias's gaze did not waver. "Not war. Not blood. Choice. The Brotherhood learned long ago that only those who can hold both light and shadow without breaking may touch the heart of the Synchronization."

Amara stirred, her eyes fluttering open. Her voice was hoarse but steady as she asked, "And if we fail?"

Elias stepped closer, the silver glow of the heavens bathing his weathered features. "Then you will know enough to fear. But you will never know enough to save. And the world will fall to whomever remains standing."

The farmhouse shuddered at his words, a low hum rising again in its beams. The sigils carved into the ruined stones flared faintly, as though echoing his decree.

Amara rose shakily to her feet, Sebastiano at her side. She met Elias's eyes, her voice trembling but resolute.

"Then test us. Whatever it is—you won't find us turning away."

Elias inclined his head once. "So be it. The trial begins now."

Chapter One Hundred and Eighteen
The Vision Trial

The farmhouse walls shimmered, their fractures knitting into streams of light. One by one, the beams dissolved until Amara and Sebastiano were no longer standing within stone, but within a vast expanse of radiance. The air pulsed with currents of gold and silver, the heavens themselves woven into living fabric.

Elias's voice echoed all around them, though his form was gone.

"The Convergence reveals. The Convergence tests. Stand as you are, and as you were, and as you will be. Only then may you bear its truth."

Amara gasped. Before her eyes, shapes gathered in the light—versions of herself. One cloaked in Renaissance silk, eyes sharp with rebellion. Another in rough homespun, her hands scarred from work but her gaze filled with quiet wisdom. Others—countless others—forming a circle of incarnations, all of them watching her.

Across from her, Sebastiano staggered, his own circle taking shape. A soldier with blood on his sword. A scholar in ink-stained robes. A weary sailor with salt-streaked hair. All of them bore his eyes, steady and fierce.

Amara clutched his hand, trembling. "Sebastiano... are they us?"

His grip tightened. "Yes. Every shadow we've walked through. Every life we've forgotten."

Elias's voice rolled like thunder. "Your trial is not to fight. It is to choose. Will you embrace all that you were—

even the darkness—or will you deny it and shatter beneath the weight? For the one who cannot carry themselves cannot carry the world."

The incarnations began to step forward, their eyes burning with memory. One by one, they raised their hands, palms alight with fragments of forgotten lives.

Amara's breath caught. She saw a younger self—a healer burned at the stake—step close, whispering, "Will you bear my pain, or cast me aside?"

Beside her, Sebastiano stiffened as his Roman self drew near, blood still dripping from his sword. The soldier's voice was a low growl: "Will you claim me, or turn from me in shame?"

The Convergence light flared. The trial had begun.

Chapter One Hundred and Nineteen
The Trial of Lives

The Convergence light thickened around them, no longer only a glow but a woven veil, shimmering as though it were spun from starlight itself. The farmhouse walls melted into haze. The earth beneath their feet dissolved into radiance.

Amara reached for Sebastiano's hand, terrified she would lose him in the brilliance. His fingers closed tight around hers. Together they stood as the veil of light parted, and the first vision unfolded before them.

A battlefield.

Sebastiano's armor glinted with dust and blood beneath a searing sun. His sword arm trembled with exhaustion, yet his eyes—still his eyes—burned with the same defiance she knew. She watched him fall, pierced by a spear. His last sight in that life had been a woman across the chaos, her face half-veiled but her tears shining—Amara, though she bore another name.

Amara gasped, covering her mouth. He had died looking at her.

The light rippled, shifting—her turn.

A monastery cloaked in winter silence.

Amara knelt in simple robes, her hands raw from tending the sick. The plague raged, but her healing touch carried whispers of something greater. Sebastiano, then a weary soldier who had stumbled to her door, saw her not only as a healer but as salvation. He died in her arms days later, whispering thanks for a kindness she had always thought too small to matter.

Sebastiano's breath hitched as he watched himself wither in her care. "It was you," he whispered. "Even then, it was you."

The Convergence light pulsed, the next vision unfurling. A renaissance court.

Sebastiano stood cloaked in velvet, a blade hidden beneath the folds, a man of intrigue and shadows. He had been ordered to kill—but when his target turned, it was Amara, radiant in silks, a duchess whose smile disarmed the assassin's hand. He spared her, though it cost him his life. His body was thrown into a canal that night, yet he carried her name into death.

Amara's tears spilled freely now. She turned to him, clutching his hand tighter. "Always you," she breathed.

The next vision unfurled—a marketplace, a gallows, a ship at sea. Each life laid bare, alternating like the beating of a great cosmic heart. In one, he died for her. In another, she bore sorrow for him. In another, they found fleeting joy, stolen days that ended too soon.

With each vision, their bond deepened, not forged but remembered. The Convergence was showing them not only trials, but proof—undeniable, unshakable—that they had always been one flame carried across the span of ages.

When the final vision ebbed, the light contracted inward, leaving only the two of them standing hand in hand, their foreheads pressed together.

The Guardians' voice thundered through the radiance, a resonance that shook bone and soul alike:

"The Key is not one life, nor one death. It is remembrance of all. Pass this trial, and no force can break you."

Sebastiano cupped her face, his eyes fierce through tears. "We've already passed it," he said.

Amara's lips trembled into a smile. "Yes. We have."

The Convergence light flared once more—awaiting their next step.

Chapter One Hundred and Twenty
The Breath Between Lifetimes

The farmhouse was gone, the battlefield erased. Around them stretched only light—vast, eternal, folding into itself like a sea without shore. Amara and Sebastiano stood suspended within it, the visions of past lives still burning in their eyes.

Her chest rose and fell, uneven, as if she had run through centuries without pause. His hands, calloused and scarred, cupped her face, anchoring her to this one breath, this one moment.

"Did you see it?" she whispered, voice trembling. "Every time… every time, we found each other, only to be torn apart."

Sebastiano's thumb brushed away a tear tracing her cheek. His dark eyes glistened, fierce and unbroken. "Yes. And I saw more." He drew her closer, their foreheads touching. "I saw that even death could not end us. I saw that every vow, every sacrifice, was a thread pulling us here. To this life. To now."

Her breath caught. The weight of all those endings pressed upon her—drowning, burning, execution, exile—but in his arms, the endings became something else. Not final, but bridges. Not loss, but proof.

She placed her palm flat against his chest, over the steady thunder of his heart. "Then let this be the last time we are torn apart. No more flames, no more gallows, no more exile. Not again."

His grip tightened at her waist, his voice low and raw. "No more." He kissed her—slow, searing, not with hunger but with the ache of centuries undone. The light around them seemed to pulse, as if the Convergence itself leaned closer to witness the vow.

When their lips parted, his breath was unsteady. "Amara… even if the heavens fall, even if the world turns to ash, I will not let go. In this life, and every life after, I choose you."

Her tears broke free, but they were not only sorrow. They were release. She pressed her face against his chest, her arms locking around him. "Then I will be your light, no matter the darkness. Your flame, no matter the night."

For a long while, they simply held each other, the silence not empty but alive—full of every vow they had ever spoken across time, and the vow they sealed now.

And when at last they lifted their eyes, the Guardians were there once more—looming, radiant, their forms etched in gold fire.

Their voices thundered, not in demand this time, but in solemn recognition:

"The Key and the Hand are bound. The Convergence has not ended—it has only begun. Now you must choose not for yourselves, but for the world."

The light shifted, darker currents stirring within it, and the promise of what came next pressed upon them both.

Chapter One Hundred and Twenty-One
The Trial of the World

The Convergence light rippled, shifting from gold into a darker spectrum, hues of indigo and iron threading through the brilliance. Amara and Sebastiano felt the ground beneath them dissolve, replaced by a vast plain of shadows that stretched without end. Above, the heavens churned, constellations colliding and reforming into sigils neither had ever seen, yet both instinctively understood.

The Guardians encircled them, colossal forms flickering in and out of being, their eyes like suns eclipsed.

"The Key and the Hand are bound," their voices boomed, shaking the plain itself. "But binding is not enough. Love alone cannot guard a world. Love must choose. Will you wield power for dominion... or for sacrifice?"

At their feet, the shadow-plain split into two paths—one paved in black marble veined with fire, leading toward a throne of obsidian that rose higher than mountains. The other path was rough, uneven stone, vanishing into a mist that concealed all beyond it, yet from within came a pulse of life, fragile and insistent.

Sebastiano's hand closed around Amara's, his grip unyielding. His jaw clenched as his gaze swept the paths. "One road promises control," he murmured, voice tight. "The other asks us to walk blind."

Amara trembled, her breath shallow. "And only one leads to salvation."

The Guardians extended their blazing arms, and the plain erupted with vision. On the throne-path, Amara saw armies kneeling, satellites falling into alignment, nations bent by invisible chains. Her own face shimmered upon the throne—radiant, terrible, crowned by power absolute.

On the mist-path, she saw no crown, no armies, only herself kneeling in the dirt beside children, beside the broken and the forgotten, her hands glowing as she lifted them up. The cost of each act carved into her body, but her eyes were clear, unshaken.

Her voice cracked. "Sebastiano… they're asking if I will save the world, or rule it."

He turned to her, anguish raw in his features. "And they're asking me if I will follow you, no matter which you choose."

The Guardians thundered again, their forms blazing brighter, the plain quaking beneath the weight of their words:

"Choose now. For the Convergence bends to will. The Key will awaken either to bind the world… or to free it."

The paths pulsed, waiting.

Amara's breath trembled as she looked into Sebastiano's eyes. He squeezed her hand, his voice low, steady, breaking through her fear:

"Whatever you choose, I am with you. In this life and every one after. But remember—Amara, love, remember who you are."

Her gaze flicked from his face to the two paths, the throne and the mist, dominion and sacrifice.

And in that breathless silence, the Convergence waited.

Chapter One Hundred and Twenty-Two
The Choice

Amara's chest rose and fell, her breath catching as the two paths pulsed before her—one blazing with dominion, the other veiled in uncertainty. The Guardians' voices rumbled like thunder behind her, pressing, demanding, inexorable.

Sebastiano's hand still gripped hers, steady, his warmth the only anchor in a world of shadows. His words lingered in her heart: Remember who you are.

Her gaze shifted one last time toward the obsidian throne. The vision shimmered—herself crowned, worshiped, feared. The surge of power called to her, whispering of ease, of control, of ending all threats forever by bending the world beneath her will. It was intoxicating.

Then her eyes turned to the mist-veiled path. She saw only fragments—a woman lifting the fallen, binding wounds, pouring herself out like flame into darkness. No glory. No crown. Only sacrifice. Yet her spirit recognized it instantly.

Amara's lips parted, her voice shaking but sure. "I was never meant to rule. I was meant to protect."

She stepped toward the mist.

The plain trembled. The throne cracked like glass struck by lightning, fissures racing across its towering frame. From its core came a scream—not human, but the howl of dominion itself dying. The black marble path shattered, collapsing into an abyss that swallowed its own promise of power.

Sebastiano followed without hesitation, his hand never leaving hers. His voice rang like iron: "Then I walk with you—through mist, through fire, through every lifetime."

The Guardians' forms flared, their eyes blazing suns. Their voices crashed over the plain like a tidal wave:

"The Key has chosen! Not to bind, but to free. The Hand has bound himself to her path. Together, they awaken the world!"

From the mist rose a light unlike any Amara had seen— neither fire nor storm, but the steady radiance of countless lives interwoven. It wrapped around her, seeping into her bones, her very breath. For the first time, she felt the true heart of the Convergence—power not as dominion, but as restoration.

Sebastiano sank to one knee before her, not as servant, but as vow fulfilled. His eyes shone, fierce and unyielding. "Amara Savard, you are the Key—and I am your hand. Now and forever."

Tears blurred her vision, but her smile was steady. "Then let us awaken the world together."

The Convergence blazed in answer, and the shadows fell away.

Chapter One Hundred and Twenty-Three
The Quiet Between Worlds

The night was impossibly still. The farmhouse walls, cracked and scorched from the battle, stood like ancient sentinels, their silence deeper than any words. Beyond the shattered windows, the sky still shimmered faintly with the fading strands of the Convergence—like threads of starlight reluctant to let go of the world below.

Amara sat on the floor beside Sebastiano, her back against the cool stone. Her head rested against his shoulder, her eyes half-closed, her breath slow. The glow that had poured from her only hours before was gone, leaving her body heavy, almost trembling from the drain. Yet she clung to his presence, her hand resting against his chest, feeling the steady beat of his heart.

Sebastiano turned his head slightly, pressing his lips into her hair. The taste of ash and salt lingered on his tongue, but beneath it was her—the warmth, the life he thought he might have lost. "You saved us," he murmured, his voice hoarse, still ragged from battle.

Her fingers curled into his shirt. "No," she whispered. "We saved each other."

The farmhouse creaked softly as though in agreement. Dust floated lazily in shafts of pale moonlight, drifting down like falling embers. Somewhere outside, a night bird called, its cry carrying across the quiet hills.

For the first time since the storm began, there were no shouts, no thunder of boots, no clash of steel. Only the two of them, and the echo of what they had endured.

Sebastiano reached for her hand, lifting it slowly, his thumb tracing a faint line along her arm. he said, his eyes dark, searching hers, "We will find each other in every lifetime forever."

Her eyes brimmed with tears, not of fear but of release. "I never want to live a life without you my beloved," she whispered.

They leaned into each other, lips meeting not in the desperation of survival but in the tenderness of a vow they had made long ago. The kiss was slow, reverent, unhurried—two souls finding their place after lifetimes of loss.

When they pulled apart, the farmhouse pulsed faintly once, a heartbeat in stone and timber. Then all was still again.

Neither of them noticed at first the shadow at the doorway—the figure who waited, silent, watching with eyes that carried the weight of centuries.

Elias.

Chapter One Hundred and Twenty-Four
The Keeper Speaks

The floorboards groaned softly under his step. Sebastiano's head snapped up, his hand instinctively reaching for the dagger at his side, but the tension in his body stilled when the figure emerged fully into the light.

Elias stepped forward—no longer cloaked in shadow, but revealed. His face was worn with the kind of age that was not counted in years but in centuries, every line etched by burden and memory. His eyes, though, were clear—silver pools reflecting both sorrow and hope.

Amara rose slowly to her feet, though she swayed slightly from exhaustion. Sebastiano steadied her with a hand at her waist. Together, they faced the man who seemed to fill the room with a presence as vast as the sea.

"You've walked far into the fire," Elias said, his voice deep, resonant, as if carried from the walls themselves. "And yet the greater flame lies ahead." Elias's gaze settled on Sebastiano. "I am Keeper of the Covenant. Long before Marchetti twisted prophecy to his will, before Leone betrayed the Brotherhood's vow, we stood guard. We watched, we waited—for this hour, and for her."

His eyes shifted to Amara, and though she felt a chill run through her, there was no malice in his gaze. Only recognition. "You are the Key—not because of bloodline alone, but because the world itself bends toward your awakening. Every cycle, the Convergence comes. Every cycle, a choice must be made."

Amara's voice trembled. "We saw it… the light, the vault opening. But I don't understand—why would it grant such power? Why would anyone be able to use it to enslave the world?"

Elias inclined his head, stepping closer. "Because the Convergence is not merely celestial—it is systemic. It is the moment when earth and sky, machine and spirit, align. The Brotherhood once swore to protect that knowledge: that in the hours of synchronization, the invisible threads that bind humanity—satellites, networks, currencies, even the quiet rhythm of the earth's magnetic field—become vulnerable. Whoever holds the Key does not just open an ancient vault."

He paused, his eyes glinting with sorrow.

"They rewrite the code of the world."

Sebastiano's hand clenched into a fist. "That's why Marchetti wanted her. Not just to rule, but to control everything. Every movement, every life."

Elias nodded once. "And why Leone sought the same— for chaos, for destruction, for power born of fear. Both saw truth, but neither bore wisdom."

Amara's throat tightened. "And me?" she whispered. "What am I meant to do?"

Elias studied her for a long moment, and then, slowly, he bowed his head. "To choose. Not with weapons, not with fire—but with your will. The Key awakens not only to guard or enslave, but to reveal. When the seven lights converged, it offered the world to whomever dared claim it. But it is not power that decides the outcome—it is the heart of the one who stands in the center of the storm."

His voice deepened, reverberating like a bell: "You are not chosen because you are strong. You are chosen because you are seen. And what you choose now will echo through every age yet to come."

The farmhouse pulsed faintly, as though affirming his words.

Sebastiano's hand tightened around Amara's, his eyes fixed on hers. "Then she won't stand alone," he said fiercely. "Elias's gaze softened. "No. She was never meant to.

Chapter One Hundred and Twenty-Five
The Keeper Speaks

The farmhouse lay in silence, its stones still thrumming faintly with the aftershocks of power. The air shimmered with the remnants of the Convergence, threads of gold and silver light weaving in and out of shadow like breath. Amara and Sebastiano stood side by side, their hands still clasped, their bodies weary yet unbroken.

From the fading glow at the heart of the farmhouse, Elias stood in the shadow. The hood of his cloak was lowered now, his face illuminated by the waning strands of celestial fire. He carried with him not menace, but a quiet gravity—the weight of centuries borne in a single frame.

"The choice has been made," Elias said, his voice deep and resonant, yet touched with warmth. His eyes lingered on Amara, then Sebastiano. "You chose to guard, not to enslave. And so the path of the Brotherhood bends to you."

Amara swallowed hard, her voice soft but steady. "Then it's done? The world is safe?"

A faint smile ghosted Elias' lips, but his gaze sharpened. "Safe... for now. But understand this, child of the Key: the Convergence is not a single event, but a cycle. Once every age it returns, aligning the heavens with the vaults below. Those who hold the Key at that moment can direct the flow—toward freedom, or toward dominion."

Sebastiano's jaw tightened. "That's why Marchetti hunted it. Why Leone spilled so much blood."

"Yes," Elias said. His hand lifted, and with a sweep of his fingers, the air itself parted. A vision unfurled before them—satellites drifting in orbit, golden filaments weaving through their signals like living veins. Networks flared, bank systems flickered, governments trembled beneath unseen threads. "At the height of the Convergence, all systems of man bend—technology, commerce, even the rhythms of the earth itself. Oceans shift, storms rise, nations collapse or endure depending on who commands the stream."

Amara stared, her breath catching. "And we… we stopped it from falling into Marchetti's hands."

"You did more," Elias corrected gently. "You redirected the stream. You bound it to guardianship. That vow, sealed in blood and light, ensures the knowledge cannot be turned toward dominion again—unless the Key itself is corrupted." His eyes pierced hers. "And that Key is you."

The farmhouse grew still. The weight of his words pressed against Amara's chest. She felt Sebastiano's hand squeeze hers, grounding her even as the enormity of what she bore sank deeper.

Elias stepped closer, lowering his voice. "This was only the first battle. The Brotherhood fractured long ago. Some still wait in shadows, loyal to nothing but their own ambition. Marchetti will not be the last. Leone will rise again. The Key will be tested—again, and again."

Amara's voice shook, but her resolve did not falter. "Then we'll be ready."

Elias' eyes softened, flicking toward Sebastiano. "Together, you are stronger than the sum of your parts. Alone, the Key may falter. But bound to the Hand that chose love over chains…" His gaze returned to Amara, glinting with something like reverence. "…you are unstoppable."

With that, he lifted his staff. The last glow of the Convergence flowed into the farmhouse walls, sealing cracks, knitting fractures, leaving the old stones stronger than before. The chest downstairs dimmed to a quiet pulse, its secrets locked once more—waiting for the next cycle, the next guardians.

Elias' form began to fade into the afterglow. His final words lingered in the farmhouse like an oath:

"Guard well. For history is not written in stone, but in the choices of those who remember."

And then he was gone, leaving only silence—and the sound of Amara and Sebastiano's breathing, steady in the stillness.

Chapter One Hundred and Twenty-Six
Echoes of Tomorrow

The silence after Elias' departure pressed close, not oppressive but profound—like the hush of a cathedral after the last note of a hymn. The farmhouse breathed around them, its walls no longer radiant but steadied. The chest sat quietly now a slow heartbeat beneath the floor. Its secrets locked inside—waiting for the next cycle, the next guardians.

Amara stood still, her hand still entwined with Sebastiano's. The weight of what she carried—what she now was—settled over her shoulders like a mantle. She could almost feel the currents of the Convergence still humming through her blood, whispering of power vast enough to change the course of the world.

Sebastiano turned, his thumb brushing the back of her hand. His eyes burned with a clarity she had never seen before. "It's over."

Her throat tightened. She leaned into him, resting her forehead against his chest. "Yes, we did this together" she said, His arm came around her holding her tight against him. "We are free to leave," she whispered. "We can stay or we can disappear. The farmhouse will guard itself as it has done for hundreds of years."

He pressed his lips softly to her hair, a quiet benediction. "You've fulfilled the vow you made lifetimes ago—to protect the integrity of the Earth," he whispered. "The energy bound to these walls is finally free. When the next guardian arrives, the Brotherhood will rise again, granting the new Key the full power to choose once more—for the fate of the Earth."

Her breath trembled, though she knew his words were truth. Slowly, she lifted her gaze to meet his. In his eyes, she no longer saw the man forged by shadows, but the soul who had chosen love over power, freedom over control. His hand rose, fingertips brushing her cheek—a touch that felt like a promise written across time.

"Wherever we land," he said, voice low and steady, "I'm with you. In this life—and in every life to come."

Her heart caught at the words. They had been spoken before—words that tied them across centuries, whispered in other lives, in other battles. She realized then that their bond was more than chance. It was part of the weave itself, as integral to the Convergence as the stars above.

The farmhouse seemed to stir at her thought, its stones creaking faintly, a whisper carried on the beams: Not alone. Never alone.

She closed her eyes for a few minutes, letting the truth of it sink deep. When she opened them again, she pressed her forehead once again to his, her whisper soft, "Whatever tomorrow brings, we face it together."

Outside, the night sky had settled into a strange stillness, as though the heavens themselves paused before the next turning of fate. The Convergence had passed, but its echo lingered—an unseen tide shifting the world beneath their feet.

Inside the farmhouse, Amara and Sebastiano held each other as if anchoring themselves against that tide. They did not yet know where the path would lead, only that they would walk it together.

And for now, in the quiet after fire and storm, that was enough.

Chapter One Hundred and Twenty-Seven
The Threads of Tomorrow

The farmhouse no longer trembled with battle, no longer pulsed with fury. Instead, a deep stillness settled over its stones—as though centuries of breath had been exhaled in a single sigh. Moonlight poured through the shattered rafters, painting silver paths across the floor. The night was no longer heavy with war but tender with release.

Amara and Sebastiano sat side by side at the kitchen table, its surface scarred by ash and flame yet miraculously intact, as though the house itself had chosen what to preserve.

"It's over," Amara whispered. Sebastiano's gaze met hers, steady, filled with love.

As if in answer, the farmhouse sighed—a slow, resonant sound that seemed to come from its very foundation. "The Key has turned. The vow fulfilled," a voice murmured, distant yet near, echoing through their hearts. "The next guardians shall rise four centuries hence, when the circle turns once more."

A radiant light burst from the chest unseen in the chamber below, the great room flooded with brilliance—and then, just as suddenly, the chest dimmed then disappeared. The pedestal beneath it shimmered and dissolved, followed by a low, harmonic chant, many voices singing as one—a final blessing. Mist began to unfurl across the floor, curling around the walls, soft and luminous.

One by one, the chamber's details began to fade—the stones, the stairs leading downward—until there was nothing left but stillness and air. Sigils flared to life across the walls of the farmhouse each burning gold for a heartbeat before winking out.

Amara exhaled a trembling breath. "It's gone," she said softly. Sebastiano nodded, his fingers entwining with hers. "We've fulfilled the vow we made long ago."

Outside, the first light of dawn crept across the horizon, touching the farmhouse walls with warmth. The land felt different now—lighter, alive. The house would sleep, dream, and protect itself until the ones destined to follow would awaken it once again.

And for the first time, Amara and Sebastiano knew they were free.

Epilogue
The Dawn Beyond

The farmhouse stood quiet now as Amara stepped into the garden, her bare feet brushing against the dew-wet earth. The air smelled of salt and earth and something more—an energy that clung to the stones of what had happened there. She tilted her face to the lightening sky.

Sebastiano walked beside her, his arm bandaged, but his posture carried no weakness. Only resolve. His eyes followed hers to the horizon, where the first rays of sun gilded the sea.

"This place will never be the same," she said softly.

"No," he agreed, his voice low, roughened by both weariness and certainty. "Neither will we."

For a moment, the world was just that—two souls standing in the quiet aftermath, bound by what they had endured, by what they had chosen.

Sebastiano's hand found hers, strong and steady, as though anchoring her to the path that stretched unseen ahead.

Amara tightened her grip. "Whatever comes," she said, her voice steady now, "we'll face it together."

The sea shone brighter as the sun broke fully across the horizon, scattering the last shadows. And with that light, they turned toward it—not as fugitives of the past, but as keepers of the future.

Their story is not an ending. It's a beginning.

About the Authors

Elian Lumis and Vickie Acklin are the co-creators of, *The Brotherhood: The Key*, a work that moves between mystery and remembrance, fiction and deeper truth. Lumis writes from the current of ancient memory and symbolic vision, while Acklin brings grounded insight, intuition, and lived human experience to the page. Together, their voices weave a narrative that is both intimate and expansive—designed not only to tell a story, but to awaken something quietly familiar within the reader.

What began as a single novel has opened into a larger unfolding. The Brotherhood: The Key is the first book in a developing series that explores hidden histories, timeless connection, and the possibility that destiny is not discovered... but remembered.

At'an Sekhem
Thothar'na

To the reader who journeyed this far—May the keys whispered between the lines awaken something ancient within you. May you remember that what you seek in shadow was always encoded in light. And may the fire sparked within these pages guide your steps forward—not just into the next chapter, but into the truth that lives within your own soul.

With reverence and remembrance,—E.L. & V.A.